FLYAWAY VAC. SWEEPSTAKES!

This month's destination:

Exciting ORLANDO, FLORIDA!

Are you the lucky person who will win a free trip to Orlando? Imagine how much fun it would be to visit Walt Disney World**, Universal Studios**, Cape Canaveral and the other sights and attractions in this area! The Next page contains tow Official Entry Coupons, as does each of the other books you received this shipment. Complete and return *all* the entry coupons—**the more times you enter, the better your chances of winning!**

Then keep your fingers crossed, because you'll find out by October 15, 1995 if you're the winner! If you are, here's what you'll get:

- Round-trip airfare for two to Orlando!
- 4 days/3 nights at a first-class resort hotel!
- $500.00 pocket money for meals and sightseeing!

Remember: The more times you enter, the better your chances of winning!*

*NO PURCHASE OR OBLIGATION TO CONTINUE BEING A SUBSCRIBER NECESSARY TO ENTER. SEE BACK PAGE FOR ALTERNATIVE MEANS OF ENTRY AND RULES.

**THE PROPRIETORS OF THE TRADEMARKS ARE NOT ASSOCIATED WITH THIS PROMOTION.

VOR KAL

FLYAWAY VACATION
SWEEPSTAKES
OFFICIAL ENTRY COUPON

This entry must be received by: SEPTEMBER 30, 1995
This month's winner will be notified by: OCTOBER 15, 1995
Trip must be taken between: NOVEMBER 30, 1995-NOVEMBER 30, 1996

YES, I want to win the vacation for two to Orlando, Florida. I understand the prize includes round-trip airfare, first-class hotel and $500.00 spending money. Please let me know if I'm the winner!

Name_____

Address _____ Apt. _____

City   State/Prov.   Zip/Postal Code

Account #_____

Return entry with invoice in reply envelope.

© 1995 HARLEQUIN ENTERPRISES LTD.   COR KAL

FLYAWAY VACATION
SWEEPSTAKES
OFFICIAL ENTRY COUPON

This entry must be received by: SEPTEMBER 30, 1995
This month's winner will be notified by: OCTOBER 15, 1995
Trip must be taken between: NOVEMBER 30, 1995-NOVEMBER 30, 1996

YES, I want to win the vacation for two to Orlando, Florida. I understand the prize includes round-trip airfare, first-class hotel and $500.00 spending money. Please let me know if I'm the winner!

Name_____

Address _____ Apt. _____

City   State/Prov.   Zip/Postal Code

Account #_____

Return entry with invoice in reply envelope.

© 1995 HARLEQUIN ENTERPRISES LTD.   COR KAL

The baby was part of the bargain

Sex would be nothing more than fulfilling the terms of their contract, Angel knew. That was the deal.

"Shouldn't I carry you over the threshold?" he asked.

"Why, Stuart, I do believe you have a romantic streak."

"Never let it be said that I shirked my duties as a bridegroom."

Before she could protest, he scooped her up into his arms, carried her to the bedroom, brushed aside the sheer mosquito net suspended from the ceiling and set her down on the edge of the bed.

"We want to conceive a baby. So it makes sense to perform the necessary tasks often, don't you think?" He slid his hands up under her hair and guided her head toward his.

"Perhaps," she answered. Although deep down inside she already knew.... *We wouldn't have to do this*, Angel thought to herself as she succumbed, *but it's so much fun....*

ABOUT THE AUTHOR

Bestselling author Pamela Browning, who has written forty books for adults and teenagers, grew up in South Florida, where she had more than a passing acquaintance with palmetto bugs like the one that terrorizes Stuart, the hero in *Angel's Baby*. She presently lives in South Carolina with her husband and their cat, Elizabeth Barrett, who, unlike Angel's six-toed cat, Caloosa, has only the normal five toes on each foot.

Books by Pamela Browning

HARLEQUIN AMERICAN ROMANCE

Don't miss any of our special offers. Write to us at the following address for information on our newest releases.

Harlequin Reader Service
U.S.: 3010 Walden Ave., P.O. Box 1325, Buffalo, NY 14269
Canadian: P.O. Box 609, Fort Erie, Ont. L2A 5X3

Pamela Browning
ANGEL'S BABY

Harlequin Books

TORONTO • NEW YORK • LONDON
AMSTERDAM • PARIS • SYDNEY • HAMBURG
STOCKHOLM • ATHENS • TOKYO • MILAN
MADRID • WARSAW • BUDAPEST • AUCKLAND

ISBN 0-373-16600-1

ANGEL'S BABY

Copyright © 1995 by Pamela Browning.

Prologue

The man stepped off the biweekly mail boat onto the dock at Halos Island. A pelican dived for a fish behind him, flapping away across the rippling clear ocean after scooping up its prey. The man's eyes were deep-set and shadowed beneath his brows. Angel couldn't determine their color.

"I'm Stuart Adams," he said, his husky voice cutting through her last-minute doubts. "I'm ready to make a baby if you are."

Angel lifted a trembling hand and brushed a gossamer strand of pale yellow hair out of her eyes.

"I think we'd better go up to the house and talk," she said.

The man, looking determined and not the least bit wary, hoisted a battered sailor's duffel over his shoulder and followed her up the dock, the silvery old boards creaking beneath his feet.

Angel had never seen this man before in her life, but she already knew that she'd marry him—if he'd agree to her terms.

She wanted him to father her child, and then she never wanted to see him again as long as she lived.

Chapter One

He was big.

He was handsome.

He'd look great in the nude.

And he didn't look like his picture. In fact, he looked a whole lot better.

Angel McCabe shot a quick glance in her visitor's direction. His skin was tanned a rich, golden bronze, which wasn't surprising, considering that he'd interrupted a sailing trip around the world to answer her ad.

He must have seen her looking at him. "The picture I sent was a couple of years old," he said apologetically.

Angel shrugged. "When I placed my ad in the personals column, I didn't specify that the picture should be recent," she said. She didn't add that she wasn't at all disappointed in his looks. She didn't want to tip her hand until she was sure he wasn't disappointed in hers, and she was afraid he might be. Howard had always said that she was too short, that her hips were too wide and her face too round, and even though she tried not to think about his constant denigration, sometimes it came back to haunt her. Like now, when she desperately wanted to make a good impression.

She moved into the lead as the path narrowed, and Stuart Adams swung easily along behind her as she led the way to her humble dwelling on a rise of land overlooking Halos Island's wide bay. He certainly didn't seem disappointed in her appearance. At the moment, she was wholly aware that he was watching the motion of her hips with obvious interest. She tried to tone down her walk, but the swaying was natural.

"So this is Halos Island," he said. "Angels *should* have halos."

She glanced back at him out of the corners of her eyes. "The name of the island has nothing to do with mine. This key was named Halos Island long before I arrived. *Halos* means *salt* in Greek."

"I like my idea better," he said, grinning.

She did, too, and she gave him a few points for originality.

The low bungalow where Angel lived crowned the rise of land; it sheltered beneath two huge banyan trees. A thicket of gumbo-limbo trees and buttonwoods hid the tiny outhouse and another small brick building that had once been an icehouse.

Stuart Adams looked around him with interest in his eyes. "All the other islands between here and Key West look uninhabited. This seems like the last place I'd expect to find a house," he said.

"The house was built during World War II for unspecified defense activities. Judging from the hundreds of brown bottles that I've found on the island, those activities included a lot of beer drinking," Angel said.

"Not much else to do in a place like this, is there?"

She swiveled her head to look at him, and he had the good grace to look away first. If he decided to stay, there would be plenty for them to do. If he decided to stay.

The screen door to the porch creaked when she opened it. "Come on in," she said, and as he mounted the steps she got her first real glimpse into his eyes. They were fringed by a double row of dark lashes, the longest she had ever seen, and they were blue, a pale, pale blue, like the sky seen from underwater. A person could drown in those eyes.

In sudden confusion, she preceded him through the door. Since she was hoping for a businesslike discussion, she didn't want to think about Stuart Adams's considerable physical attributes. She forced herself to take a deep breath before turning to face him.

He was appraising his surroundings, registering no particular expression as he took in the recently swept porch and the scarred wooden table, a relic of a past owner. When he sat down, his frame dwarfed the bent-twig porch furniture.

He was a big man, much bigger than Angel had expected from the picture, which had made him seem of average size. He was well over six feet of solid muscle. His hair was black and unruly, tumbling over a high forehead and grown too long at the sides and back. His faded jeans were slung low, and a skintight black T-shirt hugged his torso. He exuded an air of masculine sexuality so blatant that it literally took Angel's breath away.

Stuart Adams made no secret of the fact that he was looking Angel over from head to toe. His gaze took in her hair, tousled by the brisk breeze on the dock, and her face, now frozen into a noncommittal mask that was meant to match his lack of expression. After lingering on her face for much too long to suit her, his eyes fell to her breasts, which were generously outlined by the soft fabric of her blouse. He also refused to stint on the curve of her hips or the shapely outlines of her legs. Even her feet didn't escape his scrutiny.

"Well," he said at last. "Your picture didn't do you justice."

He was probably only being polite. Angel knew plenty about her physical shortcomings, having had them pointed out to her often enough. But she liked to think that she had recovered from her disastrous prior relationship, and she wanted to reply to his compliment; the problem was that she found herself completely unable to speak. All she could do was stare at him.

"Won't you sit down?" he said, and she knew from the sparkle in his eyes that inside he was laughing at her.

She sank onto a chair on the opposite side of the table, her heart pounding for no reason other than the fact that Stuart Adams couldn't seem to take his eyes off her.

"Oh, almost forgot," he said, handing over a stack of envelopes. "Toby the mailman sent you some mail."

Sent me some male, Angel thought inadvertently at the sight of his sinewy hand extended in her direction, and then she wondered, *What's wrong with me?* She'd known that Stuart Adams was a handsome man; his picture had shown her that. Maybe he was emitting such a vast quantity of pheromones that they had scrambled all her brain signals. She could only hope for a quick recovery. Had anyone discovered an antidote to male pheromones? It was a branch of research that definitely ought to be explored.

Tangled jasmine vines shaded the broad, screened-in porch and permeated the air with a heady fragrance, which Angel tried to ignore as she pretended to leaf through her mail.

"The way I understand it, you want a husband to father your child, and you don't want him hanging around

afterward. Is that right?'' her guest asked bluntly before
she had finished.

"Right," Angel replied, meeting his eyes reluctantly.
She was painfully aware that she hadn't been able to utter a polysyllabic word since she'd laid eyes on this man.
Merely looking at him, his strong physique so clearly on
display in that T-shirt and those tight jeans, tied her
tongue into knots. She knew she had been too long by
herself, sequestered on this island, away from civilization, but she ought to be able to manage *talk,* for goodness' sake.

"Why?"

Angel prayed for a sensible reply to leap to her lips.

"My lifestyle, which is one of scientific inquiry, doesn't
leave room for a man," she said.

"So how does a child fit into the picture?"

"Halos Island is a wonderful place for a child to grow
up," she said. "Swimming and fishing and nature
study—what could be a more wholesome environ-
ment?"

He studied her for a moment. "How long is research-
ing the habits of solitary bees going to interest you? Will
you want to live here on this island for the rest of your
life?"

"Maybe. The more I learn about solitary bees, the
more interested I am. The species I study exists nowhere
else in the world but on this island," she said.

"And you've been here how long?"

"Only three years."

"*Only* three years?" he repeated with a tinge of irony.

"It seems like less time," Angel said slowly.

"What did you do before that?"

"I came here from the University of Florida, where I
did my dissertation on solitary bees, and—well, you don't

want to know every detail of my professional career. Suffice it to say that I earned my bachelor's, master's and Ph.D. without catching my breath. When the opportunity landed in my lap to live here and study bees, I grabbed it."

"Why?"

"I consider the island to be an entomological laboratory for the study of living insects. My objective is to study solitary bees' instincts and habits. I can't imagine a more fascinating place."

"But aren't you lonely?"

"Being alone makes me self-reliant," she shot back.

"There's a difference between alone and lonely," he said.

"I'm never lonely," she said evenly.

"A child should have playmates," he said.

"When the child is ready for school, I'll resume teaching at the university nine months out of the year. During the summer months, the child and I will live here, where I'll study bees and the child will learn about Florida fauna and flora. The child's playmates will be the fish in the ocean, the birds in the air."

He made a sound that sounded like *Hmpfh*. What he said was "That's an awfully poetic notion, coming from a scientist."

She lifted her chin. "The point is, Halos Island is one of the best playgrounds in the world."

He looked her over. "Is it?" he said, making it perfectly clear that he was looking for a playmate of his own.

"Look, um, Stuart... My ad in the *Miami Singles Shopper* outlined the circumstances under which I want to bear a child. I want this to be a straightforward deal, complete with a contract, leaving nothing to chance. I need to know why it suits you to father a child under these unusual restrictions and requirements.''

Stuart shrugged one of his magnificent shoulders, sending a fascinating ripple undulating through his pectoral muscles. "Let's say I'd be intrigued by any ad that starts out 'Let's make a baby together,'" he said, obviously suppressing a grin.

With that, her businesslike façade crumbled. She blushed furiously, the flush starting in her face and radiating downward.

"You must have had a lot of replies," he offered.

"Enough," she said, thinking of the shoe boxes full of letters stacked under her bed.

"And why did you agree to meet me?"

Several answers came to mind, including the cleft in his chin as pictured in the photo he'd sent. His face had intrigued her, it was as simple as that. Only in a scientific way, of course. A dimpled chin was a worthwhile asset to pass on to one's offspring.

But she wasn't about to be sidetracked into talk about physical attributes. "You said you're rich," she said. "You said you'd have no trouble supporting a child financially if something happened to me."

He laughed. "At least you're honest," he said.

At least she *sounded* honest, but she was becoming less truthful by the minute. If she'd been telling the truth, she would have told him that she was completely swept away by those eyes, the set of those shoulders, his sheer masculinity.

"Back to why you answered my ad, other than the shock value of the wording," she said.

"I want a child, same as you."

"Why?"

"Undoubtedly for some of the reasons you do."

"I want a child to nurture and to cherish," Angel said, as her mind conjured up golden pictures of a curly-haired moppet chasing butterflies and tumbling with puppies.

"That's the way a mother should feel," he said.

"But not the father?" She held her breath, knowing that Stuart's answer was crucial to whether they would continue this conversation. She wanted to be a single mother. She did not want a man hanging around after the conception of their child and criticizing her child-rearing skills. She didn't want criticism, period.

He looked her in the eye and said, "Circumstances in my life are such that I won't be available to take care of a child. I require a woman who doesn't expect anything of me."

"And why, exactly, do you want a baby in the first place?"

"As a guarantee of the only kind of immortality that we humans can create in this lifetime." His eyes had turned to blue glass—brittle and hard.

"And how do you see your role in the child's life?"

"I'll provide financial support, of course. I'll send birthday and Christmas gifts. I'll send for the child once or twice a year. That's all, and that's what you wanted, right?"

Angel breathed a sigh of relief. "Right." Curiosity made her ask, "You could father a child without being married. What's in this for you?"

"I want him or her to carry my name, Stuart Adams."

"Even if it's a girl?"

"In that case, Stuart would be her middle name. A boy would be Stuart Adams, Jr. Can you live with that?"

Angel planned to name a girl *Elizabeth*. She liked the sound of *Elizabeth Stuart Adams*. And *Stuart* was a fine name for a boy. "I have no objections," she said.

His expression softened. "Why would someone like you get involved in something like this?" he said.

"Why do you think?" she said.

He watched her carefully, assessingly. "Maybe you're tired of life on this boring little island out in the middle of nowhere and you want an adventure," he said.

"No," she said emphatically. "No, no, and no again."

"Advertising for a man seems out of character for you. You're intelligent, beautiful, and you seem to have a good head on your shoulders, and—"

"A good head on my shoulders except for cooking up this crazy scheme, right?" She dismissed the fact that he'd called her beautiful; of course he would flatter her.

"All I'm saying is that you wouldn't have to advertise for a man. All you'd have to do is walk into a bar in Key West and—"

She bristled. "I don't hang out in bars in Key West. As for why I want a child, it should be obvious. I'm over thirty—"

"Only thirty-one," he interjected.

"At thirty-one, I'm ready to have a baby."

"So why not be artificially inseminated?"

"I want the child to result from marriage, so that if something happens to me, the father will take responsibility for it. I have no family, nor could I ask any of my close friends to take on the care of another child."

"So you decided to find a rich husband?"

"The ad didn't specify rich. I wanted someone who would be responsible, and people with money can afford to be responsible."

Stuart dug a sheaf of papers out of his duffel and slid it across the table. "If we both decide to go through with this, I'll set up a trust fund for the child as soon as the baby is born. This is my financial statement, notarized and signed by an officer of a well-known Boston financial institution. You'll see that I can afford to support a wife and child very well."

"I don't want anything beyond reasonable support for the child," she said.

He lifted a shoulder and let it fall. "As you choose," he said.

Angel scanned a few pages of the financial statement. According to the figures, Stuart Adams was wealthy indeed.

"Where'd you get so much money?" she asked.

He seemed amused by her directness. "I inherited most of it. My family builds boats, a lucrative field in New England. Take a lot of big navy contracts, a brisk business supplying luxury yachts to the rich and famous, and steady production of the fishing boats that made my family famous back in the days of whaling, and you have the foundation of a family fortune."

"A whale of a fortune," she murmured.

"Yes, well . . ." was all he said.

"So what brings you to the tropics?"

"I'm currently on leave from the family firm," he said. Something dark flashed across his expression for a moment, but it disappeared so fast that Angel thought she had imagined it.

"What do you do there?"

"I'm a naval architect by profession."

"Why did you take a leave? You're a little young to be having a mid-life crisis," she said. She knew from his letters that he was thirty-three.

"I needed a vacation."

"So you signed on to sail around the world on a sail-boat?" Her voice held a note of incredulity. She couldn't imagine leaving her work behind and taking an around-the-world cruise. Work was too important to her.

"A succession of sailboats. You can imagine how I re-acted to your ad when I'd been at sea for almost a month." His mouth quirked upward.

The humorous twist he was putting on the conversa-tion didn't distract her from the fact that he was provid-ing so much detail about his immediate past. This seemed odd to her; perhaps it was a tactic to keep her from ask-ing questions. Why would Stuart Adams be taking time off from a venerable old family firm? Well, it was none of her business, and probably irrelevant to the matter at hand.

She couldn't help being curious about his profession, though. "Exactly what does a naval architect do?" she asked.

"I design ships. The last one I designed was a floating palace for the sultan of Borju. It's being built now at our shipbuilding facility on Cape Cod."

"I should think you'd have wanted to stick around to see how things are going."

"Not necessarily. My brother's overseeing the pro-ject. About my financial status, if you need further as-surance—"

"I don't," she said, tossing the papers aside. As they stared at each other across the table, she took in the sharp planes of his face, the prominent cheekbones, the lips drawn into a firm line. Something sizzled between them, threatening to overload her circuits. Beneath what she hoped was a calm veneer, her heart was beating much too rapidly. And, she realized helplessly, she would have had exactly the same reaction to Stuart Adams if he were penniless.

"While you're thinking this over, could I please have a drink of water?" he asked on a note of apology.

She rose abruptly. "I made lemonade," she blurted before fleeing into the kitchen.

Inside, she leaned against the counter and struggled to regain her composure. All Stuart Adams's millions aside, the folly of having placed that ad in the personals column was beginning to be apparent. But since she left this otherwise unoccupied island only once a month or so, how else would she meet a man?

Still, what could she have been thinking of, to want to have a child with a man she didn't even know? How could she, a responsible and respected scientist, have come up with such a zany idea in the first place?

Suddenly she was no longer caught up in the bravado of choosing her own destiny. This was no longer a clear-cut business deal, the details outlined in impersonal correspondence. Now that she had met the man she had selected to be the father of her child, there was a distressingly human dimension to the scheme she had hatched months ago, when she realized that if she were ever going to have a baby, it had better be soon, before it was too late.

She reached for glasses in the small cabinet above her head and slammed the door. And then, without warning and while her back was turned, the kitchen cabinet crashed to the floor.

Glass sprayed out across the rough wooden planks, and Angel uttered a terrified squeak and stared in horror. Dishes spilled out of the fallen cabinet even as she watched; Caloosa the cat, hair standing on end, danced into the doorway on her six-toed feet with her back arched, hissing at the damage.

Stuart Adams shot through the door as if fired from a cannon.

"Are you all right?" he asked, looking rattled at the sight of the cabinet on the floor, surrounded by broken glass and pottery. Caloosa took off like a shot.

"Y-yes," Angel managed to say, scarcely able to remove her gaze from the wreckage of glassware and dishes, including her great-grandmother's heirloom china teapot, which had arrived in the United States from Ireland in the 1800s along with seven members of the McCabe clan.

"You're not all right at all. You've cut your foot," he pointed out. Glass crunched under his feet as he crossed the kitchen in two giant strides and bent to look. Sure enough, a thread of blood snaked down Angel's slim ankle. Angel couldn't feel a thing, and she was becoming more unnerved by the minute.

"It's nothing," she said, staring down, not so much at the cut as at Stuart's back, which was defined by ropy muscles that filled out his shirt in the most arresting way. Why was it that she couldn't feel the cut on her leg but was all too aware of the shiver of desire rippling up her spine?

"Don't move," he warned. He straightened and walked swiftly to the sink while Angel stood helpless amid shards of glass, china and pottery, then ripped a paper towel from the roll. He held it under the faucet for a few seconds and then returned to blot gently at the cut.

"The cut's not serious," he said, sounding relieved. "What made the cabinet fall?" He straightened so that he towered above Angel's five feet four inches. In an attempt to distance herself from any trace of erotic interest, Angel rapidly calculated what height their offspring might attain at maturity. Let's see— Stuart was over six feet, possibly six-two. Average that with her height of five foot four, which was sixty-four inches, and you got—

"I asked you what happened," he said, peering down at her.

"It just fell," she said. "Things around here keep disintegrating, partly because the house was built around 1940 and hasn't been properly maintained. I don't know how to fix things and don't have the inclination to keep things up." The mathematical calculations, and having to answer his question, had yanked her back to normal, sort of.

"Where's the bathroom? I'll get some antiseptic, and if you have Band-Aids—"

"The bathroom is located about fifty feet to the south, outside," she said.

"Oh," he said, and clamped his mouth shut.

"Band-Aids are in the drawer behind you," she told him.

He found the Band-Aids and reached out his hand. "Here, I'll steady you while you step through the debris. Careful, don't cut yourself. Those sandals you're wearing don't provide much protection."

After a moment's hesitation, she took the hand he offered and clung to his strength, stepping carefully over the broken glass.

She dropped his hand before reaching into the open drawer behind him and locating a bottle of hydrogen peroxide. She bent to dribble some on the cut, and her hair fell forward to hide her face.

"Aren't you upset about this?" he asked, looking around at the mess.

"I figure there are worse things," Angel said. "The house is still standing, anyway." She slapped a Band-Aid on the cut.

"Is there a broom around? I'll start sweeping up," he said.

"In that closet," Angel said, gesturing. Perhaps the fall of the cabinet had been a kind of blessing. It had certainly made them both concentrate on what needed to be done, instead of what they both, by this time, knew they'd be doing in the future.

They would be making a baby together. Soon, she hoped.

Stuart found the broom, and as Angel self-consciously busied herself with picking salvageable items out of the clutter on the floor, he pushed the debris into a corner.

"I have just enough carpentry skills to tack this cabinet back on the wall," he said. "By the way, a cat poked its head around the corner and took off at a run when it saw me."

"Oh, that's Caloosa," she said with a dismissive wave. "She'll get used to you."

He leaned on the broom for a moment. "And so I'm to stay?"

Angel inhaled a deep breath. "If you think I'll do," she said, trying not to think of the other women this handsome and well-connected man must have met in his lifetime, every one of them much more desirable and much more beautiful than she.

To her surprise, Stuart Adams tossed his head back and laughed. It was a long full-throated sound that brought Caloosa scampering in from the living room.

"You'll do, Angel McCabe," he said, his blue eyes crinkling at her. "And will I?"

"I should think you would do very nicely," she said stiffly. Her hands were trembling, and she clenched them into tight fists behind her back so that he wouldn't see.

The ensuing silence became so protracted that it grew awkward.

"I guess you'd probably like to see where you'll sleep until we're married," Angel said finally.

"Won't I be sleeping with you?"

"No sex until after marriage. You'll have to promise me that," she said. She couldn't make her eyes meet his.

"Why? If we're going to be married, what's the difference?"

"You could leave after... after..."

"After we sleep together?"

Angel cleared her throat. "Yes. And I could be pregnant. Then my child wouldn't have the security I want."

"Would you mind telling me why it's important? Other women, single women, have babies all the time."

She inhaled a deep breath. "I never knew my father, and I'm not sure my mother did, either. Growing up was a struggle, and I don't want any child of mine not to know who his or her father is, or to be financially deprived, like I was."

He studied her face for a long moment before nodding abruptly. "All right," he said. "I agree to your conditions. The contract between us becomes active immediately after we marry. I start a trust fund for the child as soon as the baby is born. Shall we shake on it?"

After a moment's hesitation, Angel held out her hand, and he gripped it between his two larger ones, all the while smiling at her.

Angel yanked her hand away. "There's a pullout bed in the couch," she said, brushing past him toward the living room, which she now noticed, in her distraction, looked even more frumpy than usual. She didn't pay much attention to decor, since she never entertained and since she herself preferred to spend most of her time outside with her bees. Now the chintz upholstery of the couch appeared more faded than ever, and the lamp shades more outdated.

"You can keep your clothes in here," she said, indicating a small closet.

"When can we be married?"

Angel made herself face him, hoping that she looked calmer than she felt. "This is Tuesday. When the mail boat comes back on Thursday, we can go to Key West, get our marriage license, and be married the same day in a civil ceremony in the county courthouse."

He nodded slowly. She realized belatedly that they were standing very close, almost touching, in front of the tiny closet, and she stepped backward in a hurry. Stuart Adams did something to the air when he was around, made it difficult to breathe—or maybe it was his scent, which was overwhelmingly masculine and fragrant with the tang of brine.

"I never got that lemonade," he reminded her as she turned to go. He followed her back into the kitchen.

"It's in the fridge," she said.

"I—" he began.

"A few ground rules, for the record," she said. "I won't wait on you. I won't do your laundry. You're on your own for breakfast and lunch. I like to cook a good dinner, and we can eat together if you like."

"Maybe we could go out sometimes," he said.

"There's hardly anyplace to do that."

He shifted uneasily from one foot to the other. "It was kind of a joke," he said.

"A joke," she repeated slowly. "I see."

"Lighten up, Angel. You're much too serious," he said, but he said the last couple of words to her back, because Angel was already out the back door and into the liberating freedom of sunshine and sea air.

Jokes, she thought to herself as she walked purposefully past twin banyan trees and on toward the west end of the island. *What next?*

She made herself think of the baby that would result from their marriage, and she grinned to herself. She'd better keep reminding herself that she needed Stuart Adams for one reason only. Next year at this time, she'd be a mother.

Caloosa scampered alongside her, chirruping in happy anticipation of a long walk to the beach. The cat knew from past experience that this was Angel's customary time for an afternoon swim.

"Well, he's here, Caloosa," Angel said to the cat. "And better than we expected, don't you think?"

Not that the cat paid any attention. She had already chased a chameleon into the brush.

Chapter Two

Stuart Adams found an unbroken glass on the kitchen counter and poured himself some of Angel's lemonade. It was slightly too tart for his taste; it was a lot like her. Not that Angel didn't have compensating attributes, he reminded himself.

When he stepped onto the dock an hour or so ago, he hadn't been prepared for a woman whose sexuality simmered so seductively beneath the surface. Whose big brown eyes were of the bedroom variety. Whose gently rounded curves of breasts and hips and buttocks seemed sculptured for the purpose of making a man want to make love to her.

A scientist, she had written. Studying bees. A loner who lived by herself on this small island slightly west of Key West and seldom came into contact with other people.

He had translated this information to mean that she was something of a misfit in society, albeit a highly intelligent one. Now he knew that his long-distance assessment had been incorrect. There was nothing about Angel McCabe that wouldn't fit in anywhere. In fact, he had an idea that she'd fit very well, and he grinned. The sexual chemistry was there, and he couldn't be happier.

And, he reminded himself, the best thing about the deal was that he would become a father. He'd given up on that idea since Valerie's death two years ago, thinking that the child she would have borne, had she lived, was his last link to immortality, and that when she died, all hopes of having a child had died with her. He'd known in the aftermath of that tragic night on Nantucket that he would never care about another woman enough to marry her. Never.

And yet here was Angel McCabe—someone he had met through a personals ad in a singles newspaper he'd picked up at a Miami marina on his way to another hemisphere—and she was willing to bear a child with no strings attached.

He'd almost passed up the ad in the first place. Who could take such an advertisement seriously?

Let's Make A Baby Together, it had said in bold type. Intrigued by the possibilities, he'd written to her, and Angel had replied right away. Her letter had so piqued his interest that he'd told the skipper of the racing yacht on which he was crewing at the time to go on without him, so that he could wait for Angel's next letter. As he'd exchanged letters with Angel and as it appeared that the two of them might be able to strike a mutually beneficial deal, Stuart literally couldn't believe his luck. And now he was sure he had stumbled into a fantasy.

Angel McCabe was the most beautiful woman Stuart Adams had ever seen, more beautiful even than Valerie had been. With that long hair slipping and sliding around her tan shoulders like strands of gold washed in silver, with those wide eyes holding just the slightest hint of surprise, with that firm, lithe body— Angel was the kind of woman most men saw only in their dreams.

Stuart had been unlucky in life and love. But the unlucky part was over and done with, and he didn't want to
think about it now that he was finally recovering and on
the way to making a new life for himself. It was hard,
though, really hard, not to think of what might have
been, especially now that he was actively pursuing fatherhood.

He sauntered over to a framed map on the kitchen wall
and saw that it was a map of the island. He'd looked up
Halos Island on a nautical chart earlier, but it hadn't
shown as much detail as this map. The crescent-shaped
twenty-square-mile island was one of a cluster of coral-
reef atolls flung west of Key West across the Gulf of
Mexico like a scattering of emeralds.

Embracing a wide bay, Halos Island was surmounted
by a huge oyster-shell Indian midden and bordered by
wide pink-sand beaches. There were caves on the north
shore overlooking the Straits of Florida. The surround-
ing water was turquoise in its depths, and so clear in the
shallows that you could probably see George Washing-
ton's face on a quarter lying twelve feet below the surface. It pleased Stuart that for however long it took, he
would live on Halos Island. With Angel McCabe.

After he drained two glasses of lemonade, Stuart decided that his carpentry skills, honed the summer that he
and his brother Fitz had undertaken the building of a
boat in their shed on Nantucket, were equal to hanging
the cabinet back on the wall. He'd get started on that
chore tomorrow. But first he wanted to look around.

As a former outpost of the U.S. Navy, the house—if
you could call it that—was spartan in the extreme. Fur-
thermore, it looked as if it would crumble to sawdust if
the termites stopped holding hands. Out of curiosity, he
peered into Angel's bedroom first. The small cubicle was

almost fanatically neat, the double bed, with its graceful folds of mosquito netting, pushed into a corner, and the shutters at the windows folded back to admit as much sunlight as possible. The bed was covered with a white plissé coverlet, and the hand-hooked rugs on the floor were white, too. There were no pictures, no frills, no furbelows.

"Doesn't look as if Angel McCabe has much of a personal life," he muttered to himself. Maybe that was good. She'd have plenty of time to devote to a kid. As a child who had often been left in the care of lackadaisical servants, Stuart thought he'd rather be smothered than ignored. A child, he'd always thought, deserved thoughtful, caring attention from the significant adults in his or her life.

He resisted an urge to peek into Angel's dresser drawers and went into the living room. Here there was a bouquet of fresh wildflowers on the rattan coffee table, and an overhead fan stirred the air into a sultry breeze. As Angel had pointed out, there was no inside bathroom. And he had already seen what was left of the kitchen. So the place was just three rooms—four, counting the porch.

He let himself out of the house, inhaling a long, deep breath of clean sea air. He could hear the sound of the surf from here; in fact, he'd be willing to bet that there wasn't a place on the island where you couldn't hear the ocean. That suited him superbly.

The old brick icehouse between the bungalow and Angel's small garden was a dank and unwelcoming three-foot cube. A glance inside the slant-roofed outhouse told him all he needed to know—the toilet facilities were even more primitive than he had expected. This was the typical one-holer, with a bucket of lime in one corner, a cobweb in the other. He wondered how Angel, who looked like a woman of taste and refinement, could stand it.

He followed a sandy path through a thicket of pesky sandspurs that clung to the hems of his jeans. Once he heard the scurrying of some creature nearby and was startled when Caloosa the cat leaped out from behind a palmetto tree. She pounced on his shoelaces before he reached down and caught her in his arms.

She was a dainty, pretty little thing, white with gray spots. Looking blissful, she closed her eyes and purred as he scratched her under her chin. When the purring seemed to intensify rather than abate, Stuart slung the cat over his shoulder like a baby, and she laid her throat against his neck so that he felt the vibration of her purring as he headed inland. Before long, he realized that on this inner part of the island, where the sea breeze did not penetrate the thick scrub, it was very hot. He paused to wipe the sweat from his forehead and set the cat down. He would head for the beach, where it would be cooler.

The cat followed him for a hundred yards or so before disappearing on a mission of her own. Stuart emerged from the brush into a grove of coconut palms and caught his breath at the sight of silvery waves breaking upon a wide curve of sand. Without further thought, he stripped off his shirt, shoes, jeans and underwear.

He sprinted barefoot across the hot sand but skidded to a stop halfway to the water. Angel was swimming close to the sunken coral reef, and too late he saw her clothes stacked in a neat pile at the water's edge.

If she had spotted him where he stood, he would have brazened it out and waded in to swim at a respectful distance. Weren't they going to be married as soon as possible? Weren't they going to share the same bed, conceive a child together? What could it hurt if they swam naked in the same body of water at the same time, feeling without touching, communicating without words? But she didn't see him, and he didn't want her to think he was spying.

Angel rolled over on her back and began backstroking in the opposite direction. The soft mounds of her breasts rose from the water, the nipples glistening in the bright sunlight. He imagined seawater coursing through the wedge between her legs, the pale curls as salty as seaweed. He shouldn't be watching. He knew that. But she was so beautiful. So sexy. And it had been so long since he'd been with a woman.

He groaned, feeling his body begin to respond to her. He backed into the palm grove, willing himself to calm down, but he still couldn't take his eyes off her. He held his breath, thinking that he had never seen anything as beautiful as Angel McCabe as she languidly emerged from the sea and waded slowly toward the pile of clothes on the beach, shaking the water out of her long golden hair in myriad droplets that glittered like tiny diamonds. She still had no idea that he was watching.

Her breasts were tanned and globular, with pink nipples perfectly centered and tip-tilted upward. They swung slightly when she walked, and water dripped off the tips. Her hips curved outward from a narrow waist, and her pelvis was wide—good for childbearing, Stuart reminded himself. Her body was tanned all over, and it gleamed like oiled silk. As Stuart thought about touching her, sleeping beside her, his mouth went dry and he was aroused again.

He didn't want her to see him as she made her way toward the path, so he sank to the ground and tried to meld into the shadowy trunk of a palm tree. Angel took her time putting on her clothes, starting with a sliver of lace that she shimmied up over her hips and ending with her blouse, which she slipped over her head in a single fluid motion. She was unconsciously seductive in her movements; he was sure she had no idea how the way she moved incited a healthy, red-blooded man to want her.

By this time, Stuart had decided to wait until she had gone and then cool his ardor by plunging into the sea and swimming as far out as possible. But as Angel started to walk gracefully toward the palm grove, he heard a loud "Meow," followed by Caloosa's mad dash down the sloping trunk of a coconut palm.

The cat headed straight for Stuart, her whiskers twitching. He pushed her away, but she only butted insistently against his hand and purred.

"Meow," said the cat, plaintively and loudly. Stuart shrank away, hoping that Angel wouldn't hear. She was closer now and, hearing the cat, she looked around in puzzlement.

Stuart took the chance to speak to the cat. "Go away," he growled.

"Caloosa?" said Angel. She was standing no more than twenty feet away from Stuart, the rays of the sinking sun tipping her eyelashes with gold.

"Meow," said the stupid cat, bounding toward her.

Stuart clutched his clothes over his most vulnerable parts, which at least had subsided. He could only hope that by remaining motionless, he would be invisible. With the sun in her eyes like that, Angel probably wouldn't be able to see very well.

"What have you been up to?" she said. For one heart stopping moment, Stuart thought she was talking to him.

But she wasn't. She bent and picked up the cat, stroking it gently. Caloosa struggled to get down.

"Okay, then, if you'd rather walk, fine," Angel said resignedly. The cat leaped from her arms and bounded through a thicket of sea grapes. She headed straight for Stuart.

Angel chided the cat in a playful voice. "What have you found, you silly cat? You haven't tangled with another crab, have you?" she said. Stuart looked around for an escape route. There was none.

Angel rounded a palm tree and stood openmouthed as Stuart stared up at her with a sick feeling in his stomach.

"Well," she said slowly, after a moment of speechless astonishment, "look what the cat dragged in."

Stuart could think of absolutely no reply. He stared at her, separated from her by nothing but a few feet of air and the foolish look on his face.

"You'll learn not to walk around Halos Island without clothes as soon as you get your first sunburn. The sun is very hot here," she said. "Come along, Caloosa. There's fish for dinner." She turned to go.

The cat switched her tail and, feckless creature that she was, slinked toward the path without a backward look. Angel followed with her nose in the air, and she didn't look back, either.

That suited Stuart just fine. He had turned red all over, and it had absolutely nothing to do with the sun.

IT WASN'T ANGER that Angel was trying to control as she stalked away from Stuart. It was laughter. She knew she probably should be furious with him for spying on her. And she probably would have been, if the man hadn't looked so *funny,* cringing against the trunk of the palm tree with his clothes bunched up against his private parts.

But as soon as she got her amusement under control, she realized that Stuart had probably had a good look at her—*all* of her—a mortifying thought. She didn't like anyone looking at her too-large breasts, or the hips that were too rounded, and as for her stomach, it was firm and flat, but could have been flatter. Or at least that was what Howard had always said. She hadn't let a man look at her—all of her—since she and Howard had broken up. She knew that baring her body was unavoidable in Stuart's case, but she was determined to remain one step removed from the process; somehow, she'd get through it. She was willing to do anything—anything at all—to have a baby.

Back at the bungalow, Angel started to prepare dinner. There was still no sign of Stuart Adams by the time she had squeezed the juice of a key lime over a snapper fillet and tossed a couple of potatoes in the microwave oven. She couldn't blame Stuart for staying away, she supposed. It was a way of saving face—not to mention other parts of his anatomy.

Holding the screen door open with her elbow, Angel carried the fish outside into the gathering dusk and lifted the hood of the grill. She slapped the fillet on the rack, sure that the mouth-watering smell of fresh fish cooking would bring Stuart back to the house in time for dinner. She was a little worried about what they would say to each other when he finally appeared.

She finally heard Stuart approaching. To her ears, unaccustomed to other people walking about the island, he sounded like a rhinoceros crashing through the shrubbery. She could only hope that by this time he was fully clothed. At least she thought that was what she hoped. After all, the first time she set eyes on him, she'd known he'd look great in the nude. And, aside from the preposterousness of today's revealing little incident, she hadn't exactly been disappointed. But then, she hadn't seen all of him—exactly.

She looked up from turning the fish, schooling her expression carefully.

"You can wash up at the kitchen sink," she told him. "Dinner's almost ready."

"Okay," he said. He started into the house, then turned on his heel.

"Do you, uh, want me to help with dinner? Set the table or anything?"

"Sure, that would be nice," she told him, keeping her tone aloof. "We'll eat on the porch. There are dishes in the china closet in the hall between the bedroom and the living room."

He went on into the house, and Angel breathed a sigh of relief. So far, so good, she thought as she slid the snapper onto the platter. Caloosa mewed and followed Angel up the steps. Angel adjusted Caloosa's pet door so that the cat couldn't get into the house.

"You stay outside," she told Caloosa, finding it easier to talk to the animal than to the man who was to be her husband. "I'm sure Stuart would agree that you've caused enough trouble for one day."

"Meow," said Caloosa disconsolately.

Stuart was making china-and-cutlery noises on the porch. In the kitchen, Angel quickly assembled on a tray baked potatoes, fish, stewed tomatoes from her vegetable garden, and pickled okra.

"I'll carry that for you," Stuart said, appearing suddenly and taking the tray from her.

"But—"

"No buts. Come and see if I've set the table decently. I don't have much experience along those lines."

He had located her good china and set two places at the table on the porch. He had put the forks to the right of the plates instead of to the left, and he hadn't used the place mats, which she'd forgotten to mention.

"Well?" Stuart waited anxiously.

"Very nice," she said. She wondered if he would be so eager to please if she hadn't caught him red-handed in the palm grove. Well, not exactly red-handed . . . but red.

They both sat down, and Angel picked up her fork. Stuart picked up his fork. Angel stuck her fork into her baked potato. He stuck his fork into his baked potato. Angel conveyed a bit of potato to her mouth. He conveyed a bit of potato to his mouth. She chewed and swallowed. He chewed and swallowed. Angel helped herself to the fish and passed the platter to him. He helped himself to the fish.

Suddenly he stood up and pushed his chair back. It wobbled and fell against the screen, punching a fist-size hole in the mesh. Stuart stared at the damage, then looked down at Angel helplessly.

"I didn't mean to do that," he said.

"I'll light a citronella candle so the bugs won't bother us," she said. She got up to get one.

When she set the candle on the table, Stuart started pacing to the end of the porch and back again. He looked at her from beneath his heavy brows.

"This afternoon was a mistake. I shouldn't have watched you on the beach. As soon as I realized you were there, I should have come back to the house, left you alone. All I wanted to do was go for a swim, and I'd already taken my clothes off before I realized—" He sounded genuinely distressed.

"Stuart," she said gently, interrupting him. "It's okay. I wasn't offended." She blew out the match she'd used to light the candle.

"Why not? Wasn't it a direct violation of the privacy you've come to expect on Halos Island?"

"I suppose it was," she said slowly, refusing to look at him, staring into the candle flame instead. "But if you're going to live here, too, I'll have to get used to not having the privacy I'm accustomed to having, won't I?"

"And I'll have to get used to blundering in where I shouldn't be, won't I?"

She stood up. "Stuart, we'll manage. This is an unusual set of circumstances. We can make it work."

He ran an impatient hand through his hair so that it sprang up between his fingers. "All right," he said dismissively. "Consider the subject closed." He sat down and began to eat.

Watching him, avoiding eye contact, Angel was suddenly overcome with regret. Her island had for so long been a peaceful retreat, a safe haven from the rest of the world, and she had destroyed it by allowing Stuart Adams to come here. Sudden tears at her own shortsightedness stung the back of her eyelids.

She stood up abruptly. "You go ahead and eat," she said. "I'm not hungry." She whirled and walked swiftly through the doorway into the house, leaving him to stare after her in bewilderment.

She fled out the back door, where Caloosa greeted her enthusiastically on the stoop. Angel sat down on the top step and stroked the cat's head, staring moodily out into the night. After a while she got up and scraped the specks of fish off the cooled grill into a saucer for Caloosa. She heard Stuart inside, running water into the sink.

If he noticed her sitting hunched over on the back steps while he rinsed his plate, he gave no sign. Eventually she heard his footsteps retreating, and she went back inside.

She found the remains of the broiled snapper in the refrigerator. She heard sounds from the porch that made her think that Stuart must be repairing the hole he'd made in the screen. A good thing he was, too, or they'd have a pack of mosquitoes whining around their ears all night.

Angel wondered how long it would take her to get pregnant. Two weeks? Two months?

No matter how long it took, she thought, it would seem like a very long time.

THAT NIGHT, the first night with Stuart under her roof, Angel decided that sleeping in the same house with him was an impossibility. Usually she loved lying in bed under her mosquito netting at night, lulled to sleep by the wind whispering in the palm fronds and the surf on the shore. But on this night, she couldn't go to sleep.

While Angel lay stiffly in her bed, unable to get comfortable, she heard Stuart furthering his acquaintance with Caloosa, who should have been on *her* bed, warming *her* feet, which were, for some reason, stone-cold in the middle of May.

Finally Angel heard the plunks and thumps that meant Stuart was unfolding the couch. She heard him shaking out the sheets that she'd unceremoniously dumped there while he was still on the porch fixing the screen.

Soon he made his own trip to the outhouse, and she felt a twinge of guilt when she realized that she hadn't told him where she kept the flashlight. But evidently he found his way there and back without mishap, because after a few minutes, she heard the protest of flimsy bed-springs as he lowered his weight onto the thin mattress.

The faithless Caloosa must still be hanging around him, since Angel heard Stuart murmuring in a low voice. Wouldn't you know that a cat would desert you for somebody else? Angel thought with annoyance. Next time she brought a pet to this island, it would be a dog. Dogs, at least, understood loyalty.

Angel punched her pillow again and rolled over. She was finally falling asleep when she heard an unearthly shout. She froze for a moment, then leaped out of bed and ran into the hall.

"What's wrong?" she cried as she flicked on the light.

Stuart was standing in the middle of the living room, wearing nothing but a pair of narrow black briefs. Caloosa was gleefully chasing a huge brown insect around the room, pouncing on it and then letting it go again for the sport of it.

"You didn't tell me the roaches around here fly and are as big as hummingbirds and crash-dive at people's heads at night," Stuart said accusingly.

"That's not a roach. It's a palmetto bug. And I'm very sorry, Stuart, but I don't think I can go through with this," Angel said, before bursting into tears.

Chapter Three

"Maybe you've got PMS," Stuart said.

Angel, who was standing in the middle of the room and sobbing softly, suddenly stopped. She looked as if she couldn't believe she had heard him correctly.

"What?" she said.

"Premenstrual syndrome. It makes women emotional at a certain time of their menstrual cycles," he said patiently, as if explaining to a very young child.

Angel only stared.

"Well, you have to admit that I have an interest in such things, now that I'm committed to getting you pregnant," he said.

"Good grief," Angel muttered. "I don't know whether to be amused or insulted."

"I vote for amused," he said. "If I'm allowed a vote, that is."

She looked around helplessly. "I don't suppose you have a handkerchief, do you?"

Stuart glanced down at his black briefs. "Not on me," he said.

Angel lifted the puffy sleeve of her nightgown and dried her face. "It can't be PMS," she said. "I'm only ten days into my cycle."

Stuart calculated rapidly. "That means that this week is the optimum week for you to get pregnant," he said.

"You're extraordinarily informed," she said, not without admiration.

"My favorite subject in middle school was sex ed."

"And I suppose you were a prodigy?"

"Well—"

"Never mind. Maybe I'd rather not know." Angel heaved a sigh. Her face was still damp, and her eyes were red and swollen from crying. She was still gorgeous, though, and Stuart's heart went out to her.

"Angel..." he began, hoping to offer some words of comfort, but she waved him off.

"Forgive my lapse of decorum and chalk it up to temporary hysterics. That's all it was," she said.

"I don't know why you should be hysterical. The palmetto bug wasn't trying to fly up *your* left nostril," he reminded her.

"It probably wasn't trying to fly up yours, either, unless it thought you were harboring a possible mate in your sinuses." Angel walked primly to a lumpy armchair and sat down, looking as if she intended to stay awhile. Stuart thought that maybe he should pull on his jeans, though after the episode that afternoon, it seemed pointless. And it wasn't as if his underwear revealed anything. Well, nothing but a quiescent bulge, that is.

Cautiously, he sat down on the edge of the bed. "As a native of New England, I guess I wasn't prepared for the size of the bugs in this part of the world," he said.

"The bugs in this part of the world are why I'm here," she reminded him.

"I don't think of bees as bugs, somehow," he said.

"Neither do I. To me, they're special."

"Want to tell me a little bit about your work?"

"I might as well. It looks as if you're as wide-awake as I am."

"Yeah," he said, with a glance at Caloosa, who was finishing off the palmetto bug's legs with a satisfied smirk.

"Well, the type of bee that I study doesn't live in a hive, nor are there queens, workers and drones, as there are in colonies of social bees. My bees are called solitary bees. The species I study nests in existing hollows in the ground or in trees, and Halos Island is the only place where the species exists."

"That hardly seems like enough of a reason to stay here for three years," he said.

"We weren't talking about that. I thought you wanted to know about my work," Angel said in a hurt tone.

Stuart had spent most of the last year crewing on sailboats. The kind of women he'd met in waterfront dives along the way weren't exactly the sensitive type. He'd almost forgotten how to get along with your average, ordinary, all-American girl.

"Go ahead," he said. "I'm listening."

Angel, after a long, penetrating look, went on to speak of bees and pollination, and he made himself concentrate on her low musical voice.

"And," concluded Angel with a wry twist to her voice, "if all this information about bees doesn't put you to sleep, probably nothing will." She stood up, and he caught a tantalizing glimpse of one rounded breast through the opaque fabric of her gown.

He didn't want her to leave. "Do you know that when you talk about your work, your face lights up and your eyes shine? You manage to make the most tedious facts interesting."

Angel blinked at him. "I do?" she said.

"Rehearsing those vows, are you?" he said, meaning to tease her out of her seriousness.

She bit her lip. "I'm glad you can joke about it. I can't. At least not yet."

He stood up. To give her credit, she never let her gaze drop below his shoulders. He, on the other hand, could barely keep his eyes off the curvaceous lines of her figure, outlined by the hall light behind her. He wanted nothing so much as to touch her at that moment, to run his fingertips down the soft skin of her neck, to cup her chin and turn her face toward his.

"Thinking about marrying each other is bound to be difficult at this stage of the game. We hardly know each other," he said softly.

"Neither do bees. They mate and never see each other again. The female lays her eggs, and then they hatch," she said, talking so fast that he knew she was nervous.

"Birds do that, too. And now I suppose we've had the requisite lecture on the birds and the bees," he said.

"You're making fun of me," she said.

"All I'm making is conversation. If you don't like it, we can sit here and stare at each other, feeling more uncomfortable by the minute."

"I'm going back to bed," she said.

"Not so fast," he said, his arm shooting out to bar her way.

"Stuart, it's late. I have to get up early in the morning to go out to the east meadow, where I'm tracking pollination," she said, but she didn't meet his eyes.

"I'm aware of the time. I—well, I only wanted to say that I have no qualms about what we are going to do. You'll be a fine mother for my child. I'm sure of it." He waited to see what she would say.

Finally she looked at him. "You're not just saying that? You mean it?" Her eyes searched his face.

"I mean it," he said. "And—"

"And what?"

"And as for the mating, or whatever you want to call it, well, I want to. I desire you, Angel. But you already knew that, didn't you?" He wanted to put her at ease, but his words seemed to make her more agitated.

Her chin shot up. "That makes it easy, then, doesn't it?"

"I hope it won't be difficult for you, either," he said. He desperately needed assurance that he was as desirable to her as she was to him.

She didn't give it to him, and he instantly regretted showing her how needy he was.

"No problem," she said succinctly before pushing past him.

He heard her close and lock the door to her room, shutting him out.

He wouldn't have gone to her, anyway. Stuart had every intention of waiting until they were married. He had promised her there would be no sex before marriage, and an Adams was, above all, a man of his word. It was an attribute that had been dinned into him by virtue of background and training ever since he was a small boy.

All the same, he lay awake on the uncomfortable couch bed until the early-morning hours, thinking about Angel sleeping only a few feet away, thinking about sleeping beside her, and thinking about all the ways he knew how to pleasure her when he finally did.

In the meantime, he'd have to figure out some way to get a good night's sleep on this miserable bed.

After a good bit of thrashing about, he finally curled up in as small a ball as possible, figuring that this position would minimize the damage to his spine. It wouldn't do to be incapacitated on his wedding night.

PARADISE.

Halos Island was paradise, so of course it had an Angel.

And angelfish, swimming in the limpid depths of the green-glass water near the coral reef.

These were Stuart's pleasant thoughts as he plunged into the surf the next morning, snorkel in mouth, flippers on feet. He'd found the gear in the closet in the living room and, for lack of anything better to do after rehanging the kitchen cabinet, he'd decided to explore the coral reef.

He'd been immediately glad he had. Here on the west side of the island, the water was so clear that the myriad colors of the reef were incredible. Lacy branches of coral undulated with the motion of the waves; fish swam past him, flicking his skin with their cool, silvery fins. Another world, beautiful and mysterious, existed beneath the surface of the water.

He hadn't gone snorkeling since he and Valerie had explored the wreck of a fishing boat on the rocks off Nantucket years ago. Valerie had always been up for anything he suggested, always ready to take a dare. Once, when they were children, she had leaped off a high bluff into the crashing breakers below. Another time, in Boston, when they were teenagers, she had led them into one of the city's most crime-ridden districts on a scavenger hunt; they had barely escaped being mugged.

And, on the night she died, she had dared him to accelerate over the sand dunes. Or at least that was what his brother, Fitz, who had been the only witness to what happened that night, said. He couldn't remember, didn't know why he'd even been driving Valerie's brand-new Takawa Tsunami, a notoriously unstable vehicle, over such steep and soft terrain. He only knew that when he woke up in the hospital after days in a coma and with no memory of the accident, they had told him that Valerie was dead.

His well-hidden anger at this unfair twist of fate seethed inside him, and he kicked out forcefully, propelling himself into deeper water, purging the past in a sudden burst of energy. The past was over and done with, and he was on his way to someplace far away where he could start a new life, make new friends, and forget the whole nightmarish experience.

His sudden spurt of activity startled a school of creole wrasses, sending them flashing toward the open sea. He swam harder, wanting to swim until his muscles ached, until he was totally exhausted, but water seeping into his mask and stinging his eyes with salt finally made him lift his head. That was when he heard Angel's urgent shouts from the beach.

When his eyes cleared, he saw that she was waving both hands and jumping up and down, and he couldn't understand a word she was saying. Whatever it was, it seemed important enough to head for shore, employing the powerful crawl stroke that had made him a collegiate swim champion in his younger days.

As he waded onto the beach, Angel regarded him with her hands on her hips and an impatient scowl.

"Did you see the moray eel?" she said.

He pushed his hair back from his face. "Is there one?"

"Yes, a big one. He lives in a cave near the place where you were swimming."

"I missed him. Or he missed me," Stuart said, trying not to concentrate on the soft sensuality of Angel's lower lip.

She was oblivious to the way he was looking at her. "The eel won't bother you unless you disturb him. If you'd stirred him up, you'd have regretted it, and so would I. My limited first-aid skills don't extend to coping with the results of eel attacks."

Stuart tossed the mask and snorkel aside and flung himself down on the damp sand, where he proceeded to remove the flippers. He took care to keep his back turned away from Angel so that she wouldn't see the narrow scar to the left of his spine; he didn't want to have to explain it, at least not today.

"Maybe you'd better take a minute to fill me in on the dangers of this island," he said. "Moray eels and flying cockroaches have convinced me that the whole place is a hazard."

"They're not flying cockroaches. They're palmetto bugs," Angel reminded him. After a moment's hesitation, she sat down beside him.

Stuart exhaled an exasperated sigh and studied the curvature of her hip, which was only inches from his. "Palmetto bugs, then," he conceded.

Angel had assumed a matter-of-fact tone, the kind he imagined she'd employ when lecturing a group of students. "The island is as safe as anyplace when you know how to live here," she said. "For instance, sharks seldom penetrate past the coral reef, so don't go swimming outside."

"Okay," he said.

"Then there are the dive-bombing mockingbirds. They're nesting, and when their young are nearby, they'll chase you unmercifully. I saw one ride on Caloosa's back all the way down the dock the other day.''

"I'm not as worried about birds as I am about snakes," he told her.

"You mostly have to watch for rattlesnakes on this island. You could possibly run across coral snakes and their lookalikes, the king snakes. Coral snakes are poisonous, and king snakes aren't, but they both have black, red and yellow stripes in a different order, depending on which kind they are. The way to remember is, 'red touching yellow, dangerous fellow.' ''

"Red touching yellow, dangerous fellow. All right, anything else?"

"Keep an eye out for scorpions—they're arachnids with curved tails, and their sting is painful and toxic."

"Do I need to worry about the bees?"

"If you stay away from them, they'll stay away from you."

"Is that what you do?"

"I spend almost all my time observing them."

"Ever been stung?"

"I've been hurt worse by contact with humans."

He stared at her for a moment. She was serious. He'd touched a nerve, but he decided not to pursue it.

"Anything else I need to worry about?" he asked.

"The weather. It changes fast in the tropics. You'll see waterspouts—tornadoes over water—regularly. We have horrendous thunderstorms at this time of year, continuing all summer. And, of course, we have hurricanes, but there's usually plenty of time to leave the island before one of those hits. Far more dangerous are tropical storms, because they can spring up without much warning, but as long as you're not in a boat when one arrives, it's usually not too big a deal."

"I've been thinking about getting a sailboat while I'm here, just for the fun of it," he said.

She shook her head. "You may not be here long. I plan to get pregnant right away." She scooped idly at the sand, raking it into whorled patterns; her fingernails were short and curved, like pink shells.

"Oh? And what makes you think you will?" He was frankly mystified by her certainty that it would be so easy.

"Maybe that's what I prefer to think," she said.

"So I'll get the hell out of here?" he shot back, regretting it immediately when he saw how it affected her.

She stared at him for an instant before jumping to her feet. "I didn't say that. You did," she said before dusting the sand off her shapely derriere and flouncing up the beach.

Stuart watched her until she disappeared into the trees. She struck him as a bit touchy and definitely temperamental. Well, maybe he'd been off base saying what he had, especially since she'd obviously come here to get away from people. Sometimes when he let his own guard down, his anger erupted unexpectedly, and besides, he was impatient with her standoffishness, which, under these admittedly peculiar circumstances, seemed ridiculous.

But what did it matter? As soon as Angel was pregnant, he'd be off for another port. Tahiti, maybe. Or New Zealand. Somewhere in the South Seas.

One thing he knew for sure. If Angel McCabe didn't get pregnant right away, it wouldn't be for lack of trying on his part.

As A PEACE OFFERING, Stuart decided to provide dinner. He spent the early afternoon waist-deep in water under the dock, chipping oysters off the dock pilings with a hammer and chisel. Caloosa, curious in the way of cats, kept him company, peering down at him between the boards and occasionally poking one of her large paws through a crack.

When they returned to the house, there was no sign of Angel, but the cat seemed agreeable to following the bag of oysters with its interesting scent to the rocky beach below the bungalow, where Stuart proceeded to build a driftwood fire. He nursed the dry tinder, shielding it from the wind with his body, until a tiny flame licked at the dry wood.

Once the fire grew to the point where it no longer needed tending, Stuart walked the short distance back to the house and rummaged around in the pantry until he found a large, flat piece of metal that would work admirably for roasting oysters. He noticed that Angel's bedroom door was closed, and he was sure it had been open earlier.

"Angel?"

She replied with a cautious "Yes?"

"Come down to the beach. I'm cooking dinner, and we can eat there," he said. He took two baking potatoes from the pantry and stuffed them in a paper bag, along with leftover three-bean salad and half a stick of butter. Plates, plates . . . he recalled seeing paper plates on the shelf of the closet where he kept his clothes, and he went to get them.

"You're cooking dinner?" Although she sounded intrigued, Angel still didn't come out of her room.

"Yes. My turn," he said. With the plates was a package of plastic forks and knives; he dropped several of them in his shirt pocket.

Silence fairly screamed from the other side of Angel's door, so he picked up the bag and the sheet metal and left, taking along a big piece of burlap he spotted hanging from the railing of the back stoop.

Maybe Angel wouldn't show up. If she doesn't, do I care? he asked himself as he made his way down the overgrown path. He didn't have to care about her. She certainly didn't care about him, except as a means to an end.

But he did care; he couldn't help it.

The sun was setting on the west side of the island, bathing the beach in a mellow golden glow. Caloosa scampered here and there, chasing tiny crabs into their burrows as Stuart tended the fire.

"Better watch it, or you'll get bitten," Stuart warned, but the cat only glared at him for a moment and sat down to wait for an elusive crab to reappear.

When the fire had subsided into a bed of hot coals, Stuart balanced the piece of sheet metal over the fire on four hefty rocks and buried the potatoes in the ashes. As he was washing his hands off in the surf, he glimpsed Angel walking down the path carrying a cooler and a tote bag. She looked determined, as if meeting him for dinner were something that she felt honor bound to do.

He felt a quick surge of anger. She was as aware of the sexual chemistry between them as he was, and he wished she'd stop pretending that it didn't exist. If they didn't make headway soon in establishing a personal relationship, their wedding night was doomed to be as awkward as hell.

Take it easy, man, he told himself as he watched her picking her way through clumps of sea grape bushes. *You won't get anywhere by making her angry.* He figured he'd better temper his annoyance and establish a congenial atmosphere; otherwise, the whole deal could be scuttled.

Angel's greeting was subdued, although her clothes were anything but. She was wearing a bright red blouse tucked into very short plaid shorts, and her hair was drawn back into a high ponytail to expose the white nape of her neck.

"I brought dessert," she said. "It's half a chocolate cake that I put in the freezer about a month ago." She pulled a package out of the tote bag and handed it to him.

He adopted a genial expression that he hoped would put her at ease.

"We'll set the cake here, on top of this log," he said, taking it from her.

She opened the cooler. "And here's a bottle of wine that I didn't know what to do with. I brought plastic glasses, too."

Wine. He wished he'd thought of it. A few good swigs might help her to loosen up.

"Where'd you find the oysters?" Angel walked over and looked at the bag.

"On the dock pilings," he said. "There are a lot of them."

"I know, but I never thought of eating any," she said. Looking as if she weren't sure what to do with herself, she finally sat down and stretched her legs out toward the ocean so that the waves spilled their foam near her feet.

"Don't you like oysters?" he asked.

"Sure, but when I'm hungry, it's easier to open a can of something," she said, wiggling her toes in the sand and stretching back so that the long line of her neck was exposed. Stuart swallowed and looked away. He was sure that she had no idea how it affected him when she so unconsciously struck a seductive pose, as she often did.

"Well. This is pleasant, Stuart. I should take time to relax like this more often," she said, gazing out at the breaking waves.

"Why don't you?" he said, still not looking at her. He uncorked the wine with the corkscrew on his Swiss army knife and poured each of them a glass.

She lifted a shoulder and let it fall, a study in movement and grace. "I don't know. I never think of it, I guess."

He handed her the wine and sat down beside her, keeping a careful distance between them. "Sounds to me as if you're a workaholic. Busy as a bee," he said conversationally.

She took a sip, considering. "Maybe my bees' industriousness rubs off on me. Like pollen," she answered.

"I'd like to see that you have a little fun before the baby comes," he said after a moment's thought.

She turned to look at him, focusing her wide-eyed gaze on his face. "Why?"

"You'll spend the next twenty years or so caring for my kid. It seems as if the least I can do is encourage you to enjoy yourself beforehand."

"I don't think you understand, Stuart," she said slowly, her finger tracing lazy doodles in the sand. "What could be more exciting than watching a baby grow?" She lifted her eyes to his, and he saw that she really meant what she was saying, she really believed it. He felt bewildered, seeing the passion in her eyes. He couldn't imagine feeling so committed to a child; the idea was foreign to him.

"I never thought about it," he said honestly. To him, the baby that the two of them were planning to create was an abstract thing, not real. By the time it became a reality, he would be long gone. For the first time, he felt slightly uncertain about stepping so easily out of his child's life.

"I've thought about the baby a lot," she said, staring out over the ocean with a dreamy look on her face. Stuart noticed that her shirt gaped open in the front where a button had come undone. Through the opening, he saw the softly rounded curves of her breasts, the shadow of a nipple visible through the lace of her bra. He looked away. Should he tell her that her blouse was open? Or would it be better to keep his mouth shut? He decided to keep his mouth shut.

Angel went on talking. "I'll go to Key West for the birth," she was saying. "Maybe I could stay with Toby the mail boat captain and his daughter for a week or so before the baby is born. Or maybe the doctor will want to induce labor so I won't be taking the chance of delivering the baby here on the island, where there won't be anyone to help."

Stuart knew he shouldn't give a flying fig where Angel planned to give birth, but with a sense of surprise, he discovered that he did.

He reached around the log for the wine bottle and topped off her glass. "You can't live on Halos Island during the last part of your pregnancy," he said in a reasoning tone.

"Of course I can," she said.

"It's too far away from everything. You don't even have a short-wave radio for communicating in case of an emergency. Why don't you have one, anyway?"

"It's never seemed important. I'm young, I'm healthy and I know how to cope with emergencies," she said.

"Not with childbirth," he said.

"I didn't say I was going to have the baby on Halos Island, did I? I told you I'll go to the hospital in Key West, didn't I?"

He wished she wouldn't bristle at his suggestions. He was only trying to point out the deficiencies in her plan. He was pondering whether to point out to her that he was being as agreeable as he could, but he'd barely shaped his thoughts into unspoken words when Angel said, "I thought you promised me some oysters."

Glad to have something to do, he stood up. "Why don't you set out the plates and forks?" he said, indicating a large, flat rock near the high-water mark.

To cook the oysters, Stuart heaped them on the heavy steel plate over the fire. Then he waded into the ocean and scooped up water with his hands, throwing it over the shells until steam rose in billows, the fragrance of the oysters mingling with the pungent scent of seawater and wood smoke. Finally, he covered the mound of oysters with the wet burlap sack until the heat from the steam began to crack the shells open.

While he was doing this, Angel watched attentively but made no attempt at conversation. When they sat down uneasily across from each other to eat, he had to show her how to shuck the oysters with the large blade of his pocketknife and dig out the succulent meat.

"The oysters are good, Stuart, really good," she said. He watched her making short work of the oysters and wished that he wasn't sitting across from her. It was impossible to take his eyes off her face as it expressed pleasure and even bliss. What, he wondered, would her face look like at the height of lovemaking? Could a lover evoke those same rapt expressions, those same sighs of pleasure? He found himself focusing on her mouth, rosy and flecked with a bit of potato. He had the reckless desire to reach over and brush it off; thankfully, she did it first. Still, he couldn't stop looking at her mouth, studying her delicately rounded chin, thinking that she had a face and a physique obviously made for pleasing a man. For pleasing him.

"Stuart," Angel said, as if from a long way off, "is anything wrong?"

He blinked his eyes, bringing Angel back into perspective. "Uh, no," he said. And after that he couldn't make himself look at her mouth; it would have given him away, had she seen the look in his eyes that betrayed his hunger—which at this point was not for his dinner, but for her.

Later, he tossed more wood on the fire and poured the rest of the wine into their glasses. They watched the moon rise over the ocean, turning the sand into a blanket of glittering diamonds and casting a silver-sheened path on the water. Stuart nursed the last of his wine, trying to think of something to say that would get him on Angel's good side, if only for the sake of their feeling comfortable around each other.

The baby, he thought. Her pregnancy. He focused his eyes on the lights of a distant freighter moving slowly across the horizon. "I was thinking," he said carefully, "that we ought to buy one of those home pregnancy test kits when we're in Key West getting married."

Angel shrugged it off. "Maybe we won't need one," she said.

He looked down at her, thinking that perhaps she could be teased out of her too-serious mood.

"You'd rather kill a rabbit?" he said.

Angel looked up, unsure how to take his remark. He wasn't being smart-alecky, she decided after taking a split second to register his good-humored expression.

"Doctors don't use rabbits to diagnose pregnancy anymore. It's determined by more sophisticated tests."

"Fine, but a home pregnancy test sounds like a good idea. It's not that easy to get to a doctor from this island. Why wonder, when you can know for sure?"

She sighed. "All right, we'll buy the test kit when we go to Key West to be married, but I'm sure I won't need any home pregnancy test, because I'll be able to tell when I'm pregnant as soon as it happens," she said in a soft voice.

Even in the darkness, she could see Stuart's eyebrows fly up. "How?" he said.

She'd have to be very careful how she answered. She leaned forward, looping her arms around her upraised knees and gazing up at the stars, magical pinpricks of light shining through the vast velvety curtain of the sky.

"Oh, there's this mystical feeling that I imagine a woman must feel as soon as she's harboring a new life," she said vaguely. *Not to mention nausea, swollen breasts, and the urge to sleep all the time,* she thought to herself.

"Coming from a scientist, that sounds a little flaky," he said. She turned to look at him and realized that he didn't mean that in a derogatory sense; he was looking at her with an expression of openness and what he probably hoped would pass for understanding. The trouble was that he thought the experience of getting pregnant was as new to her as it would be to him. And he was dead wrong.

"I was a woman before I became a scientist," she reminded him.

"And you think women have some inner sense that tells them, 'Hey, guess what, you're pregnant'?" He gazed thoughtfully at the phosphorescent glow of the waves as they tumbled on the beach.

"Absolutely." She allowed her surreptitious glance to fall on his long, muscular legs, knowing even as she did so that it wasn't a good idea.

"Why do you think that?" he said.

"It's really not as farfetched as you think. It's scientific as long as you keep in mind that, like other animals, humans have instincts. Solitary bees know to build nests and store pollen for their young, even though they can't know intellectually or experientially that they are going to mate and lay eggs. I have a very strong mating instinct, for instance, and—"

"Oh, you do?" he said, his eyes lighting up.

"That is to say... Well...I mean..." she stammered. She had meant to say that she had a very strong *mothering* instinct; chalk it up to a Freudian slip.

"I can hardly wait for this mating instinct to manifest itself," Stuart said dryly.

"That wasn't what I meant to say, and if you don't mind, I'd like to drop the subject," she said. She stood up, thinking it was high time she went back to the house.

Stuart stood, too, blocking her way to the path. The flickering flames of the firelight were reflected deep in the pupils of his eyes.

Angel was trembling, even though from where she stood she could feel the warm glow from the fire. There was another, longer path to the house to the north, and she sidestepped Stuart and veered in that direction, walking with her head down, her arms wrapped around herself to ward off the chill.

"I find this whole process of making a baby very interesting," Stuart said, falling into step beside her.

"No doubt," Angel muttered, but now she was thinking, *How am I going to get rid of him, short of telling him to get lost?*

"Would you mind not walking so fast?" he said.

"I didn't ask you to follow me," she said.

"No," he allowed.

"In fact, it would suit me if you'd go back to the house. I'd like some privacy, Stuart."

"Why? Because of what I said?"

"You could take this situation more seriously. The conception of our baby isn't something to joke about."

"You've been living apart from people for too long. This is how people talk to each other, Angel. Real communication isn't accomplished by talking the way words are written in books. It's give-and-take, it's silly banter."

"What's your point, Stuart?"

"Talking is how we get to know each other."

"We don't necessarily have to know each other," she said.

Stuart grabbed her arm. "Angel, when we're married, we're going to be doing the most intimate thing two people can do. Don't you think it makes sense for us to be more than acquaintances?"

She shook his hand away. "Why? Many members of the animal kingdom never know each other, never see each other again after the act that impregnates the female."

"We're human beings, Angel. I hate to be the first one to break the news to you, but human beings are a higher life-form than animals."

"Some are. On the other hand, I've known a few men who occupied a spot on the evolutionary ladder that is several orders beneath pond scum," she said.

Stuart stuffed his hands in his pockets and walked slightly behind her for a time. "I'd sure like to know where you're coming from," he said.

Her breath caught in her throat. "It's no business of yours. All you are required to do is father a child by me. I don't expect you to know me or understand me or care about me. I made that clear from the beginning, and I don't want to confide in you or tell you about my past or be friends with you," she said in a rush.

"You don't have to confide in me, and if you won't talk about your past, I won't talk about mine. I think we at least ought to try to be friends, though, for obvious reasons."

Caught off guard, she regarded him out of the corners of her eyes. "Friendship wasn't in the bargain," she said.

"I thought it was implied."

"You thought wrong."

"All right, Angel. I get it. You're the queen bee of this island."

"I'm a solitary bee, Stuart. I live alone, like the female of the species of bee I study."

"Okay. And you've got this misguided idea that you can do your own work, like the female solitary bees. You build your own nest and you store your own pollen. The male bee, after he does his duty, is never around. That's me."

"If you say so," she answered. This whole conversation was so off-the-wall that she was beginning to wonder if she was hearing it correctly.

"Tell me, Angel. How are you going to manage to be long gone by the time your little larva hatches? That's what the female solitary bee does, isn't it?"

"Don't be ridiculous. You know I'm eager to be a mother."

"Nevertheless, I see certain parallels between you and the bees you study. I think they've bee-fuddled you."

"You're very clever with words, Stuart. Now will you please fall off the face of the earth? At least until tomorrow morning?"

Stuart seized her shoulders and whirled her around to face him. With his back to the full moon, his features were shadowed. His fingers bit into her flesh. "Listen, Angel, we're going to live together on this island until you're pregnant, but I can't live with you if you're antagonistic. And it seems damned unnatural for us to climb into bed together on our wedding night without sharing so much as a kiss beforehand."

"All right," she said, giving up. "Go ahead and kiss me."

He dropped his hands. "Not like this," he said with distaste.

"Like what?"

"To get it over with. In my opinion, a kiss should be spontaneous." He started to walk back in the direction from which they had come.

Angel refused to let him have the last word. "Right now I'm thinking that you might have a point," she said.

"About your similarity to solitary bees?" In the moonlight, he looked grim and angry.

"About—about our wedding night," she said. "About its being difficult . . . to . . ." She couldn't say the words.

"To have sex?" he supplied, with a humorless smile.

"If that's what you want to call it," she said.

"I prefer to call it making love, but you can't make love to a person you barely know. Sex is an instinct, while lovemaking is an art. It takes a caring human being to elevate the act to its highest purpose, as opposed to insects, who are only doing what comes naturally," he said, figuring that he might as well speak his piece in terms she'd understand.

She stared at him.

"So am I finally getting through to you?"

"I understand what you're trying to say," she said carefully, but she was thinking that he was according the act of intercourse more importance than it was due. She could never tell him how unimportant sex was to her, except for the purpose of procreation.

"Good," he said, though he must have seen her confusion written on her face, because he laughed under his breath and walked back to where she stood.

His eyes glittered. "I have an idea, Angel, that under that calm, cool veneer, you're a passionate woman," he said.

She wanted to scream, *But I'm not! I never have been! I don't even know what passion is!*

Failing that, she wanted to fling a curt answer in his direction and run. But she couldn't move. It was as if she were rooted to the spot. Her stomach felt as if the bottom had fallen out, and all she could do was stare at him.

He reached out a hand and cupped her chin, turning her face so that the moonlight shone in her eyes. She twisted away from him, but he only laughed under his breath.

"Mating in the human usually begins with foreplay," he said softly. "Foreplay begins with touching. It can be something as light as a finger on the lips, like this," and he demonstrated, drawing the tip of his forefinger across her parted lips so that they began to tingle.

"Or it can be a nuzzle, like this," he said, before lowering his lips to the sensitive spot just below her ear.

"Or it can start with a kiss." And he touched his lips lightly to hers.

Her breath caught as his mouth took possession of hers. She felt his tongue outline her lips before exploring her mouth. Angel stood motionless, her head spinning with the shock of being kissed by a man who knew exactly how to go about it. As her astonishment was replaced by sensation, she actually felt desire curling up from the pit of her stomach. The sensation was so unexpected, so amazing, that time halted, the world stopped spinning, and all she could do was center down into it, experiencing it, and—much to her surprise—liking it. Her self-control ebbed away as if borne by the tide.

Without touching her anywhere else, Stuart deepened the kiss. His lips were soft yet firm, moving against hers with a sensitivity that weakened her knees. She was acutely aware of his body so close to hers that its heat seemed to surround her. His male scent swirled to envelop her, filling her senses.

Her heartbeat throbbed like the beat of a drum in her ears. If he would touch her with his hands, settle them at the hollow of her waist, move them slightly upward, she would surely be unable to breathe. She imagined him curving his fingers around her breasts, his fingers tracing their contours, caressing her nipples. The thought of it brought a warm, liquid feeling to the juncture of her thighs so that she was restlessly aware of a longing to be touched by him, to be filled by him.

Only an inch remained between them, and she arched toward him, willing his arms to go around her. He didn't oblige. He held her only with his lips, teasing her with desire. How had he learned to make a woman want him by only using his lips and teeth and tongue? What was it about kissing him that made her have to fight for breath and thought and even her own sanity?

When she thought that she could not sustain the kiss for one more minute, when she thought that she must throw her arms around him and cling to him in sheer wanton pleasure, he abruptly removed his lips from hers.

"A preview of coming attractions," he said.

She caught her breath. "Coming. Attractions," she said woodenly.

The corners of his mouth turned up. "You're really terrific at this, you know. We're going to be good together."

Her heart seemed to plummet all the way to the pit of her stomach. She knew she wasn't capable of pleasing a man who so clearly regarded the sex act as something more than mere mechanics. Oh, she was sure he didn't want love from her; that was their understanding. But, at the very least, he seemed to expect a good time in bed. This was bad news. Definitely bad news.

No point in letting him see her utter lack of self-assurance. Nor could she afford to let herself become emotionally involved with this man. She turned away, afraid that the expression in her eyes would reveal her painful vulnerability.

Stuart reached out a hand and tipped her face back toward his. "Don't try to make an enemy out of me, Angel. We *are* going to be friends, you know. It will be so much better for the child."

"Why don't you go back to the house, Stuart?" she said. "I'd really like to be alone." She looked him directly in the eye, as difficult as that was, and tried to stare him down.

He reached out his hands and touched the front of her blouse, startling her so that she jumped backward as if she'd been stung.

"I was only pulling the two sides of your blouse together. The button's undone."

She looked down, and as she watched, he slowly and deliberately pushed the button through its loop.

With that, Stuart wheeled around and walked briskly up the beach, leaving her staring after him. In that moment, she realized that he was wearing a red-and-yellow striped shirt.

Red touching yellow, dangerous fellow. She couldn't stop herself from thinking it.

What was it he had said? *Don't try to make an enemy out of me.*

Angel certainly hadn't invited Stuart Adams to the island with that purpose in mind. But, given her past history with relationships, she was afraid that was exactly what was most likely to happen.

Chapter Four

Angel woke up early on her wedding day. She lay quietly in bed, thinking of how her life would change after she had her baby.

Her life had almost changed in that way once before, and even though she'd almost stopped thinking about Howard, today he intruded into her thoughts and wouldn't go away.

But this was the day she was going to be married to someone else, and she counted her blessings. Howard was only a painful part of her past now, but in the life she had shared with him up until three years ago, he had often criticized her in public, and he'd also complained long and loud about her looks in private. "Can't you do something with your hair? Isn't there a bra that will minimize your breasts? Can't you find a pair of higher heels, so your ankles won't look so fat?" he would say, tearing down her fragile self-esteem without regard to the pain he was causing in her soul.

She hadn't realized that this qualified as emotional abuse until after they broke up. Now she knew that Howard had controlled her by demeaning her. By making her think that she wasn't good enough for anyone else, he had made sure that she stayed with him. And his strategy had worked. During the time that they were together, Angel's opinion of herself had fallen so low that she was terrified of leaving the relationship. Who else would want her?

In the end, Howard hadn't wanted her, either, and so all her appeasing and all her groveling and all her pain had been for nothing. Howard, who was a professor at the university where Angel had been an associate professor, had left her to live with his research assistant. And, stricken with grief, Angel had lost his baby, the baby he'd furiously told her that he didn't want.

Angel had healed on Halos Island. Healed to the point where she could think about restructuring her life, this time around a child—a baby who would take the place in her heart of the one she'd lost, and who would love her unconditionally forever. Who would admire her and look up to her. Who would fulfill her longing to be a mother, finally.

And this baby would be Stuart's baby. Perhaps it would look like him. Considering how she felt about her own looks, she *hoped* it would look like him. Angel couldn't wait to be pregnant again, to marvel at the miraculous swelling of her body to accommodate the baby, to feel the joy of knowing that she was really and truly with child. Stuart's child.

The thought of carrying Stuart's baby within her excited her and made her feel distinctly erotic. She touched her abdomen, trying to imagine its slight concavity becoming convex. Her hands slid over her breasts, reliving the changes she had felt when she was pregnant before, imagining them swollen with milk. She well remembered how early pregnancy had made her feel highly sexual, how she had, for the first time in her life, really wanted sex. And how Howard had sneered and rejected her advances, telling her she was acting like a common whore.

Her pregnancy had been the only time in her life when she had a climax. Howard had been so intent on his own pleasure that he didn't even notice.

Why was she thinking about that? What did it matter?

It did matter. It mattered very much. Because she didn't want to disappoint Stuart Adams, and she was very much afraid that she would.

Well, she thought as she got out of bed, at least somebody wanted her. Not for herself, but for the baby that she could provide. And that was perfectly okay with her. It wasn't as though she were interested in anything permanent. She'd been soured on permanent relationships for life.

Outside, the sun was shining and the birds were singing, but Angel already suspected that this day would be unbearable. It was her wedding day, a day that should be the most wonderful ever, and she was already wishing it was over. She would have to greet Stuart this morning as if nothing were amiss. Then she would somehow have to make small talk with him until the mail boat came, on which they would sit stiffly, side by side. Finally, they'd have to go through the whole rigmarole of the marriage license and wedding. She couldn't imagine how she was going to get through it.

She wanted, suddenly, to cry, but instead Angel made herself pad into the kitchen in her nightgown and pour both Caloosa and herself some milk. Stuart wasn't stirring yet, and she took care not to disturb him. She had no desire to encounter him this morning, had no wish to risk letting him see how she really felt.

Caloosa went outside, and Angel headed for the shower. Hastily she assembled soap, towel and shampoo and hurried outside to the novel arrangement for keeping oneself clean while living on Halos Island.

The shower was located beside the kitchen window and had a rusty nozzle leading from an equally rusty pipe, which connected to the rain cistern on the roof. By pulling a chain, you ensured that an indeterminate amount of water, which was heated by the sun, would be dumped over your person. There was no shower curtain, there never having been a need, and besides, there was no apparatus on which to hang one.

Very simple, very clever. Except for its unpredictability.

You might pull the chain and get no water at all, if it hadn't rained lately. Or you might pull the chain and be deluged. And sometimes you got a nasty surprise, in various forms of island wildlife, which found the cistern hospitable for a number of activities—including procreation, which could result in a shower of tadpoles.

On this day, Angel found the water to be warm and clean and soothing. She pulled the chain to get herself wet all over and, while she was standing under the running water, she heard a sound. Her eyes flew open to see Stuart standing stock-still beneath one of the banyan trees. He wore a pair of corduroy shorts and nothing else.

Angel froze. For a moment, the birds stopped singing and all she could hear was the blood rushing in her ears. She should have grabbed her towel, but she couldn't. She should have run, but she didn't.

He didn't say a word, only stood there with the sun on his face, his eyes taking in every inch of her. He started toward her. For a moment she thought he was going to walk past her into the house, but he stopped when he reached her. Silently, his eyes never leaving hers, he reached for the soap.

Slowly he picked it up, slowly he moved his lips toward hers. She lifted hers to meet them, keeping her eyes wide open so that she could watch the expression on his face. He kissed her, sliding one hand up the side of her neck to bring her closer, and with the other hand he began to soap her body.

She thought she might swoon. Tenderly he spread a thin film of soap across each of her breasts, slid his fingers across her nipples, soaped her neck and her back. Suds sluiced across her ribs, her stomach, her softly rounded backside. He lifted each arm, sliding the soap along the insides, massaging until ropy skeins of bubbles dripped from her fingertips.

He lifted her legs one at a time and soaped behind her knees, reverently touched her ankles, ran his fingers between her toes. And all the time he spoke not one word. The music of the water trickling down upon the mossy slab, the fragrant soap, Stuart's cool, slick fingers sliding across her wet skin—all combined to create a rapt state of mind and body that seemed only once removed from pure magic.

When Stuart finally finished, he pulled the chain to drench them both with water; his eyelashes were beaded with misty, jewellike drops in the sunlight. Angel was still stunned by what he had done, and all she could do was look at him. When she finally opened her mouth to speak, he silenced her with a finger over her lips and shook his head. And then he slipped away toward the path, the cool, dark shadows of the banyan tree closing around him, leaving her staring after him in a state of shock.

Numb and trembling, she reached for her towel. What had possessed Stuart to do such a thing, she didn't know. Nor did she know why she had let him. But it had been one of the most intimate acts she had ever engaged in, and she felt uncommonly sexual and sensual, like a womanly woman. Like someone who had regained her lost sexuality.

Talk about the unpredictability of showering on Halos Island! Never again would she complain about it, even to herself. She wrapped herself in the towel, not daring to look toward the woods, and went inside to dress for her wedding.

IF ANYONE HAD BEEN AROUND to ask Stuart why he had done what he had, he couldn't have given a reason that made sense.

All he knew was that he had awakened early and gone for a stroll on the beach for a few silent moments of contemplating what he was about to do. Marriage. Fatherhood. Big steps in anybody's life, no matter what the reason.

Not that he had come to any earthshaking conclusions, other than that he was ready to go ahead with the plan. And then, when he came out of the thicket into the clearing behind the bungalow, he had seen her.

No one who had ever seen Angel McCabe standing wet and naked in the pale light of morning could avoid realizing that she was beautiful. No one could deny her radiant presence. All Stuart knew was that when he saw her, he had to touch her. Had to feel her soft, silky skin beneath the palms of his hands, had to be close enough to feel her breath on his cheek and to look deep into her eyes.

Maybe it was just sex. Sex was a physical need; everyone needed it, some more than others. All right, so he needed Angel McCabe the way he'd occasionally needed other women since Valerie, to slake a thirst, to curb a desire. He couldn't recall being so aroused by any other woman, though. Angel had a certain indefinable something, a special quality that pegged her as beddable. A beddable woman. One who looked as if she'd like sex. Thrive on it. Hunger for it.

Maybe it was those eyes, wide and lustrous and glowing with a barely concealed sensuality. Or maybe it was her breasts, large for such a small woman, the nipples firm and pouty. Or maybe it was the way her buttocks tapered delectably into the back curve of her thighs, making him want to shape his hand to that contour and urge her close to him.

And there she had been when he came back from his walk, standing under the shower. If she had objected, he wouldn't have touched her. He would have gone into the house and put her out of his mind, but only for the moment, because tonight she would be his.

But from the instant she lifted her lips for his kiss, he had known that she craved his touch as much as he wished to give it. And so he had picked up the soap, and he had let his hands slide freely across her body, over every contour, into crevices, along her limbs, moving with a lassitude that was usually foreign to him. Mesmerized, totally under her spell, he had let his hands mold to the shape of her body, anticipating making love—*really* making love—to her.

He had made love to her so many times in his mind that, in a way, touching her seemed like a recapitulation of all his fantasies since he'd arrived on the island. He thought about taking her to bed in . . . let's see . . . ten or twelve more hours. Would she drop her barriers once she spoke her marriage vows?

He didn't know. All he could do was hope.

After a time in his life when hope had seemed impossible, when his future had seemed bleak and loveless, he was encouraged. The promised heat of his relationship with Angel McCabe might be exactly what he needed to melt away the coldness of the past two years.

He shucked off his wet shorts and plunged into the ocean, swimming with clean, swift strokes toward the coral reef in the distance.

ANGEL, still moving as if in shock after her intimate encounter with Stuart, put on a white linen dress that she had been saving for a special occasion. It was a long-sleeved, scoop-necked princess-style sheath that flared at the bottom like the petals of a morning glory, fluttering slightly as she walked. Her shoes were new white high-heeled pumps that she had bought to go with the dress.

With trembling fingers, she French-braided her hair high off her neck; the heat at this time of year could be fierce in Key West, and maybe a cool hairdo would compensate for the dress's long sleeves, she thought. Soft tendrils escaped, framing her face in gold. All the while, she was thinking how much she dreaded seeing Stuart again. How would he act? How would *she* act? It would be impossible to act normal around him after this morning.

"I haven't heard him come back into the house," she said to Caloosa, who had wandered into her room and was sniffing curiously at her new shoes. Caloosa only favored Angel with a blank look before jumping up on the bed and sitting down to watch these unusual proceedings; Angel in a dress was totally beyond her ken.

Angel nervously checked the time. Toby was due with the mail boat in less than half an hour, and if they weren't ready to leave, he wouldn't wait. Stuart had been wearing shorts—wet shorts, at that; he'd have to get ready. What would he wear for the ceremony, anyway? They'd never discussed it.

Angel pulled on a pair of panty hose, then took them off again, deciding that it was too hot to wear them. She pushed the neckline of her dress lower, then hiked it back up. *It doesn't matter how I look,* she told herself, knowing that she didn't mean it. This was her wedding day.

When Stuart still hadn't appeared, Angel went and peeked into the living room. The couch bed had been folded up and the coffee table set squarely in front of it. There was no sign of her intended bridegroom.

Angel was beginning to be concerned. Stuart knew what time the mail boat came, because he'd arrived on it himself on Tuesday. She peered through the porch screen, past the spreading branches of the royal poinciana tree to see if by any chance he was on the dock. The only thing she saw there was a lone seagull preening its feathers.

At that point, she stopped worrying about what they were going to say to each other when he showed up and started to worry about whether he'd actually show up at all. What if Stuart had taken off for some part of the island where he didn't know the territory and had met with misfortune? Despite her warnings, a snake could have bitten him, he could have wrenched his ankle in a gopher tortoise's hole—had she thought to mention the dangers of gopher tortoise holes? He could have even gone swimming and forgotten to look out for the moray eel that lurked in the depths of the coral reef.

After a mere two days, Stuart wasn't accustomed to living on this island, that was the truth of it, and anything could have happened to him. Anything.

Not knowing what else to do, Angel ran down to the dock. She scanned the bright blue-green expanse as she shaded her eyes against the fiery sun with one trembling hand.

He couldn't get off the island, she told herself. Without prior arrangement with one of the other boatmen who sometimes provided transportation to and from Key West, the mail boat was the only way to leave Halos Island. But maybe Stuart had arranged a way to be picked up before he arrived, in case their arrangement didn't work out. Maybe he didn't want to go through with their plans after all. Maybe he had left her.

Just like Howard.

A cold chill swept through her as she remembered.

Stuart wouldn't do that, she told herself as she slowly climbed the rise back to the house. He wouldn't. He just wouldn't.

Would he? Especially after this morning?

Uneasily she climbed the steps to the back porch and made sure that the pet door was operative so that Caloosa could go in and out while she was gone. Then she busied herself setting out enough food to tide Caloosa over during their overnight absence. Caloosa mewed and rubbed against Angel's ankles, already sensing a separation.

"Where's Stuart? Where's he gone?" Angel asked Caloosa, just for something to say.

If Caloosa knew, she wasn't telling. She was much more interested in her Kitti Bitti-Bits than in the whereabouts of the new human on the island.

Then, out of the corner of her eye, Angel caught a glimpse of Stuart as he emerged from the shadows beneath the banyan tree.

Her first emotion was one of relief. And her second, more unexpected feeling was pure joy. Without thinking what she was doing, Angel dropped the box of cat food and flew down the steps. She rushed to meet him, her heart in her throat. Dappled sunlight filtering through the banyan leaves above them shifted and shimmered over Stuart's even features, making Angel's head swim. He was wet, his hair curled into ringlets falling across his forehead. His arms were heaped with flowers from the meadows—pink periwinkles, oleanders in vivid shades of red, and a fragile species of wild white orchid, as delicate as lace.

"These are for you," he said, and she gathered them into her arms, enveloped in the heady fragrance.

"Stuart, it's almost time for the mail boat," she said.

"I know. I'll hurry," he replied.

He made a move to brush past her, but she stood in his way. "I was so worried," she said.

For a moment, Stuart wasn't sure how to react. He took in her flushed cheeks, her heaving bosom, the full lips that he had never seen brightened with lipstick until now. He also saw how her elaborate hairdo made her neck look thinner and more vulnerable. The tendrils escaping from her braid framed her face in gold.

"I only went for a swim," he said. "And to get these flowers."

"They're lovely. Thank you. But I—I thought something had happened to you."

It was a complete surprise to Stuart that Angel didn't seem to expect an apology for the way he had touched her when she was taking a shower. "Nothing happened," he said, not knowing what else to say.

"Oh," she said. "I just wondered."

"Guess I'd better get ready," he said.

"Yes." She stepped aside, and he hurried into the house. She tagged along, feeling foolish and not knowing what to do with herself. Should she follow him inside? Watch him get ready? Go into her room until the mail boat arrived? Finally she walked around the house to the front porch and decided to stay there.

She was touched that he had brought her flowers. It made the day seem more festive, and she wasn't sure how she felt about that. To celebrate this occasion seemed wrong, misguided. But not to celebrate it seemed even worse.

As she wound the orchids through her braid with trembling fingers, she heard Stuart moving around inside, running the water in the kitchen sink to wash his face and hands, opening and closing the closet door. She imagined him moving around inside her house, taking up too much room, making too much noise, filling up the rooms with his belongings. Thinking about the changes he would bring—had already brought—to her easy life, Angel felt edgy and jittery. She felt overdressed. She definitely did not feel like getting married today.

When Stuart emerged fifteen minutes later, Angel was arranging the oleanders and the periwinkles in a vase on the porch table. Stuart smelled of shaving cream, and his hair was still damp so that it curved over his ears in shiny dark waves. He wore an open-throated white dress shirt and a pair of dark trousers. In deference to the heat of the day, he carried his suit jacket.

He looked at her as if he expected her to say something. "You look very... nice," she told him.

"Thanks" was all he said before sitting down, and as she dropped to the chair across from him, she had the fleeting impression that Stuart was not as ill at ease about getting married as she was. He was acting as if people got married every day. Well, of course, they did. But not these two people under these very special circumstances.

To hide her nervousness, Angel bent down and gathered Caloosa into her lap, rubbing the cat behind her ears until she subsided into a floppy, purring dead weight. Stuart had made it clear last night that he didn't think she knew how to converse, and she thought now that maybe she really *had* lost the ability. She could think of nothing to say to him. What did people talk about when they were about to be married? Were all brides and grooms so self-conscious? Or was she unable to talk to him because of what had happened when she was taking a shower? Because she was thinking of the firm, cool touch of his hands upon her body? Of his kiss on her willing lips?

When she looked up, Stuart was watching her. "What were you thinking a moment ago?" he asked sharply.

She bowed her head over the cat again. "It's not important," she said.

"Tell me," he demanded in such an imperious tone that she found the words spilling out before she could stop them.

"I don't know what to talk to you about," she blurted, thinking that was the least of it.

"Don't worry about it," he said so dismissively that her spirits took a dive.

"I suppose that other people who are going to be married have plans to look forward to, and that's what they talk about," she said, momentarily envying couples whose futures together were assured and inevitable.

"You didn't want to have plans," he pointed out, not unkindly.

"I know," she said, and then sighed.

For a long time, the quiet was punctuated only by the purring of the cat. It was Angel who broke the silence. She wanted to talk, wanted to chatter, wanted someone to listen.

"When I was a child, I thought I'd have a big wedding. A huge wedding, in a church. With bridesmaids, flowers, all of it," she said.

"Life," said Stuart, "doesn't always live up to our expectations." He leaned back in his chair, studying her dispassionately. "Did you ever come close to the wedding of your dreams? Ever think about getting married?" he asked.

This was cutting much too close to the bone. "Once," she said, biting the word off short.

"What happened?"

She leveled a steady look at him. "It didn't work out."

When it became clear that she was reluctant to elaborate, he lifted an eyebrow. "So what do you want? For things to be different than they are?" he said.

Angel thought about it for a moment. "No," she said firmly. "I'm doing what I wanted. I'm getting married for the sole purpose of having a child."

"Want me to propose? To make this a little more conventional?"

She was afraid that he was making fun of her. "Absolutely not," she said stiffly.

"Well, I offered," he said.

She had no idea whether he was joking or not. They stared at each other for a long moment.

"Don't I hear the boat?" Angel said hopefully. The drone of the engine was still far away.

Stuart stood up. "Shall we go to our wedding, Angel?" he said, his expression inscrutable. He held out his arm, and after a short hesitation she stood up and looped her hand through it. His skin beneath the thin cotton of his shirt sleeve felt warm, distracting her, making her think of things she'd rather not think about. Before twenty-four hours had passed, she would know Stuart Adams's body intimately. Was it possible to have sex with someone, anyone, without being changed by it? At the moment, Angel doubted it.

As they made their way down the slope to the dock, the mail boat eased through the inlet channel in the coral reef. It approached slowly, pulling a curving white wake, and soon Toby was tying up at the dock.

"Halloo!" he called at their approach. He leaped from the boat to the dock, taking in Angel's white linen dress.

"What's the special occasion?" Toby asked.

"Nothing elaborate," Angel said. "Just a small wedding. We're getting married."

Toby's eyes nearly popped out of his head as his stare darted from her face to Stuart's.

"Married?" he squeaked in disbelief.

"Right," Angel said as Stuart handed her onto the boat and tossed their overnight bags over the gunwales.

Toby followed Stuart onto the boat, forgetting to give Angel her mail, staring at Stuart in his starched white shirt. Finally he disappeared into the wheel house, shaking his head and muttering to himself.

"I think Toby is shocked," Stuart whispered.

"I think it's none of Toby's business," Angel managed to whisper back, but Stuart only laughed.

THE PUBLIC MARINA where Toby docked the mail boat in the island town of Key West was a hubbub of activity. Stuart stood up as Toby made the lines fast.

"Might as well get this show on the road," he told Angel.

She bit her lip. "You don't have to sound so...so..." Her words trailed off.

"Well, go on," he said.

"You sound so nonchalant," she finished.

This only caused Stuart to shrug before turning to Toby and arranging for him to drop their overnight bags off at the Kapok Tree Resort Hotel.

"You going to stay in Key West for a while?" Toby asked.

"Overnight," Angel said.

"Well, I guess I should offer my congratulations or something," Toby said, scratching his head.

"Or something," Angel agreed, making her way nimbly over the side of the boat despite her high heels.

"Congratulations, then," Toby said, as if as an afterthought.

"I don't think he likes this idea," Stuart said under his breath once they were walking up the dock.

Angel shrugged. "Does it matter?" she said.

"Toby's a nice guy. Maybe he deserves some sort of explanation."

"You explain it. I can't," Angel said, thinking that the world of seeking mates through the personals columns would be anathema to the ultratraditional Toby.

Their progress along the dock was impeded while a fisherman scooped a flopping fish into a net and dumped it into a water-filled bucket. A group of children clamored to board a sleek speedboat. Nearby, two old men sat playing dominoes, slapping the tiles down on the bottom of an upended fish barrel and cackling loudly with each slap.

"That looks like fun," Stuart observed.

"They play every day," Angel replied.

"How would you know? You said you don't come to town often," he said.

"I come once a month or so to buy groceries. Whenever I do, those fellows are playing dominoes."

"Ever challenge them to a game?"

"No. I always go back to Halos Island as soon as I buy my supplies. Key West is a touristy kind of place, and all the sightseers get on my nerves."

"The tourists seem like a friendly group to me."

"They block intersections and slow traffic on the sidewalks."

"In your white dress and heels, you look like you could be a tourist yourself today," he told her.

"Great," she muttered.

Stuart thought maybe he had said the wrong thing. He tried to think of some way to put Angel at ease. "I didn't get to spend any time here when I got off the commuter flight from Miami. I caught the mail boat as soon as we landed. Tell me a little bit about Key West," he said.

"I'm not good at travelogues."

"You're really nervous, aren't you?"

"Just because I'm not good at travelogues doesn't mean I'm nervous," she retorted, regaining a bit of her usual equilibrium.

"All right, all right. Don't tell me anything. Never mind that I've spent very little time on this island, never mind that I want to know a little about its history, never mind—"

"All right," Angel said, deciding that she might as well humor him. "The Spaniards called this island Cayo

Hueso, or Island of the Bones, because they found human bones lying around when they came here," she said. She took a devilish pleasure in relating this grisly detail; still, it was more interesting than the usual tourist-guide fluff.

"Whose bones?"

"No one knows. Maybe pirates' bones, or Caloosas' bones."

"Caloosa's?"

She couldn't help smiling at the horrified look on Stuart's face. "Not my Caloosa's. I named my cat after the Caloosa Indians, who lived in the Keys, maybe even on Halos Island. They were all either killed or they died off due to encroaching civilization. No remnants of the tribe exist. Anyway, the name Cayo Hueso was eventually corrupted to Key West, or so the story goes."

"Pretty gruesome history, which makes me wonder why I've only heard of Key West as a haven for artists and writers."

"They came along later. Caloosa—my cat Caloosa, I mean—was born in Ernest Hemingway's house. She's a descendant of his own cat and, like many of her brothers and sisters and aunts and uncles who still live in the house, Caloosa has six toes on each foot."

"Six?"

"Six. You'll notice if she ever claws you."

"No chance of that. We're friends, Caloosa and me," he said, recalling too late how she had betrayed him in the palm grove.

If Angel was thinking of that episode, she gave no sign. "Anyway," she said, "President Harry Truman found Key West so pleasant that he established his winter White House here, and Jimmy Buffett got his start here singing about Margaritaville, and Tennessee Williams lived here, too. That's Key West in a nutshell, and I haven't begun to do it justice.''

They were walking past yards lush with hibiscus, frangipani and mango trees; the houses were fine and ornate. With a distinct air of taking charge, Stuart took Angel's elbow when they came to a curb.

"Maybe I'll get to know this place better while I'm here. Now, back to business. First we'll buy the ring. Do you know a good jewelry store?"

"I don't want a ring," Angel said.

"We can't get married without a ring," Stuart insisted.

Angel went over the wedding ceremony in her mind. "There has to be a witness. A wedding band is probably optional," she said.

"The wedding ceremony says, 'With this ring I thee wed.' How can there not be a ring?" he reasoned.

Angel sighed. "All right, so there has to be a wedding ring. It could be a nose ring or a belly-button ring, for all I care," she said.

"As far as I know, you lack the proper apertures for one of those. Unless you want me to find someone who will oblige us by piercing your navel in time for the ceremony," he suggested, the corners of his mouth twitching.

"Thanks, but I'll pass on that. Couldn't we find a gum-ball machine and hope to win a nice plastic ring?"

"Those aren't exactly made to last."

"Neither is this marriage," Angel said.

That shut him up. They walked in silence for a block or two before turning onto a main thoroughfare in the historic Old Town district, where they immediately encountered a jewelry store. Stuart slowed his footsteps, peering through the polished plate-glass window.

"Let's go in and take a look," he said. He marched Angel into the store, where the air-conditioning hit her in the face like a blast of arctic air and where the unctuous jeweler was only too happy to trot out his wares.

"Now here's a lovely wedding band," the man said, setting it reverently on a midnight-blue velvet pad. "It's eighteen-karat gold and has eight channel-set diamonds, each of them an eighth of a carat." He turned the ring this way and that so that the diamonds flashed in the light from the well-placed overhead spotlight.

"Nice," said Stuart in instant approval.

The jeweler turned to Angel. "Would you like to try it on?"

"It's too fancy," she said bluntly.

"Too fancy?"

"The stones. They're gaudy," she said, wishing that she was anywhere but here. She didn't like jewelry; she never wore it.

"Perhaps you'd like something in brushed gold," the jeweler said. "I have a lovely wide gold band with small diamonds set in a swirl pattern." He took it out and displayed it. Angel hated it.

"Maybe something more classic," Stuart suggested after a glance at her forbidding expression.

"This is a charming Victorian-style band, carved with roses and lilies of the valley," the man said, pulling out a case and flipping open the top.

"Very attractive," Stuart said. "Don't you think so, Angel?"

"I was thinking of something in plastic," she muttered.

"I beg your pardon?" said the jeweler, but Stuart's eyebrows drew together in a silent warning.

Angel escaped to another section of the store. The jeweler hurriedly began to put away his display items as Stuart joined her.

"You're embarrassing me," he hissed.

"There's no point in spending a lot of money on a ring I'll never wear," she hissed back.

"Pick one out and let's get out of here," Stuart said. He sounded completely fed up.

The jeweler joined them. "See something you like?"

Angel looked down and pointed blindly. "I'll take that one," she said.

The jeweler removed the ring from the case. It was a wide filigree gold band with beaded edges, stunning in its craftsmanship. He held it out so that she could try it on.

"Put it on," Stuart said.

She looked at him. "I don't—"

"Angel," he said, and, unwilling to make a scene, Angel held out her third finger, left hand. The jeweler slipped it on and beamed. "Such a wise choice," he said approvingly. "So perfect for your finger."

Angel studied the ring and admitted to herself that it did look nice. The gold of the ring complemented the golden tones of her skin, and the wide band was attractive. It was the kind of wedding band she would have chosen to wear for a lifetime. *If* she'd intended to stay married for a lifetime.

"I like it," Stuart said. "Angel?"

"It's fine," Angel said, tugging the ring off her finger and replacing it in the velvet slot in its box. The jeweler gave her an odd look, but she didn't care. If she'd ever stopped to consider what other people thought, this plan would never have progressed this far.

"There, that's done," Stuart said, sounding pleased as they emerged from the jewelry shop. The heat and glare of a Key West afternoon hit Angel full force, and she found that she had nothing to say. But, of course, Stuart did.

"You're the first woman I've ever had to force to let me buy her a piece of jewelry," he said.

She shot him a sidelong glance. "And do you go around buying jewelry for women on an indiscriminate basis?"

"Never. I'm very discriminating," he said lightly.

"No girl in every port?"

"No" was all he said, and when she ventured a look, his lips were drawn into a firm line and his overall expression could only be described as closed and shuttered.

He changed the subject. "Where to next?"

"The home pregnancy test kit. We can buy one at the drugstore," she said. Stuart took her arm again as they crossed the street.

Angel traded at this particular drugstore often, but this was the first time she'd ever been here on an errand remotely resembling this one. "I wonder where they keep those things, anyway," she said, looking around once they were inside the door.

"Home pregnancy test kits? Maybe they're with the baby stuff," Stuart said, leading the way down an aisle marked Baby.

He stopped in front of a rack full of pacifiers, baby powder and infant formula, and Angel felt a little thrill at the thought that soon she would be buying these things for her very own baby. The round, angelic faces of the babies on the packages enchanted her with their sweetness and good cheer. Her baby would look like these, she mused, touching a finger to the picture of a blond cherub on a box of disposable diapers. But maybe her baby would have dark hair, like Stuart.

"The pregnancy test kits must be someplace else," Stuart said, wandering in another direction. Angel followed, but only after a lingering, longing look at a pair of cunning yellow booties in a cellophane box. She could imagine her baby wearing them, the little legs bicycling energetically, the tiny rosebud mouth emitting gentle coos from time to time.

"Angel? Here they are," Stuart called.

The pregnancy test kits were shelved with the contraceptives. Angel glanced covertly at Stuart, who had bent down to pick up one of the packages from a lower shelf. If he had noticed the company the test kits were keeping, he gave no sign.

"Hmm..." Stuart said. "There are lots to choose from. I had no idea there was so much variety in these things."

"Neither did I," Angel said. She felt more than slightly embarrassed to be browsing through these products with a man she'd only known for three days.

Stuart picked up a blue-and-white package and studied the directions. Angel read them over his shoulder, realizing that there were tremendous gaps in her knowledge about such things. Finding out if you were pregnant seemed to involve a bodily process that she would rather not think about in the company of Stuart, and when she realized that the whole procedure would have to be conducted in the drafty outhouse in the presence of its resident spider, she began to think that waiting a week or two after a missed period and making an appointment with a gynecologist was a much more sensible idea.

"This one has a stick that turns blue if the results are positive. Imagine that!" Stuart said.

"Let me see," Angel said. He handed her the package and picked up another one, skimming through the instructions quickly. "Here's one that gives the results in three minutes and turns green. How long does that one take?"

"Four minutes," Angel said. "I think I'd rather see a gynecologist and let a nice nurse take care of all this." She put the package back on the shelf, ignoring the teenage boy who skulked past, carefully not looking at the vast array of condoms.

"*You* might not want to know as soon as you're pregnant, but what about *me?*" Stuart said indignantly.

"What about you, Stuart?" she said evenly.

"I'll want to know immediately. In three minutes. Let's take this one." He waved the test kit in front of her.

It was perfectly clear to Angel that Stuart wanted to know as soon as possible when she was pregnant because then he would be free to leave Halos Island. She made a show of arranging the packages on the shelf, making them neat. Should she mention her distaste for the procedure involved? Should she mention the spider in the outhouse?

"Angel?"

"I don't care which one you get. Suit yourself, Stuart. While you're mulling it over, I'll be waiting for you in the toothbrush section," she said, fleeing to the far wall.

When she had wasted enough time reading the labels of various dental products, she steeled herself to face the inevitable and met Stuart at the checkout counter, where he was in the process of paying for six home pregnancy tests. She thought of pointing out that six was far too many, that one—maybe two—would be plenty. However, for once she didn't want to think about the pregnancy. All she wanted to do at this point was get on with the wedding.

The clerk bagged their purchases and, her cheeks burning in embarrassment, Angel preceded an all-too-chipper Stuart out the door.

"All right. County courthouse, here we come," Stuart said with an air of lightheartedness that she couldn't hope to match. Angel wished that she could adopt some of his enthusiasm, but it had turned into a long afternoon, her dress was wilting in the humidity, and a blister was raising on her left heel.

When they reached the courthouse, they were directed to the marriage license office where a lackadaisical clerk shoved the proper forms across the counter and handed them pens. "Fill in the blanks, sign, and pay the fee. If you wish to be married in the courthouse, you must go next door and request an appointment with the proper person," she said.

"Appointment?" Angel said. "No one said anything about an appointment when I inquired about the license."

The clerk eyed her balefully. "Key West is a popular place for people to elope, which is why all the people who are qualified to perform the marriage ceremony around here keep real busy. See all these other couples waiting in here? They're in line ahead of you," she said.

A quick survey of the room's occupants told them that the place was doing a brisk business today. They turned to look at each other at precisely the same moment.

"I'd better run next door and make the appointment," Stuart said.

"Good idea," she said, glad that she didn't have to do it. She felt like she was on display here, with several couples standing and sitting around and all of them seemingly interested in her. Or maybe they were interested in Stuart, who was, after all, extremely handsome.

After Stuart left, Angel ignored the stares of the other couples and bent over the form, diligently filling in the blanks. *Current street address.* Now that was a toughie. Angel thought of putting "Sail due west for several nautical miles, walk up the dock and past the royal poinciana tree, house is ten paces from the left-hand banyan," but thought better of it. The clerk did not look like one who would let that pass without making a problem.

Stuart returned quickly, looking harried.

"Did you make our appointment?" she asked without looking up.

"Don't be disappointed, Angel," he said soberly, "but there's no way we're going to get married today, at least not here. Every time slot is taken."

Chapter Five

They couldn't possibly postpone the wedding, not during the few days of the month that comprised her most fertile period.

"We'll have to go somewhere else, then," Angel said, starting to feel panicky. She turned to the clerk. "Where else can we be married?"

The clerk responded in an indifferent drawl. "You can get married right here at the courthouse. If you wait until tomorrow morning, that is."

"We can't. You see, it's urgent," Angel said, not thinking.

The clerk's mouth formed into an O, and her gaze dropped to the gentle curve of Angel's abdomen. "I see," she said, as if she really didn't.

"Oh, no," Angel said unconvincingly, "it's not like that. I live—I mean, we live—on an island, and we came in on the mail boat, and we have to get back before too late tomorrow, in case Caloosa runs out of food."

Stuart, having filled out his form by this time, sized up the situation. "And," he said, taking Angel's hand and gazing deeply into her eyes, "we're very much in love."

Angel yanked her hand away. "What we need to know is, where else can we get married without waiting until tomorrow?" She kicked Stuart in the ankle to make him stop looking at her like that.

"A notary public or a minister can marry you. I heard tell that a captain of a boat can marry you, but probably not the captain of the mail boat," the woman said.

Looking more than a little annoyed with the clerk, Stuart shoved a handful of bills across the counter in payment for the license. "Come on, Angel, we'll find somebody," he said. He took her hand.

They were halfway out the door when the clerk called after them. "Hey, you two, don't you think you'd better wait for your marriage license? It ain't ready yet, but it will be."

Sheepishly they returned and sat down on the edges of two of the wobbly plastic chairs, enduring the avidly curious glances of the other couples, who had heard the whole conversation. Finally the clerk beckoned Angel over to the counter and handed her the license.

"Let's go," said Stuart, and when he stood up, all six of the home pregnancy test kits fell out of the bag and clattered to the floor. The other couples stared, and one middle-aged woman held a hand to her mouth and tittered.

Angel fled, leaving Stuart to pick them up and stuff them into the bag.

Stuart caught up with her in the hallway, but it wasn't until they were outside the courthouse that they finally dared to look at each other. When she saw the red flush on Stuart's cheeks, Angel couldn't help it. She started to laugh.

He bit his lip, and then he was laughing, too. They laughed together, in a marvelous tension-breaking cascade of mirth that left them gasping so hard that they collapsed onto a nearby bench.

When he was able, Stuart slid an arm around Angel's shoulders. "You know what the guy next to me said?"

"What?"

"He said, 'No wonder you're in a hurry to get married.'"

"I wonder what he'd say if he knew the truth," she said, growing somber.

"I'm never telling anyone the truth." Stuart said. "I wouldn't want our baby to learn that his parents didn't have a real marriage, that it was only a...a..." He couldn't think of the proper term.

"A marriage of convenience," Angel supplied.

"As far as I'm concerned, we met and married after a whirlwind courtship, and it didn't work out."

Angel met his resolute look with one of her own. "All right," she said. "I'll stick to that story, too."

They sat quietly for a moment, each lost in thought.

"You didn't have to pretend to the clerk that we're in love," Angel said after a while.

"I didn't like the way she was looking at you."

"You mean because I was making such a fool of myself?"

"No, because you didn't sound like a woman who is eager to be married. You were putting practical considerations first—like getting back to Halos Island—when what the clerk and everyone else in there wanted to hear was how much we're in love. The whole world opens its hearts to lovers, you know. I figured that if she thought we were so in love that we couldn't wait to be married, she'd find a way for us to have the ceremony then and there."

"Instead, we're on our own. So much for the whole world opening its hearts to lovers." A sudden thought occurred to her. "Stuart, would you mind...that is, would you care if we were married in a church?"

"No, of course not. Do you have a particular one in mind?"

"Any one will do. Let's just get this over with," she said.

Stuart stood up. "We'd better look for a church before they all close," he said, taking her hand in his. This time, holding hands didn't feel at all unnatural or forced.

They found a small church on one of the streets frequented by tourists, and the minister happened to be carrying a bag of groceries into the parsonage when they approached him.

He invited them inside the cool, shadowy house, looked them over carefully, and insisted on conducting a premarital interview in his study. He eased himself onto a bulky leather chair behind a large desk, and they sat on two uncomfortable office chairs, nervous and hardly daring to look at each other.

"Well," he said, regarding them affably through thick glasses, "so you've decided to get married."

Stuart cleared his throat. "Yes," he said.

"Have you known each other long?"

"Long enough to know that this is what we want to do," Angel said quickly before Stuart could give his version of an answer.

"Marriage is a big step. People often enter into it ill-advisedly without considering its consequences," said the minister.

"Not us," Stuart said. "We both know what we want. We've thought about the consequences in great detail."

"Yes," Angel agreed, and then clamped her mouth shut. She wished they could just be married. She didn't want to have to explain her reasons. She didn't want to have to defend her choice.

"And what exactly is that?" the minister shot back.

This caught Angel off guard. "What is what?" she blurted out, earning her a sharp look from Stuart.

"What you want? What you expect?"

"Children. A happy home," Angel said helpfully.

At that moment, three bright-eyed kids popped into the study. "Who's that?" asked the smallest, a girl.

"That's the bride," the minister said affectionately. The girl climbed on his knee.

"If there's a wedding, can we go?"

"Of course," the minister said, gently setting the girl down and pushing her toward the door. "Ask your mother to give you some rice for after the ceremony. We'll want to give this happy couple a nice send-off."

"Rice! Rice!" shouted the children, clattering down the hall.

"Now, where were we?" the minister asked Stuart.

"My fiancée was just saying how much we want to have children," Stuart said smoothly.

"Ah, yes. Children are a great blessing. Well, it's getting late. Would you prefer to be married in my study or in the sanctuary?"

"You—you mean you'll marry us?" Angel stammered.

"My wife would object. She'd tell you that I'm already married," he said, smiling benevolently.

Angel smiled back. So did Stuart.

"My study or the sanctuary?" prompted the minister.

"The church," Angel said. "Stuart, is that okay?"

He reached for her hand. "Very much okay," he said reassuringly.

The church was quiet and smelled of leather-bound hymnals; the late-afternoon sun shone through stained-glass windows to cast rainbow colors across the altar. The best man was the aged custodian, who grinned a big, toothless grin throughout the ceremony and dropped the ring so that it rolled under the first pew. The maid of honor was a plump, florid church member who was in the process of removing old flower arrangements from the altar when pressed into service by the minister, who seemed intent on doing everything just right.

The maid of honor, a flower enthusiast of the first degree, became indignant at the thought of any bride's going through the wedding ceremony without a bouquet. She insisted on holding up the ceremony until even the minister was impatiently tapping his foot, while she ventured into the parsonage garden. She eventually emerged with a hastily assembled clump of red hibiscus blossoms, which she shoved unceremoniously into Angel's hands.

The wedding drew a few onlookers, such as the man who had been selling Popsicles from a cart, and the minister's children, who sat quietly in a back pew and stared in awe at Angel in her white dress. At the point in the ceremony where Angel was told to join hands with Stuart, the maid of honor relieved Angel of her bouquet and proceeded to hiccup into it during the rest of the ceremony.

Angel moved through the ritual as if sleepwalking, saying all the right words, going through all the motions, but oddly enough, she didn't feel a thing.

A meaningless ritual, she told herself, *that's all it is.* But at the same time she was aware that this wedding bore only a passing resemblance to the wedding she had once wanted to have. In fact, this ceremony put her in mind of a dog-and-pony show. Instead of several bridesmaids for attendants, she had this one slightly dippy lady, and instead of a church full of friends and relatives, there were three children she didn't know and a Popsicle man. If she'd thought of it, she could have had him supply music, which was sadly lacking. If she remembered correctly from past visits to Key West, his cart played "Waltzing Matilda."

Stuart, standing at her side, looked appropriately serious, and he showed a great deal of patience with the poor old custodian when the man dropped the ring. And when he spoke the words "I, Stuart, take thee, Angel," a shiver coursed through her in spite of her lack of feeling.

In that moment, she had an inkling of what it would be like to really marry Stuart Adams—to be the one with whom he'd chosen to live his life—and she felt the sudden, unexpected prick of tears behind her eyelids.

To love somebody for better or worse, for richer and for poorer, in sickness and in health—that was a tall order. As she said the words to him, she was suddenly struck by their import. "As long as we both shall live," she heard herself say, and then she realized that indeed it was as the minister had said at the beginning of the ceremony: The state of matrimony was not to be entered into lightly, and yet, she saw now, that was exactly what she and Stuart were doing.

But were they? A baby would result. An honest-to-goodness miracle. There was nothing "lightly" about that.

"And now," said the minister, breaking into her reverie, "I pronounce you husband and wife. Sir, you may kiss the bride."

In a daze, Angel stared up at Stuart, at his eyes, gone dark with an inexplicable emotion, at his hair, falling so unruly over his forehead.

Maybe I could love this man, she thought in a moment of pure shock, as his head bent over hers and she raised her lips to his.

She was taken by surprise by the expression in Stuart's eyes as he touched his lips to hers, tentatively at first, then more surely. Had the words they'd both spoken affected him as well? He looked so—sad? Confused? Sentimental? *All of the above,* she thought.

When they kissed, the children at the back of the church cheered and the maid of honor beamed. And then Stuart released her, and Angel held his eyes for one long moment with her own. The next thing they knew, the minister was shaking their hands, the maid of honor was insisting on hugging Angel, crushing the hibiscus bouquet between them, and the custodian was cackling in toothless glee.

"Well, that's it," Stuart said to Angel, and she managed a little half smile in reply. They walked slowly down the aisle toward the door, afraid to look at each other.

To Angel's surprise, the Popsicle man and the children were lined up in front of the church, and they pelted them with rice as they ran down the steps.

"Good luck!" called the maid of honor.

"Goodbye, goodbye!" called the children.

The voices echoed in their ears until they turned the corner and stopped abruptly to stare at each other.

"Well," Angel said.

"Yes," Stuart said, loosening his tie. He pulled it off and stuffed it in his jacket pocket.

She stared at him for a moment longer, trying to keep the idea of the baby in mind as a kind of justification for the marriage. For once she couldn't imagine the baby's little face or the small fingers that would curve so sweetly around her own. The baby wasn't at all clear in her mind; what was clear was Stuart, staring at her as if he had never seen her before.

"We should have hired a car to take us to our hotel," Stuart said finally. "I didn't think of it."

"We can walk," she said.

He took her arm and drew it through his as they started down the street.

"Mrs. Stuart Adams," he said, trying to sound jolly.

Angel tried to laugh, but couldn't. She couldn't think of anything to say at all; she felt bereft somehow, and her mind was a blank. She had an idea that this was how zombies went through life, without a thought in their heads, mindlessly putting one foot in front of the other.

"How do you feel?" Stuart said.

She thought fast. "Married," she said, though she didn't at all.

"Don't you feel a sense of completion? Of taking the first step toward your goal?"

She didn't. Maybe she should. Maybe she did but didn't know it yet. "Something like that," she said, hoping Stuart was also in a state where he couldn't think, couldn't comprehend the enormity of what they had done.

"We should have dinner. A wedding feast," he said.

"That's not necessary," she said, even as she realized that, having completed the first step, it was time to move on to the second one. It was time to go to the hotel.

He was looking down at her with an appealing earnestness, and she thought that he might be as reluctant to go to the hotel right away as she was.

"I'm sure there are wonderful restaurants in Key West, and how often do you get to go to them?" he asked.

"Almost never," she admitted.

"And isn't Nouvella's considered the best restaurant in town?"

"I wouldn't know."

"That's the word I picked up at the Miami marina," he said. "I think we should go there and have a leisurely drink and dinner, maybe dance a bit—"

"Stuart, you don't have to do any of this," she interjected.

He looked hurt. "I know, Angel, but it's my wedding, too. We're going back to Halos Island tomorrow morning, and who knows when we'll get back into town?"

Suddenly Angel saw this situation from Stuart's perspective. Halos Island was the most fascinating place on earth to her, but he probably found it boring. When they returned there, she would continue her work, while Stuart would have nothing to do but... Stuart would have nothing to do but be her drone.

"Angel?"

The thought of Stuart as a drone buzzing around her honey almost made her laugh, but there wasn't anything funny about it. While he was waiting for her to get pregnant, he would probably miss being around other people, going out for a drink and eating in good restaurants.

"All right," she said. "Nouvella's it is. I *am* hungry."

He grinned. "So am I. And not only for food."

Angel's stomach seemed to take a dive, and suddenly she wasn't hungry at all.

NOUVELLA'S was quiet and elegant, and they were solicitously seated at a choice table on a patio overlooking the ocean, probably due to the fact that Stuart slipped the maître d' a sizable wad of bills. Angel ignored this by-play; instead, she listened to the floating strains of show tunes and dance classics played by the band inside. She could see dancers moving in and out of the candlelight, dark shadows ebbing and flowing with the music.

The wine steward promptly trotted out a bottle of Moët et Chandon, pouring both of them a generous glass.

"To...our baby," Stuart said, holding his glass up to hers.

At least he hadn't toasted their marriage, which would have made even more of a mockery of it.

"Our baby," Angel agreed, and promptly sneezed from the champagne bubbles tickling her nose.

Stuart smiled at her across the table. "Do you really feel married? I certainly don't."

She shook her head. "Maybe we never will," she said, with a certain amount of wistfulness.

"Maybe not," he agreed. "Although maybe after we—"

Her head shot up. "I doubt that the sex act itself is what makes people feel married," she said.

He watched her steadily. "Then, in your opinion, what does?"

Angel considered this. It wasn't easy to think with the way he was looking at her, his eyes never leaving her face. She looked away to give herself a chance to summon coherent thoughts.

"I think people must feel married when they've lowered all the barriers between them," she said. "When they've achieved real intimacy by sharing every detail of their lives, past and present, and by beginning to think of themselves as a unit. As a *we,* rather than two separate *I*s."

"Ah" was all he said, but he was still staring at her.

"Is anything wrong?" she asked.

He shook his head. "You're a beautiful bride, Angel, you turned heads wherever we went today," he said.

"Only because I'm wearing a long-sleeved dress in the middle of May," she said. Her glass was already empty, and a waiter came by and refilled it.

"No, Angel, it was because you're so pretty. I hope our baby inherits the shape and color of your eyes."

"But not my vision. I started to wear glasses when I was a kid."

"You don't wear them now," he pointed out.

"I wear contact lenses. Glasses got in my way on the island, always sliding down the bridge of my nose, or falling off, or getting smudged."

"Okay, our baby will have my perfect eyesight," he agreed.

She smiled at him, pleased that he was referring to the baby as theirs and not hers.

Dinner, broiled Florida lobster and tiny new potatoes and a big green salad, arrived, and Angel watched Stuart from under her lashes as they ate. Later, over after-dinner drinks, Stuart pushed his chair back and regarded Angel with a half smile. His dark hair gleamed with blue-black highlights, and his white shirt was open at the neckline to reveal a mat of dark, curly hair. His blue gaze took in her flushed cheeks, the low neckline of her dress, and finally her finger with his ring on it. She was unnerved by the air of pure possession that she detected in that look.

He shoved his chair back. "Let's dance," he said imperatively, and before she knew it, they were swaying to and fro on the tiny dance floor, separated by only an inch or two of space. Other people were watching, noticing, and in that moment, Angel felt proud to be seen with

Stuart. He was a handsome man; she was the envy of every woman on the dance floor.

Stuart guided her skillfully past other dancers on the floor. His sure sense of rhythm made him easy to follow, and he held her with assurance. She tipped her head back to look at him.

"Where'd you learn to dance like this?" she asked.

"At Boston's best dancing school. Dancing lessons at Miss Beatrice's Junior Cotillion were de rigueur for members of our social set."

Angel inadvertently stepped on his foot, and he winced.

"I didn't have the advantage of dancing school, in case you haven't guessed by now," she told him. In her social set, in the scrubby little town in north Florida where she'd grown up, the only lessons outside the classroom had come from the school of hard knocks.

"You're doing fine. Relax a bit." He swirled her around so that her skirt rippled around their legs. "That's it, that's better," he said.

"I've never been a good dancer," she said, thinking of Howard and how he'd always scoffed at her for having two left feet.

"You're light on your feet, and you're easy to lead. That makes a good dancer in my book. With a little more practice..." he said, his voice tapering off as he drew her closer.

It was easier to follow his lead when he held her so close; she was able to detect nuances in the direction of his body before his hand guided her. For a moment, she closed her eyes, letting herself enjoy this experience. The champagne was singing softly in her veins, the music played gently in her ears, and, with her hand resting lightly on Stuart's shoulder, she could admire the way the unwanted wedding ring looked on her finger.

She should be happy. And it was odd, but she did feel a slight intimation of happiness, as if it were right around the corner, eluding her. For a moment, she could almost believe that this was the real thing—a real marriage and a real husband—and not the farce that it actually was.

She was utterly aware of Stuart's arm around her, of his hand holding hers so strongly and so surely. He held her close, her body barely touching his, but it was enough contact to make her aware of the heat emanating from him. Her breasts brushed his chest, sending flash fires of excitement coursing through her, making her nipples tender and tight. Without warning, he pulled her closer, so that she was pressed against him from chest to thigh.

The champagne sharpened her senses, making her notice the tangy fragrance of Stuart's after-shave, making his face seem brighter, making his eyes more blue. She moved in a haze, feeling light-headed and weak, and she knew somewhere in the dim recesses of her mind that Stuart was caught up in the same feeling.

She heard him sigh, his hot breath fluttering against her ear, as he released her right hand and slid his arm around her waist. Her free hand crept up his arm until her fingers linked around his neck. They found themselves in a dark corner of the dance floor, where they danced with their bodies gently swaying, their feet barely moving. They were caught up in the music's spell, and their own.

"Angel," Stuart said, his voice a mere murmur, "let's get out of here."

It took only a few minutes to pay the check, and before Angel knew what was happening, they were outside the restaurant and Stuart was hailing a cab. On the way to the hotel, she caught herself up short, thinking about the next step.

He might find her performance in bed wanting, but she could always fake her pleasure. That was easy enough for a woman, and, in Angel's limited experience, most men seemed to fall for a few well-spaced gasps and groans, especially if in the process, the woman managed to cry out the man's name. So, okay, she could manage a phony orgasm, but what about pleasing *him?* What if she made a fool of herself? What if she didn't do everything the way he liked it? It took a long time to establish a satisfactory sexual relationship; some people never managed it, as Angel well knew. What if the experience turned out to be, well, an ordeal for Stuart?

If it happened that way, could she bear his disappointment, even his scorn? Well, she'd have to, wouldn't she? If she wanted a baby.

Maybe they would get it over with quickly. Maybe it would be nothing more than a mechanical juxtaposition of body parts, signifying nothing and meaning even less.

Think about the baby, she told herself sternly. She pictured the babies on baby food jars, in magazine ads, on disposable-diaper packages. She pictured babies in pink organdy dresses and babies in blue denim rompers and babies wearing nothing at all.

She pictured Stuart Adams wearing nothing at all, and she almost melted with anticipation.

Then they were at the Kapok Tree Resort Hotel, one of the nicest and newest in Key West, checking in amid a flurry of activity. She stood silently as Stuart signed the check-in form, somehow surprised and yet not surprised to see him write, "Mr. and Mrs. Stuart Adams."

She was Mrs. Stuart Adams. *She* was. She hadn't thought that the ramifications of her new status would affect her at all; to her, the married state had seemed peripheral to the real reason for marrying Stuart. She stood beside him, feeling one step removed, trying not to worry about what would be required of her once they were alone. When the bellman conducted them to their room, she kept her eyes focused downward, afraid that he would guess that they were not typical honeymooners.

Their accommodations turned out to be one of the hotel's honeymoon suites. The two rooms and a bath overlooked the point where the waters of the Atlantic Ocean and the Gulf of Mexico were seamed together by the silver path laid across the faintly rippling water by a three-quarter moon. While Stuart adopted an air of nonchalance, the bellman flipped switches and adjusted draperies. Angel, feeling more curious than bridelike, peeked into the bedroom to see a huge king-size bed swathed in silken draperies; the living area ended in a series of steps to a walled terrace, where a heart-shaped sunken hot tub bubbled invitingly. It was a scene of pure luxury, and she hadn't expected anything like it.

"We don't need such an elaborate room," she protested after the bellman had completed his seemingly endless chores and left.

"I know, but I told Toby to request a honeymoon suite when he delivered our overnight bags. I wanted it to be special," Stuart said.

"It wouldn't have had to be," she said.

"For you, it did," he said, his eyes bright.

Suddenly she didn't know where to look. If she focused straight ahead, she'd be staring at the cleft in Stuart's chin. If she lifted her eyelids, she'd have to look directly into his eyes, which suddenly seemed like too great an intimacy. Instead, she looked away, her mouth growing dry, her mind groping for something to say.

Nothing presented itself, and she realized that she wanted Stuart to touch her. To kiss her. To do something, for heaven's sake.

"Well," he said. "Here we are."

"Here we are," she agreed.

"Married," he said.

"Married," she repeated. A silence. "We've only known each other for three days," she said into the void.

"Longer than that, if we count the letter-writing stage."

"What was it? Two weeks? Three?"

"Long enough for me to know that this is what I wanted to do," he said.

"Do...do you still want to?" she asked him, holding her breath. What if he said no?

His eyes were the deep blue of sapphires. "I've wanted to make love to you ever since I saw you tripping your way down the dock when I arrived," he said.

"No regrets?" she murmured.

"Not yet," he replied. "How about you?"

She swallowed. "The same," she said.

"Take those shoes off. You look like they're killing you."

They were and she did, immediately becoming several inches shorter. "I suppose we should, um..." she said, indicating the bedroom with a wave of one hand.

"Or we could, um..." he said, his wave indicating the hot tub. "You decide." She sensed a barely contained impatience, but he held it in.

She managed a tight little laugh. "I guess I could test the temperature of the water," she said. She started toward the terrace.

Tiny points of starlight danced in the dark ripples of the hot tub. She balanced carefully on the edge, and

Stuart caught her hand to support her as she gingerly dipped a toe in the water.

"How is it?"

"Just right," she said. She wavered on the edge of the tub, and he spanned her waist with both hands and swung her down.

"Want to try it?"

She shrugged. A breeze from the shore rustled the palm fronds overhead, and clouds scudded across the moon.

"Don't be nervous," he said, his gaze locking with hers. "We're going to make love, and it's going to be wonderful."

"We've come this far, so we might as well finish what we started out to do," she said jokingly.

"We really have no choice," he agreed, a faint smile touching the corners of his mouth.

"In fact, in order for our contract to be valid, we must consummate the marriage," she said, staring resolutely at the knot in his tie.

"The contract be damned," he said with feeling. He wrapped his arms around her and fumbled with the buttons at the back of her dress. "Aren't you slightly overdressed for your wedding night?" he said.

She reached around, her fingers encountering his as she slid the buttons through the buttonholes. In the meantime, his hands found their way to her outthrust breasts and caressed them through the fabric. His touch sent a ripple of excitement through her.

Once she unbuttoned it, the dress fell away from her shoulders, and Stuart moved his fingers upward to hook them around the neckline. As he eased it down, she heard his sharp intake of breath at the sight of her breasts, contained in the wispy white bra.

"You are so beautiful," he said, cupping his hands around the lush lower contours of her breasts.

"No," she said, shaking her head in denial. A flutter of delicate petals from the orchids in her hair rained down upon her face, nestled in the hollow between her breasts.

"Beautiful," he said. "You are." Her eyelids drifted closed as she let her growing arousal penetrate to the marrow of her bones. With one hand, he brushed away the soft strands of hair in front of her ear, threaded his fingers through her braid and loosened it from its pins. Her hair cascaded around her shoulders, releasing its scent to mingle with the fragrance of the nearby frangipani trees and the honeysuckle arching over the high terrace wall.

His hand came to rest on the curve of her cheek. She instinctively tilted her head for his kiss. His mouth found hers, drawing her into a warm, sweet blending of lips and tongue that ignited a flame deep inside her, a flame that grew and grew until she felt consumed by its heat. Carefully he unhooked her bra and brushed it aside, along with a flurry of fallen flower petals, then unbuttoned his shirt so that her breasts grazed the curly hair on his chest. It was a delightful sensation, exquisitely arousing.

He took his time kissing her, delicately tracing her lips with the tip of his tongue and then following with a stronger thrust and parry, his mouth fierce and seeking. She found herself responding with unprecedented ardor. With a soft moan of pleasure at her eager response, he slid his hands down her body to her buttocks and pulled her to him, so that the full length of their bodies was pressed together, crushing the aching round fullness of her breasts against his chest.

She was swept away on a tide of sensation, was lost in it. Her head was swimming, floating, dizzy, and she had the unexpected sensation of drowning in his kisses. Kissing Stuart Adams was like nothing she had ever experienced before, a mad delirium fraught with possibilities that she had heretofore only imagined. And imagination was never like this, never so exquisite, never so incredibly real.

Her dress dropped to her feet, pooling in soft folds around her ankles, and Stuart continued to kiss her as he tucked his fingers into her panties. Slowly, so slowly that she almost stopped breathing, he peeled the gauzy fabric downward. Now she stood before him completely naked, terrified that he wouldn't like the way she looked.

"Angel," he said reverently, unable to take his eyes off her. "Oh, Angel."

No feeling in the world could ever compare to the way she felt when he looked at her with such adoration. She felt humility in the presence of his admiration, and she felt wonder, and joy. She pleased him.

It should have been enough to have him looking at her that way, but all she could think was that, as much as her body was for him, his was for her. She reached for his belt and began to unbuckle it.

Belt, hook, zipper, underwear, and finally hot, pulsing flesh. He gasped as she released him from his briefs. She dared to look at him, her eyes eager, her hands ready to learn the geography of this man who was now her husband, and who was kissing her, touching her, evoking her hidden sensuality. She closed her eyes and sent herself into a darkness where sensation was all; she wrapped her fingers around him, exploring the hard ridges and folds of his sex, learning him by touch, knowing the powerful exultation of possession.

His rough beard bit into her chin, his hands claimed her breasts. She heard her own breathing harsh in her throat, and she couldn't inhale enough air, couldn't get her breath, was gasping with a wildness that was totally foreign to the Angel McCabe she had been only a few minutes ago. Every fantasy she had ever had about Stuart Adams or about any other man came alive for her, and suddenly she knew what she had been missing her whole life. This. This magic, this pleasure, this unadulterated bliss.

She opened her eyes and gazed into his. They were beyond beauty, beyond lust, conveying an animal hunger for who and what she was. She knew in that instant that she really was beautiful because he made her feel that way. And she belonged to him, not only because of the vows they had spoken, but because their mission was to create a child together.

He shifted his stance and, taking her cue from him, she reached for the hard, muscular curves of his buttocks. He supported her with one arm as the other slid down and between her legs to weave his fingers into the soft curls. She closed her eyes in sheer rapture as the warmth spread from her molten center toward her stomach, toward her thighs, in ever-radiating circles.

She wanted to tell him how to touch her so that her pleasure could increase, but he seemed to know instinctively. When she had turned to liquid in his arms, when she was ready to flow into him, become part of him, he suddenly positioned her so that her pelvis rode against him, against his maleness, rocking against her in an ever-quickening rhythm.

In a surge of abandon, she thought that if this was what making love could be like, she wanted to do nothing else until the day she died. He must have sensed the depth of her mood, her utter recklessness, because he drew back to look at her, but she only pulled his head down again into a deep, passionate kiss that was meant to signal her readiness.

She felt herself throbbing with the rhythm of his body, breathing with the rhythm of his breath. It was as if her heart and her mind opened to him, making way for her body to open, as well. She wanted to become one with him, to absorb his taste and his smell and his pulse and his passion, to hold him inside her, making him hers and only hers. As she already was his.

Stuart lifted her into his arms, sliding her body upward and inward until her legs wrapped around his waist. He kissed her, deeply, hungrily, his mouth leaving hers only to murmur against her lips, "Let's make a baby, Angel."

"Yes," she said, surprised that she could still speak. "Yes, Stuart. Oh, yes."

If babies are the product of pure passion, thought Angel, *then we will make a baby for sure.*

There was nothing shy about Stuart or about her, but he seemed to want to take his time, to draw out their lovemaking. What had happened on the terrace was only the beginning; he made that clear as he stood over her after he deposited her on the silk-curtained bed, his eyes intently absorbed as they worshiped her body.

This is foreplay, he seemed to be saying to her as he made love to her with his eyes, and for the first time she understood what the prelude to the sex act was all about. It was more than kissing, more than mere touching. It was waiting and wanting and aching and knowing enough to realize that there was so much more.

She wondered if her own anticipation showed in her eyes. Stuart Adams was a magnificent specimen of man, powerfully aroused. At the sight of his body hard and beautiful in the carven perfection of his sex, she was overcome with a sudden, sharp heat in her loins. Her chest rose and fell with increased excitement, and when he took her outstretched hand in one of his, she felt a sensation so new, so incredible, that she could only marvel at it.

"Stuart," she said, barely able to articulate his name.

"I think you want me as much as I want you," he said softly.

"Yes," she said.

He stared at her for a moment, then placed his hand possessively on her breast. "You'll have to tell me the things you'd like me to do as we make love," he said.

She felt tears welling behind her eyelids. No one had ever asked her before. Even as she fought the urge to tell him this, her nipple hardened against the callus on his palm, and slowly and gently he massaged until it tightened into a knot that he drew between his fingers, evoking a tugging sensation deep in her abdomen.

"Do you like this?" he asked.

She nodded, unable to speak. He touched her other nipple. "And this? Do you like this?" Her breast swelled to fit his hand, and he laughed low in his throat before bending his head to her neck, where he blew the loose wisps of silvery gold hair aside and nuzzled the sensitive skin beneath her ear. She placed her trembling hands on the sides of his head, winding her fingers through the shiny dark curls.

"I like everything," she said, absorbing this truth into her reality. She, who had never registered more than a lukewarm response to Howard, was fully enjoying being made love to in Stuart's inimitable way.

"So do I," he said, tracing the delicate curves of her ear with his tongue. The growing heat in her belly swirled down, down, and she opened her legs to make room for him. He settled there, his weight and warmth foreign to her, and yet as familiar as if they had done this many times before. She held him between the inner white flesh of her thighs and watched as, his cheeks shadowed by those incomparable dark lashes, he took the soft pink tip of one breast into his mouth, teasing, circling, elongating her nipple and working it with his tongue until she thought she would die of pleasure.

When she was sure that she couldn't possibly be aroused any further, she caught a glimpse of the two of them in the mirrored wall opposite the bed. As he bent over her, she could see how his darker skin moved like a shadow against hers, how her fingers pressed hollows into the flex and ripple of the muscles in his back, could see the wet flash of his tongue as he abandoned one breast and with his mouth laid down a trail of liquid silver across her breastbone before drawing her other nipple between his lips. He suckled there greedily, with barely audible sighs, and she felt her self dissolving, merging, losing its separateness.

She kissed his face, his hair, his eyes, and became immediately drunk with the taste and scent of him. Still he did not touch her where she longed to be touched. This was torture, the sweetest torture of all. She undulated her hips against him and reached for his hand, guiding it to the slit between her legs. She was fully wet now, and slippery, and he pressed his fingers into her moist recesses. He swiftly located the tender tip in which her whole being was now centered, circling gently and dipping occasionally into the warm, wet heat of her until she was breathless.

She arched toward him in frustration, wanting more, gasping, aching deep inside as he finally slid his body over hers.

"Look," she said, her eyes darting toward the mirror and the two of them so passionately entwined. "Look at us."

He turned his head, and in the mirror his eyes met and locked with hers. He groaned.

"Yes," he said, and in the mirror she saw the moment he lost control, saw him driving into her, ramming into her as if he were a man demented. In that final moment, the world expanded and contracted into warm circles begetting spirals of need, and she convulsed around him in a spasm of joy and completion as their image in the mirror splintered into a hundred thousand sparkling shards of light.

In that delirious moment when he poured himself into her, when she was so primed to receive him, Angel knew that their baby would be conceived as a result of this act of love. Her body had welcomed Stuart Adams, and now her heart and mind and her very soul reached out to their baby, welcoming it into her, welcoming it home.

Chapter Six

When Angel woke up the next morning, she didn't know where she was at first. She only knew that she was somewhere other than in her own bed and that a heavy arm was thrown across her thigh. She opened her eyes, still not knowing, and then she saw Stuart's dark curly hair on the pillow beside her and remembered.

They were married.

Memories of the vows they had spoken weighed heavily on her heart. However, remembering the abandon with which they had given themselves to each other last night, for the first time she realized that she was going to find a lot to like about being married to Stuart Adams.

Carefully she dislodged his arm and turned onto her side so that she could look at her husband. He lay on his back, his body striped by the lemon yellow light sifting through the louvers at the window, bed covers kicked aside to reveal him in all his glory. Angel slowly took in the sight: the strong masculine symmetry of him, the utter handsomeness of his face in repose, the rise and fall of his chest as he breathed. He was beautiful.

And he was a practiced lover, one who took as much care about her own pleasure as he did his. From the moment he first touched her last night, she hadn't even thought about faking her response. It hadn't been necessary. With him, she thought with a thrill of happy anticipation, it probably never would be.

Stuart stirred in his sleep and rolled over on his side so that he was facing away from her, and she didn't have the heart to disturb such a deep sleep. A shred of bright sunlight touched upon the pale curve of scar tissue to the left of his spine. Was it the result of an accident? An operation? She bent to look more closely, resisting the urge to run her fingers along it, to learn this part of him as well as she had learned every other. She made a mental note to ask him about it later.

After a few minutes, she slid carefully out of bed, pulled a thin robe out of the suitcase that she'd never even had time to unpack, and walked barefoot into the living room.

It was already after nine, late for someone who usually started her day at dawn. She slid the wide glass door open and stepped out onto the private terrace overlooking the water. The scene before her was framed by the palm trees planted in lush profusion around the hotel. The newly risen sun still hung low in the sky, and when she held out her hand, its rays gleamed upon the delicate gold beading around the edges of her wedding ring.

She started to slide the ring from her finger before remembering something she'd once heard her mother, who was born and raised in the mountains of North Carolina, say. "It's bad luck to take off your wedding ring before your first child is born," Mama had told her. "Mayhap a woman never will have any babies if she takes off that ring beforehand." Angel herself had certainly seen no point in wearing a wedding ring at all, but now that she had it, why tempt fate? Slowly she pushed the ring back over her knuckle and stared at it, scarcely believing that she was really a wife.

All right. So she was really married. She might as well believe it. And soon—she knew it with every fiber of her being—she would be a mother. But for now, she would have to get used to her new status. She would have to get used to this new husband of hers.

With that thought, Angel inhaled deeply of the fresh sea breeze. For a moment, she felt a sharp pang of longing for the island and everything that it represented to her—her work, her freedom and her solitude. Her sojourn there, before the advent of Stuart Adams, had been a halcyon time, full of beauty and sunshine and a peace that she'd never achieved anywhere else. She'd had her cat and her garden and her work, and she'd had the physical pleasures of swimming and snorkeling and sunbathing.

She had been afraid that she was going to lose at least some of those pleasures with the addition of Stuart to Halos Island, but she had learned last night that she had only added another pleasure to them, that of making love with him. She was in awe of the power of the act as they had performed it; she felt changed by it. She almost felt hopeful for their relationship, but in the same moment, she was afraid for herself. This was no real relationship; it was a sham of a marriage, arranged for only one purpose—lawful procreation.

"Angel?"

She turned quickly to see Stuart, his tall frame outlined against the flaming magenta blossoms of the bougainvillea vine climbing the side of the building. He had wrapped a white towel around his waist, and he hadn't bothered to comb his hair.

Her heart quickened at the sight of him. With his hair mussed and his eyelids still droopy with sleep, he seemed boyish and vulnerable. Ah, but she knew the real Stuart now. The real Stuart was not merely the handsome, charming heir to a family fortune, he was a living, breathing, passionate human being. He was more than the father of her future child, the one that was surely being conceived even now deep within the mysterious inner folds of her body. He was a real person. And, at the moment, he only had eyes for her.

"I didn't want to disturb you," she said, suddenly shy.

He walked to her swiftly and gathered her into his arms. "I missed you," he said simply, and as if it were the most natural thing in the world, she lifted her lips for his kiss, all her doubts about him and their relationship and his intrusion into her life falling away.

She didn't expect to be transported to a state of bliss by one good-morning kiss, but before it was over, she was clinging to him, her head spinning.

"I missed you when I woke up and you weren't there," he said, his lips moving against her hair.

"I didn't want to wake you," she said.

"I wouldn't have minded. In fact, you have my permission to wake me up anytime you like," he said.

"I always get up early. I'm usually out in the field by this time," she said in a rush. She had no idea what she was supposed to say to a husband she hardly knew after a wedding night that must have broken all records for sheer sensuality. Stuart was an indefatigable lover, thorough and inventive. Remembering now how they had made love over and over, she felt a flush spreading upward from her neck. Stuart noticed and smiled, bending his head to touch his lips to her rosy cheek. He then slid the robe off her shoulders and deliberately spread his hands over her breasts, shaping them to the curves of his palms.

She closed her eyes, drawing the sensation deep inside her, using it to recall the passion of the night before. She had been a passionate person then; had it been a fluke? Or had that passionate side of her nature become part of the person she really was, the Angel McCabe she had thought she never could be? And if she was this new person—this passionate, sexy woman—what had happened to the person she used to be? Was that Angel gone forever?

Or was it the world that had changed, not her? No, she thought as she opened her eyes, the rest of the world continued as it had before. Somewhere she heard hedge clippers grooming shrubbery; birds sang as they built nests in hollows beneath terra cotta roof tiles. The world was not taking note of her response to Stuart's considerable sexual prowess. It didn't care that a few short hours after they had fallen asleep, exhausted and besotted after a spectacular wedding night, Stuart Adams was touching her, wanting her, making her want him again.

"Let me see you in the sunshine," he whispered, dropping her robe to the floor and kicking it away with one impatient foot.

She didn't like him looking at her, though she knew that, as her husband, he had every right. On the other hand, she certainly enjoyed looking at him—at the wide, muscled chest, with its two dark nipples nestled among whorls of black hair, at the taut skin of his abdomen, at the part of him that so blatantly declared his maleness.

He ran his hands over the arc of her hips. "Your body pleases me," he said, close to her ear. "You please me."

She swallowed, afraid to show him how happy these statements made her. "Shouldn't we go inside? Some-one might see us," she said.

He chuckled. "This is the honeymoon suite. We're supposed to act like honeymooners." He touched the tip of his tongue to her earlobe.

"I think I could get to like what honeymooners do," she said unsteadily as her nipples drew into hard little nubs.

He must have noticed his effect on her, because his fingers soon found those little nubs and rolled them, slowly and gently, until she tingled all the way down to her toes. He bent his head until his tongue swirled mois-ture on one uptilted nipple, then the other, and his fin-gers resumed their circling. "Honeymooners do a lot more than this," he said, in between leisurely tastes of her breasts, her shoulder, the soft skin stretched across her sternum. "By the way, Mrs. Adams, we're assured of complete privacy on the terrace, as well as in the bed-room. I read it on a placard in the bathroom."

She gasped as his mouth curved hotly into the sensi-tive hollow in her throat as if his lips were made to fit there.

"I don't know how you've found time for reading," she managed to say. "We've both been so busy ever since we've arrived in this—oh, Stuart, that feels so good—in this suite."

Stuart lifted his head, smiling at her in lazy amuse-ment. "In this suite, in this sweet bond of matrimony, in this sweet state of—oh, please touch me, Angel, the way you did last night—sweet, sweet," and he guided her hand until it curved gently around the most manly part of him.

"I never knew that what honeymooners did in complete privacy could be so exciting," she said, sliding her hand against the hot hard flesh.

"Neither did I. Oh, Angel, if you only knew how good that feels, how much it makes me want you, all of you, in every way," he said breathlessly, moving into the rhythm she set.

Was it possible to become intoxicated with lovemaking? Angel asked herself dazedly. Was it possible to go crazy from this kind of touching? To want to do nothing else but?

She certainly thought it was, because the way he was feathering his hands down the sensitive skin over her rib cage made her feel as if every cell in her body were about to burst into flame. What had happened to Angel Mc-Cabe, the calm, cool, self-possessed person she had been only a few short days ago, the person who had been psyching herself up for sex, knowing that she'd have to go through with it, avoiding the very thought of intercourse, planning to fake a climax? That person seemed to have disappeared, and a new one—this Angel Mc-Cabe who was swooping eagerly from one delightful crest of sensation to another—had taken her place.

She felt herself going soft and pliant, yielding to him with such sweet surrender that she could hardly believe it was true. But it was true, and real, and wonderful, and the two of them fit together as if they were made for each other.

He groaned, his mouth fused with hers, melding his angles to her curves, igniting a heat deep inside her. The taste of him was intoxicating, like heady wine, like the champagne they had drunk the night before, and she was giddy with desire. His mouth explored hers in a leisurely way, his tongue insistent, and she was awash in sensation, drowning in a flood of passion. He surprised her by taking her lower lip between his teeth and sucking at it gently. Her mouth opened greedily for hot, lingering kisses, her hands still full of his strength and his power and his might.

"I knew it would be like this," he said, pulling his mouth from hers, and she only uttered a soft cry and buried her face in his neck, inhaling the musky male scent of him, reveling in the scrape of his beard against her cheek.

"I didn't," she whispered. "I didn't know anything could be like this."

"Kiss me," he demanded roughly. "Let me have your lips."

She raised her head, looked deep into his eyes, was lost in his longing and made it her own.

And then he was kissing her with all his being, caressing her with his whole body. He hadn't even entered her yet, and she was frantic and straining and wondrously, joyously alive—alive as she had never been in her life— and in a rush of feeling she knew that this marvelous, unbelievable gift couldn't be happening, not to her.

But it was.

In her release, she heard him murmuring, "Angel, Angel," and she tensed in convulsive shudders that seemed to go on forever until at last, when she thought she would die from sensation, she subsided limply in his arms. She heard Stuart laugh in sudden exultation. Dimly she realized that bringing her to such a lofty peak made him happy, exhilarated him, and she felt swept away by a surge of deep gratitude mixed with totally unexpected euphoria.

Before she had entirely caught her breath, Stuart slid a hand under her knees and swung her up into his arms, staring down at her with delight and an eager, hungry passion. He was still aroused, his manhood pressing against her, showing her that he wanted her, needed her, and was not about to let his ardor subside.

"God, you're responsive," he said, and she wanted to tell him that she had never been responsive before, and that the reason that she was able to let go with him was that he knew exactly how to evoke all the best sensations. But there was no chance to say anything before he was kissing her again, his mouth covering hers with a demanding urgency.

Then he was striding into the hot tub, down the steps, depositing her in the swirling hot water and leaning over her, kissing her, pressing her back against the curved seat. His knees slid between her legs, and she lifted her own legs up out of the water to wind them around his back, pulling him down to her beneath the bubbles until their bodies effortlessly became one.

"This is more of what honeymooners are supposed to do in this private honeymoon suite," he said, his eyes laughing down at her as he sank into her warmth and softness.

"Was all of this outlined on that placard in the bathroom?" she murmured.

"The placard left a lot to the imagination," he said. "I mean, there weren't any diagrams or anything."

"Thank goodness," she managed to reply. "I'd hate to think of how busy we'd be if we had to follow diagrams."

"Especially since my imagination is working overtime as it is. You can't imagine what marvels a naval architect could dream up in a watery situation like this one," he said.

"I can't imagine anything," she gasped. "I know nothing about boats."

"All you have to know at this point is that they float," he said. "And you have exactly what it takes, Angel, to float mine."

"We wouldn't go anywhere without all your wonderful rowing," she murmured against his neck as he slowly moved in and out.

"At the moment, I would be hard put to tell port from starboard," he whispered. He held her close as he rolled over, reversing their positions so that she was poised above him.

He smiled at her and curved his hands around her breasts. "These are mighty big sails for such a small ship," he said. She made no effort at all to smother the easy laughter that came to her in that moment; she was exulting in his admiration of her. Oh, she liked this, she really did! The water buoyed her up and made it easy for her to control the depth of penetration. Without even thinking about it, she eased into a vigorous rocking motion that soon had Stuart gasping and bucking against her.

"I think we're about to go sailing over the bounding main," he said, and despite the lightness of his words, Angel was mesmerized by Stuart's intent, absorbed expression as he concentrated on his own pleasure. And something else showed in his eyes, too, an extraordinary fascination with what he saw in her own. In that moment, they shared an all-encompassing intimacy such as Angel could never have imagined if she had not experienced it.

His completion was sudden, and she was so caught up in his response, in his elation, that all she could do when he cried her name was to collapse in the circle of his arms and listen to the frantic pounding of his heart until it subsided into a steady, rhythmic beat.

His hands were wet as they caressed her hair. She rested on his stomach, still pleasurably filled by him, her head cradled against his, the bubbles eddying around them. Birds sang nearby, a steady cascade of trilling notes keeping time with the melody in her heart.

"Anchors aweigh, my darling, my wife," he whispered against her hair, and she smiled, feeling the curve of his lips against her temple.

"This water seems a lot hotter than it was a few minutes ago, and so am I," Stuart said finally, kissing her lightly on the cheek. "What do you say we go back to bed?"

"Why?" she said, not wanting to move, not wanting to uncouple. She had never felt so much at one with anyone before in her life, and she didn't want it to end.

"Why not?" he replied.

"Because... I like this," she said, with a hint of bewilderment.

"So do I," he said, laughing at her. "I like it so much that I can hardly wait to do it all over again."

"Maybe we need time to recover," she said, wriggling her hips so that he was drawn even farther inside her. "Maybe we need a rest."

"Maybe you're talking complete nonsense," he said, looking down at her with affection.

"I suppose there's only one way to find out," she replied demurely.

"Oh, there's probably more than one," Stuart said, entirely serious, and after a while, clinging together, dripping, they went inside and tumbled amid steamy sheets until they fell back exhausted, sated and suffused with well-being. And then they slept, entwined in each other's arms.

STUART, lounging back against lacy pillows after an hour's nap, said, "I could stay right here at the Kapok Tree Resort Hotel forever."

"We can't, Stuart. I told Toby to have Barky Flynt meet us in his boat at the marina at one o'clock," Angel said as she traced his spine with one lazy hand. "We can't stay another day."

"Can't you phone this Barky guy and tell him we want to postpone going back to Halos Island?" Stuart said, his words muffled by the pillow. Angel's hand swooped lower, and if they only had time, he thought he'd turn over on his back and show her exactly why he wanted to stay. Even now, just thinking about it, he felt a telltale stirring in his nether regions.

"Barky doesn't have a phone, and Caloosa will run out of food," she said. Her hand traced the scar tissue on his back. "How'd you get this scar?" she asked.

Stuart had prepared himself for the question, but even so, he had a difficult time answering. "An accident," he mumbled.

"What kind of accident?" She asked it idly, only mildly curious.

He paused before answering. "Oh, it was something that happened on Nantucket. Do you think we have time to order something from room service?"

He held his breath, but Angel only said, "I'll phone and ask room service to bring coffee. Is that okay?" Safely diverted from her line of questioning, Angel fluttered her hands up his backbone and across the back of his neck before winding them in his hair. She seemed fascinated with the texture and curl of it, twining separate strands around her fingers.

"Sure," he said, relaxing again. "And maybe a few rolls. We can stop for lunch on the way to the marina."

"I'd better call now," she said, leaning over him to reach for the telephone.

After she made the call, he reached out and brushed her hair away from her face to reveal the smooth, clean line of her jaw.

"What are you doing?" she said, her eyes again focusing on his face.

"Admiring the view," he said. He felt an unaccountable rush of tenderness toward her.

"Oh," she said, looking away as if she were embarrassed.

"You really are something special, Angel. You're a stunning woman, a fantastic-looking woman." He didn't add *my woman,* but he would have liked to. After last night and this morning, it would be hard to think of her any other way.

"I am a woman with too-big breasts and too-wide hips," she said, drawing away slightly.

"You're perfect," he said, sliding his hand up her flat stomach and cupping one of her gently curved breasts. "Your breasts are perfect."

She looked at him, clearly disbelieving, which astonished him. Someone who looked like Angel should know how lovely she was; surely other men had told her she was beautiful, hadn't they? He would have asked, but such a question seemed inappropriate.

She looked down at her full breasts. "At least I should be able to nurse a baby successfully," she said, easing away from him and pulling the sheet up over her.

Stuart tugged the sheet back down again. "I love looking at you," he said.

She stared for a moment, either refusing to comment or unable to speak, he wasn't sure which. "As for your hips," he went on, "they're perfect, too."

"You don't have to flatter me, you know," she said. "You really haven't anything to gain from it. I mean, we're going to . . . to make love until I conceive, and then you can go."

He was taken aback. He couldn't believe that she could so easily dismiss the passion they had shown each other in their lovemaking. For him, it had been spectacular— bells, whistles, fireworks, the whole shebang. Was she saying that for her the sex act meant nothing more than fulfilling the terms of their contract?

He didn't know what to say, but he didn't stop her when she got up and went into the bathroom. In a few minutes he heard the shower running, and he folded his hands behind his head and stared at the stucco ceiling, thinking over every last moment, reliving every last gasp of their lovemaking.

Angel had felt something for him each and every time they made love. He was sure of it.

Or had she?

Listening to the shower running, with last night and this morning quickly fading into memory, Stuart had to admit that when it came right down to it, he had no idea.

ANGEL'S FRIEND with the boat, Barky Flynt, turned out to be a Key West character in a battered sailor's hat and an oversize T-shirt that came nearly to his knees. He not only sat on the back of the seat of his runabout, he also steered with his bare feet. He had the disconcerting habit of spitting a trail of tobacco juice into the clear water along the way, but since Stuart had met a good many oddballs during the course of his sailing days, he took these eccentricities in stride. Barky even invited him to go fishing with him someday in the near future, an invitation that Stuart accepted.

Angel seemed subdued on the run back to Halos Island, and Stuart wasn't sure why. It might be their conversation before she'd so hurriedly gotten out of bed; it might be that she was distracted by thoughts of her work. *He* certainly was distracted by the sight of her sitting across from him in the boat, her ankles primly crossed above a pair of white sandals, her hair whipping wildly in the wind. She looked so cool and controlled that she only slightly resembled the ardent woman she had been in bed.

She was his secret, he thought to himself, and he reached over and squeezed her hand. For a moment she looked vaguely uncertain, and he thought maybe he had somehow done the wrong thing in showing her that bit of affection. It wasn't as though he could help acting affectionately toward her; after last night, he felt benevolent toward the whole world.

That included Halos Island, which was growing larger in the distance, and the cat, too. "Looks like Caloosa is happy to see us," Stuart said in amusement when he saw her, tail held high and crooked at the end, bounding eagerly toward the dock as the boat drew near.

"See you bright and early Saturday morning," Barky called to Stuart after he and Angel disembarked, and Stuart, bringing up the rear of their little procession as he carried their overnight gear, saluted him.

As Stuart followed Angel, who was carrying the cat in her arms and crooning to her, the island seemed incredibly beautiful to him. A flowering tree—a magnificent

royal poinciana—shaded the last few feet of the path to
the dock, its brilliant red-orange blossoms littering the
grass and sand beneath it. The house nestled at the top of
the rise, its green painted shingles dwarfed by the two
huge banyan trees. Stuart hadn't realized it before, but
he'd missed the place during his short absence.

Angel hadn't locked the door; it wasn't necessary,
she'd said. Now she turned to him and shifted Caloosa to
his arms, because the humidity had made the screen door
stick and she needed both hands to open it.

"It's good to be back," he said, and Angel turned, her
eyes questioning. "I mean it," he said, when he realized
that she looked dubious.

"Halos Island isn't for everyone," she said.

He smiled at her. "Depends on what everyone's looking for. Take me, for instance. I like peace and quiet. I
like the idea of living on a tropical island, far away from
the rest of the world." He was going to say, "I think I'm
really going to like living with you," but at that point
Caloosa struggled to get down, and he set her on the
floor, whereupon she immediately ran up the screen and
hung there from her claws, looking over her shoulder at
them.

Angel went over and gently dislodged Caloosa from
the wire mesh. "She's acting out her frustration at being
left alone overnight," Angel explained. She turned
around, hugging the cat to her, and Stuart thought that
they made a lovely picture, the gray-and-white cat cud-
dled close to the blue fabric of Angel's dress, Angel's pale
hair flowing over her shoulders. The flowers he had
brought Angel yesterday morning in celebration of their
wedding day spilled over the sides of a vase behind her,
their blooms a riot of color.

She moved toward the door.

"Not so fast," Stuart said. "Shouldn't I carry you over the threshold? Like a proper bridegroom?"

"I'm already over the threshold," she said.

"The porch doesn't count. I'm going to carry you over the threshold of the house proper. Caloosa, too." He scooped both of them up into his arms.

"Stuart, put me down," Angel said, but she was laughing as she said it.

"Not on your life," he said.

She gazed at him, her eyes dancing. "Why, Stuart, I do believe you have a romantic streak," she said.

"I do believe you're right," he said before ceremoniously carrying her into the house, through the kitchen, across the tiny hall and into the bedroom, where he brushed aside the sheer mosquito net suspended from the ceiling and set her down on the edge of the bed. Caloosa uttered a put-upon meow and leaped out of Angel's arms before disappearing into the living room.

Stuart bent over Angel, his arms on either side of her. His eyebrows quirked upward. "Never let it be said that I shirked my duties as a bridegroom," he said.

"Of course not."

"As to those duties, perhaps I should perform some of them repeatedly."

"You already have."

"I mean, we want to conceive a baby. So it makes sense to perform the necessary tasks often, don't you think?"

"The optimum interval between 'tasks' is forty-eight hours if we wish to achieve maximum results," she said, although she already knew that somewhere inside her, sperm had met egg and cells were dividing, creating a baby—her baby.

Stuart slid his hands up under her hair and guided her head toward his. "I'm not interested in intervals—optimum or otherwise," he said slowly, the words a mere whisper, and then he kissed her.

We wouldn't have to do this, Angel thought to herself as she succumbed, *but it's so much fun.* And then she was lost in sensation, in feeling. It seemed almost too much to hope for that they would be able to sustain the sexual excitement they'd found on their honeymoon. Maybe it had been a fluke; somehow those hours in the Kapok Tree Resort Hotel seemed unreal. She pretended for a few seconds—only a few—that this man, who still seemed to so ardently desire her, wanted more than a baby, that he actually wanted her for herself.

It's too dangerous to think that way, she thought, and then, reveling in the satiny texture of his skin against hers, she was unable to think at all.

Chapter Seven

It took Angel ten days to decide that she was definitely pregnant.

For one thing, her breasts had become sore and her nipples swollen. For another, she couldn't stand the smell of butter or bacon or salad dressing. When she cooked, she had to keep running to the open kitchen door to get a breath of fresh air. She was ecstatic about her symptoms. But she didn't mention them to Stuart.

He seemed to notice every time she bolted for the outdoors; these days, Stuart noticed everything about her. "Is something wrong?" he'd say. "Are you looking for something out there in the banyan tree?"

"Caloosa," she'd say. "The mockingbirds were chasing her again today, and I haven't seen her since." Or she'd say, "The sunset is so lovely that I had to come out to take a look."

Whereupon Stuart would say, "I'll look for Caloosa. Want to come with me?" Or "The sunset's prettier on the beach. Let's walk down and watch it."

No matter how she felt, Angel could never say no to Stuart's requests. She had lived alone on the island for so long that she'd thought she liked being alone. Now, here was Stuart, always around, always wanting her company for something or other. She'd be on her way to the meadow to spend time with her bees, and Stuart would come along and suggest something that sounded too good to pass up.

They hiked. They explored the limestone caves on the north shore. They made love.

He was good company, which was why she usually stopped what she was doing and joined him. For the first time in years, she was having fun.

How could she *not* have fun, when he made every activity so exciting? Swimming, for instance. She loved to swim, and she swam every day. But swimming with Stuart was much more interesting than swimming by herself.

One day he found an extra snorkel in the closet and asked her to come out to the reef with him.

"I can't," she told him. "I have work to do. There are larvae I'm keeping an eye on over in the east meadow."

"You're keeping an eye on larvae? Why? They're not going anywhere anytime soon, are they?"

"Of course not, Stuart, larvae don't go much of anywhere, ever. I'm waiting to see—"

He pulled her into his arms, something he did more and more often these days. "I'm waiting to see that big bad moray eel, and I don't know where to find him. I've forgotten where you said to look."

"I said not to look, if you'll remember correctly. Big bad moray eels aren't something you want to stir up."

"How will I know where he is if you don't come along to steer me away from him?" he was wheedling now, sliding his hands up her backbone and tunneling them through her hair. He smiled at her—it was a sunny smile full of pleasure—and she could hardly deny him anything when he turned on all the charm.

"All right," she said. "I'll get my swimsuit."

"I've been thinking about that," Stuart said. "There's no one to see us. We could run around this island without clothes all the time."

"Until you sit on your first sandspur," she retorted, but she didn't get her swimsuit after all.

Stuart grabbed her hand and, pulling her along with him, kept her laughing all the way to the beach. Once they got there, he helped her out of her clothes, and she pulled his shirt over his head and peeled his jeans down his thighs.

"You look like Eve in the Garden of Eden," he said in a tone of reverence when they stood naked in the bright sunlight. "You look like Venus rising from the sea."

"You look like a Greek statue," she said, unable to think of any other comparisons. One thing she knew was that he looked as if he really liked what he saw as his eyes raked her figure, lingering on what he claimed to consider her finer attributes.

"Our baby will be beautiful. I hope it looks exactly like you," he said, and she demurred until he silenced her with a light kiss on her lips.

He drew her closer. "Maybe we don't want to swim after all. Maybe we want to take the time to enjoy being together . . . like this . . . you and me . . ."

He kissed her again, more deeply now, but she was still in a playful mood, and pulled away, laughing. "You'll have to catch me first," she said as she started to run. Her feet skimmed like lightning over the warm sand, and Stuart raced after her. When she realized that she was going to be caught and perhaps even tackled, she neatly sidestepped him and bounded into the water, falling to her knees amid the frothy waves.

"Caught you," Stuart said, leaping in after her. She had to cling to him to keep from going under, and he kissed her, his lips cool and salty against hers.

"We forgot the snorkels," she said after a while.

"Who wants to come up for air?"

"We can't keep on doing what we're doing," she said as another wave washed over them.

"Why not? Deborah Kerr and Burt Lancaster did in that movie—what was its title?"

"From Here to Eternity," she said, sliding her legs around his until the two of them were entwined.

"When we make a movie, we'll call it *From Here to Maternity,"* Stuart said.

"Spare me the silly puns," she said, because her mind was trying to figure out if this was an utterly romantic episode or if it was merely a throwback to some primeval animal instinct from the time when animals crawled out of the ocean and started to live on land. As she was thinking, as she was kissing him, Stuart pressed his hardness against her thigh.

"If you're going to do that, you might as well do it where it would do some good," she said, and then she kissed him the way she knew he liked to be kissed, deeply and with feeling. It wasn't hard to enjoy this, not with the sea wrapped around them like silk and their own bodies primed for the exquisite pleasure that they had come to expect when they came together.

Angel hadn't expected to like lovemaking so much. But she did. And she liked it more and more each time. Stuart was a master of lovemaking; he played her body like a virtuoso. As the days flew by and her body started changing, albeit subtly, Angel became even more sensitive. Stuart's cool hands soothed her hot breasts, and orgasms, which she now experienced with regularity, made her nausea go away. She had not yet reached the point where she went to Stuart and by look or by touch suggested making love whenever she felt sick to her stomach, but she thought she might. She wondered how he would react if she made the first move. So far, she'd never summoned enough nerve. The way Howard had reacted to the increased libido of her first pregnancy was never far from her mind.

Angel loved being pregnant, feeling pregnant, knowing that her body was harboring a new little life. But as soon as he knew she was pregnant, Stuart would leave. More and more, she thought about his leaving with dismay.

When Stuart was gone, who would she talk to at breakfast? Since the first few days of their marriage, Angel made coffee in the morning and spread guava jelly on toast, Stuart cooked eggs or cut up a few of their homegrown mangoes to put in their cereal, and they ate companionably at the porch table. If Stuart were gone, who would beat her at rummy? Who would read her humorous fillers out of *Reader's Digest* as she trailed a bit of yarn across the floor for Caloosa to chase?

When Stuart was gone, who would make love to her and murmur complimentary things in her ear? Who would make her feel like a woman, something she hadn't felt for years?

Even though in her heart she was sure that she carried a baby inside her, Angel didn't give Stuart a clue. She couldn't, because then he would leave. As the days passed, as she began to be filled with remorse at her own duplicity, she knew she was emotionally unprepared to share her suspicions—no, her certain knowledge—that she was pregnant.

And then Stuart received a letter.

IT ARRIVED via the mail boat, courtesy of Toby, who was showing an uncommon interest in them. Before Stuart had come to the island, Toby used to toss the mail on the dock without a word; now he'd linger, looking hopefully up the hill at the bungalow until Stuart appeared to talk with him. What they talked about, Angel didn't know.

As luck would have it, Angel happened to be down at the dock on the day Stuart's letter came.

"Yo, Stuart," Toby said as he tossed a line to Stuart on the dock. "I've got something for you."

Angel, who had walked down to the dock with Stuart and was sitting with her feet dangling over the side, looked up in surprise.

Stuart took the envelope and glanced at the return address. An expression of foreboding flickered across his features.

"Something from your family?" Angel said brightly, jumping to her feet so that she could read the return address over his shoulder.

Stuart merely nodded and stuck the envelope in his pocket. Angel thought that if she'd received a letter from a family member, she'd have opened it on the spot, especially if she was on the first leg of a long journey, as Stuart claimed he was.

Stuart and Toby got into a conversation about the Florida Marlins and how their season was going, an affable exchange that ended when Toby said he had to get back to Key West. As Toby guided the boat toward the cut in the reef, Stuart started back up the dock.

"Wait for me, I'll walk with you," Angel said, but instead of the welcoming expression she'd learned to expect from Stuart, all she got was a stony look.

On the way up the path, Angel searched through her own mail and found nothing of interest. Stuart took the newly arrived envelope from his pocket and stared at it for a long time.

"Anything wrong?" she asked.

"No. My brother doesn't write often, that's all."

Angel flopped down on a porch chair. "That's too bad. If I were lucky enough to have a brother, I'd want to keep in touch."

"An only child tends to overestimate the joy of having siblings," he said, and she glanced at him to see him scowling uncharacteristically. He still hadn't opened the letter.

"I think it would be wonderful to have a family. Now that my mother's gone, there's no one."

"Maybe you should consider yourself lucky," he said.

"How can you say that? If I'd had someone—" Angel stopped herself short. She'd been about to say that if she'd felt closely connected to someone, perhaps to family members, she wouldn't have thought up this crazy scheme to have a baby. She couldn't, in all honesty, say the words. But then, why this sudden compunction about honesty? She certainly hadn't been completely honest with him. He had no idea, she was sure, that she was having symptoms of pregnancy.

"You wouldn't want a brother like my brother Fitz," he said.

"Is he that bad?"

"Bad?" he said slowly. "I don't think *bad* is the word for Fitz."

"How would you describe him?"

"I wouldn't bother. I'm trying to put that part of my life behind me," he said.

"You don't intend to return to your family firm after your leave of absence?"

"I have other things in mind," he said. He folded the envelope, stared at it for a few seconds, and stuffed it deep in his back pocket. He still hadn't opened it. He focused his eyes on her. "Don't you have work to do?"

His tone of dismissal hurt. Usually he was eager to spend time with her.

"I'll be out in the field. Do you still want to dig around in the oyster shells on the Indian midden this afternoon?"

"Some other time," he said. He threw himself down on a chair and sat staring out at a butterfly hovering over the planting of Turk's caps outside the porch screen.

After a moment, Angel went into the kitchen, poured herself a glass of cold water from the bottle in the refrigerator, and thought about asking Stuart if he wanted some. A glance through the doorway showed her that he was still sitting there, his expression thoughtful, and she decided against it.

"I'll be back in time to stir-fry vegetables for dinner," she called to him, but he gave no sign that he heard her, and she let herself out of the house quietly.

Stuart had never been so uncommunicative, and she knew it was all because of the letter from Fitz.

For the first time, she was curious about Stuart's family and the lack of affection in his voice whenever he mentioned them, which was seldom. Maybe if she took it easy, she'd find out more. It wasn't for herself that she needed to know about Stuart's elusive family, she assured herself as she swung along the crooked path to the east meadow. It was for the baby, who would be born an Adams.

WHEN HE WAS SURE that Angel had left the house, Stuart opened the letter from his brother.

Dear Mr. Adams,
Thank you for your donation to the Sailors' Home. As you know, your generous gift will help many fine sailors who have contributed so much to this nation's success.

Our mission in Boston continues to support many sailors who otherwise would have no home, and we plan to start construction on our facility on Nantucket this summer. If you're ever in the area, please stop by our Boston office so that we can thank you for your donation in person.

Very truly yours,

H. Fitzroy Adams
Chairman of the Board
New England Maritime Charitable Trust

Stuart's lip curled in derision as he crumpled the letter in his fist. A form letter from his own brother! What a joke.

Not that he had expected a personal communication from Fitz. He hadn't heard from his brother in almost two years. Not since Fitz had deserted him when he needed him most.

But what was the point of thinking about it? Fitz had gone his way after the incident on Nantucket, and Stuart had gone his. Fitz seemed eager to distance himself from Stuart; maybe he feared that Stuart's disgrace would stain his own reputation. Since that terrible night, Fitz had reportedly given up drinking and ostentatiously devoted himself to good works.

Fitz had even married and was now the father of a baby girl Stuart had never seen. Nor had he met Fitz's wife, Jeanne. When he was still living in Boston, Stuart had read about their wedding in the papers; it had been a big social event in Newport to which Stuart wasn't even invited. When he saw the announcement of their baby's birth a year later, Stuart had realized that Fitz had attained the life that he, Stuart, had always dreamed about.

That life was closed to him now. Who would want to plan a life with him after what he'd done? No one, that's who. With other avenues closed to him, shunned by his family and friends, he had thought his arrangement with Angel was the best way to marry and conceive a child who would carry on his name.

Too bad he couldn't send a clipping about his wedding to Fitz:

Adams-McCabe Nuptials, the headline would read.

Stuart Adams of Boston and Nantucket, scion of a prominent Massachusetts family whose forebears arrived in America on the Mayflower, recently wed Angel McCabe, a bee researcher from Halos Island, Florida.

The bride, whose mother is dead and whose father is nowhere around, wore a wrinkled white linen dress and carried a bouquet of wilting hibiscus. The groom's replies were barely audible in the church, which was deserted by everyone but three children, a Popsicle man and, of course, the wedding party.

The rotund maid of honor was stricken with an attack of hiccups as soon as the bride said her first "I do." The toothless custodian, who acted as best man, dropped the ring, which the bride didn't want to wear anyway.

After the wedding and a short reception at a local restaurant, the couple honeymooned briefly in Key West, where they discovered that they were unusually compatible sexually.

Mr. and Mrs. Adams will reside on Halos Island, an isolated atoll off the Florida coast. They expect their first child soon.

Stuart grinned to himself. That little news item would certainly upset Fitz and all the other Adamses who had avoided him ever since his guilty plea to a charge of manslaughter. Members of their family were supposed to live circumspect lives, stay out of trouble with the law, marry well and procreate. So far, Stuart had managed to do none of those things.

Except procreate, possibly. Angel could be pregnant already with a new little Adams. Stuart could picture the baby in his mind; it would be a roly-poly little elf, with his eyes and Angel's coloring. He or she would be a wonderful baby, he was sure of it.

He might not be able to send Fitz a wedding announcement, but Stuart would certainly see to it that he got a birth announcement, and maybe he'd even send along a copy of the personals ad that had brought him to Angel. He only wished he could see a photo of Fitz's face when he saw them.

Cheered by the thought of Fitz's almost certain consternation, Stuart began to feel much more optimistic. He wished he hadn't told Angel that he didn't want to explore the Indian midden today.

Come to think of it, maybe he ought to go find her. She might still want to go.

ANGEL, on her way to the meadow, was confronted by Caloosa, who bounded in front of her and came to a skidding stop.

"What in the world is wrong with you, Caloosa?" Angel asked, bending down to pet her, but the cat was so skittish that she jumped out of Angel's way.

"Caloosa?" Angel said. She'd never seen her cat act this way before.

The cat ran to the edge of the path and looked over her shoulder at Angel. When Angel approached, Caloosa twitched her tail and leaped into the shrubbery. Angel could have sworn that Caloosa wanted Angel to follow her.

The connecting path to her swimming beach was nearby, and Caloosa ran in that direction. Angel, unsure why she was doing it, followed along.

At the edge of the beach, Caloosa skirted the palm grove and ran out onto the sand. When Angel emerged from the brush into the bright glaring sunlight of the beach, she couldn't see the cat at first. As her eyes adjusted, she realized that Caloosa was running back and forth at the edge of the ocean, keeping just outside the reach of the surf. Angel was amused at how the cat managed to dodge the water; then she realized that Caloosa was acting highly distressed at the sight of an object that was rising and falling on the gently billowing waves.

Angel ran to the high-tide line and saw immediately that whatever Caloosa was paying so much attention to was moving and definitely alive. *Why, it's a pelican!* Angel thought with a start. The bird's feathers were ruffled and dirty, and it wasn't sitting correctly in the water, but it definitely was a brown pelican, one of a flock that inhabited Halos Island.

By this time, Caloosa was mewing distractedly, and after Angel kicked her shoes off and waded a few feet into the water for a better look, she realized that the bird was caught in a discarded six-ring plastic beer pack. It was clearly exhausted from the struggle of trying to escape it.

Angel didn't even have to think about it; she plunged into the water, clothes and all, to rescue the beleaguered pelican.

The surf wasn't high today, and she was a good swimmer. In a matter of seconds, she reached the pelican, which stared at her without much hope out of the eye on the side facing her. Angel paused to tread water for a moment or two as she planned the best way to disentangle the terrified bird, and when she realized that not only was its bill caught in one of the rings but that its feet were twisted in two others, her heart sank. This wasn't going to be a simple task.

The bird seemed to be losing strength. Angel gingerly placed her hands around it, expecting it to burst free of the plastic and nip her at any second, but the bird was apparently so worn out from its struggles that it attempted only a feeble token effort. Angel launched herself toward shore and kicked as hard as she could, pushing the pelican ahead of her.

Her hair got in her eyes, making it even more difficult for her to see, but she was making some progress. She was beginning to congratulate herself when she felt the first sting on her lower leg. *A jellyfish,* she thought. *What an inconvenience.* But then the sting became a searing pain that made her cry out involuntarily so that she gulped a mouthful of water. After that, attempting to ignore the pain, she clamped her lips shut and tried to keep kicking. It was a nasty shock when she realized that whatever was stinging her was now trailing across her thigh, scorching the skin in a kind of slow torture.

She fought to keep from crying out. She didn't dare try to brush away whatever was causing the pain for fear of what it might do to her hand. Panic caught in her throat, but she wasn't about to abandon the pelican after what she'd already gone through. The bird, however, seemed resigned to its fate. It lowered its head and heaved a great sigh.

Angel gritted her teeth against the torment and pushed the bird toward land with one last giant heave, hoping that this desperate effort would provide enough impetus to wash the pelican up on shore.

At that moment, she spotted the source of her pain: the clear blue flotation sac of *Physalia pelagica,* the dreaded Portuguese man-of-war, hulked only a few feet away from her. She knew that this member of the phylum Coelenterata, like other jellyfish, possessed a network of toxic tentacles that floated beneath it, and if she became enmeshed in its tangle, she would be in even worse straits. And where there was one man-of-war, there were usually others. She could be smack in the middle of a whole flotilla of them, unable to see them because of the rise and fall of the waves.

Keep calm, she told herself, and that was when she heard Stuart shouting at her.

"What's wrong, Angel?"

"Man-of-war!" she called back, scarcely able to speak. The pain was shooting through her whole leg, and she had to fight not to scream in agony.

Stuart started into the water. "No, stay there, it's too dangerous!" she yelled, kicking and paddling with all her might. For all she knew, she could be heading into a web of poisonous lashes, but she had to get to shore.

At that moment, a large wave bore her upward and toward shore, so that with one more powerful lunge, she was within Stuart's grasp.

"Watch...out..." she managed to gasp as he hauled her onto the sand. She knew that the tentacles of the man-of-war could be more than fifty feet long, and that they could be coiled around her leg. If Stuart touched them, he would be stung, too.

"I see them," Stuart said tersely. His eyes raked her body, taking in her sodden clothes and the red welts beginning to rise on her legs. "Where else did they sting you?" he asked, as he pulled off his shirt and used it to wipe gently at the tentacles adhering to the welts.

"Just on my legs," Angel said through teeth gritted against the pain.

She strained to see the pelican, which was lying on the sand only a few feet away, its sides heaving. "Can't you take care of the bird first?" she asked.

Stuart glanced at the pelican. "If you're up to removing the tentacles from your legs, I'll take a look at the bird."

"I can do it," she said. He handed her his shirt, and she began to swab gently at her welts. Stuart, after studying the situation briefly, grasped the pelican firmly and eased its feet and neck out of the plastic rings.

"This fellow's going to be okay," he said. He went to the edge of the water and released the bird. It looked stunned, but Stuart spent no more time worrying about it. He hurried back to Angel.

"You'd better lie back," he said. "I'll do this."

Angel gratefully allowed him to minister to her. Now she felt the toxin from the man-of-war spreading through her body, making her feel weak and woozy. As Stuart said, "There! That's the last of them," she felt a cramp in her leg.

Stuart looked alarmed. "You are okay, aren't you?"

She nodded, unable to speak. She swallowed hard against the nausea rising in her throat.

"Angel?" Stuart said, as if from a long distance away.

She realized that she had closed her eyes; she opened them again. "Is the pelican all right?" she asked anxiously. Stuart was blocking her view.

Stuart moved, and they both saw the pelican fly a short distance before coming to rest on the surface of the ocean. The bird sat there, riding the waves. Caloosa, who had been crouching nearby, watching the proceedings, suddenly got up and trotted over to Angel, where she rubbed up against her mistress's face.

"The pelican will be fine," Stuart assured her. "I'm not so sure about you."

"I'll be fine, too," Angel said, and then she lost the battle with her stomach.

"TALK ABOUT STUPID," Stuart said. "Talk about ill-advised. You should have seen the Portuguese man-of-wars. There were certainly plenty of them."

"I was worried about the pelican," Angel said from her position on the sofa where Stuart had deposited her after carrying her back to the house.

"You risked your life for that bird. Does that make you feel better?" He eyed her sternly from the kitchen, where he was diluting ammonia with water.

"I'm glad he's okay. Are you sure you saw him fly away?"

"Absolutely sure. He's probably diving for fish out past the reef right now, which is more than you're going to be doing," he said. He hurried into the living room and knelt by her side, washing the welts on her legs with the ammonia-and-water solution. His touch was gentle, and she felt a rush of gratitude toward him. Stuart was right, of course. She should have been more careful, should have seen the jellyfish floating on the surface of the water.

The ammonia stung, and she winced. Stuart glanced sharply at her face. "Some people have really bad reactions to man-of-war stings," he said. "Do you still feel nauseated?"

"No," she said, but she was lying. She always felt nauseated these days.

"If you start having trouble breathing, you'd better tell me," he said. "And you'd better get out of those wet clothes."

Angel struggled to sit up. "Bring me the robe hanging on the back of the bathroom door, will you?" she said.

He went and got the robe, handing it to her silently. "Do you want me to help you to bed?" he asked her.

She shook her head. With difficulty, she pulled her shirt up, and he helped her ease it over her head. Angel felt stifled under the wet fabric, finding it hard to breathe, and her stomach turned over. She pushed the shirt upward, but her hair was wet and tangled, and it snagged on one of the shirt's decorative buttons.

"Careful," Stuart said, cautiously unwinding the strand of hair.

Angel inhaled deeply when she was free of the shirt. Stuart was looking at her strangely.

"You still look a little green around the gills," he said.

"I'll be all right," she replied. She reached around and unhooked her bra, sliding it down her arms and setting it on top of the wet shirt. She knew Stuart was looking at her breasts, their nipples already swollen with the enlargement of early pregnancy, and though she still felt sick, she couldn't help feeling a thrill of pride that he desired her even when she looked like a drowned rat.

"Help me, Stuart," she said, trying to slide the wet shorts and panties down her legs, which were visibly branded in a crisscrossing pattern of welts that showed minute hemorrhages underneath.

He complied, expertly but carefully easing her clothes past the welts and over her feet. She slid her arms through the armholes of her robe and wrapped it around her, and Stuart helped with that, too. He was trying to look businesslike and failing miserably; in spite of the pain that she still felt from the man-of-war stings, Angel almost smiled. Even now, there was a sexual tension between them. These days, it never went away.

She felt a pleasant tightening in her lower abdomen, and it felt good but inappropriate. Ditto the way her nipples were puckering under the loose robe in anticipation of his touch. If Stuart had touched her at that moment, had given her any sign that he wanted her, she would have said yes. But, because of her unsettled stomach, Angel was glad when he didn't.

Stuart arranged a pillow behind her and tossed aside the wet bed sheet that he'd pulled over the couch to protect it from the seawater. She was surprised and yet somehow not surprised that he was so competent in handling this emergency.

She shifted onto her side and pillowed her hands under her cheek. "How did you know the proper first aid for man-of-war stings?" she asked him.

He studied the marks on her legs through narrowed eyes. "I've been around the sea all my life. I've sailed around the Caribbean enough to know what harm a Portuguese man-of-war can do."

"You have?" she said. The aspirins he had given her when they first came back to the house were making her drowsy, but she didn't want him to leave her; she didn't want to be left alone. But Stuart had been on his way to somewhere when he spotted her struggling out in the ocean; surely he wouldn't stick around once he had taken care of her. *Keep him talking*, she told herself.

Stuart sat on the floor and leaned back against the arm of the couch. "One summer when I was in college, a friend and I bummed around the Bahamas for two months. We crewed on a dive boat, and we ran into more than a few jellyfish and assorted nasty sea creatures," he said.

"Like what?"

"Barracudas. A shark or two. And once I stepped on a sea urchin."

"Mmm..." was all Angel said.

Stuart noticed her lassitude. "Would you like to sleep? Take a nap?" he asked sharply.

Angel shook her head. "No. I like to listen to you talk," she said.

"What would you like to talk about?"

"Tell me about your childhood," she said.

Probably she was merely making small talk, but he was reluctant to comply. He racked his brain, trying to think of an aspect of his childhood that he wanted to mention. The only thing he could think about was Valerie, and he didn't think that his childhood sweetheart was an appropriate topic to discuss with Angel McCabe.

She seemed to sense his hesitation. "How about your family?" she asked. "What are they like?"

His family. Certainly that was the last thing he wanted to talk about.

He started to tell her so, but one look into those interested brown eyes reminded him that she was going to be the mother of his child and had a right to know the bare essentials about that child's ancestry. He inhaled a deep breath.

"Family. Okay, here goes. My mother was of Boston Brahmin stock. My father comes from a long line of Adamses stretching back to the *Mayflower,* and he spent his whole life furthering the family shipbuilding empire. I have no sisters, and my only brother is a year younger than I am. My parents are both dead. My father died from too much drinking, and my mother died from too much smoking. I barely knew them, since I was reared by a succession of people who were paid to look after my brother and me." He was unaware of the bitterness in his voice until Angel spoke. He'd thought she was falling asleep.

"I'm sorry, Stuart," she said in a soft voice. To his surprise, she rested a hand on his arm and squeezed it in a show of support and reassurance. He was unaccountably moved by this, and he had to look away.

"When was the last time you saw your brother?" she said.

Of course. He'd known she was curious about the letter he'd received today.

"It's been a while," he said, in a tone that he hoped would put an end to her questions about his family.

She appeared to consider this for a while. He thought that if he was lucky, Angel would nod off, but she seemed more wide-awake than ever.

"I think it would be nice to have a brother or sister. It's sad when siblings aren't good friends," she said.

He managed a diffident shrug. "If you knew my brother, you wouldn't feel that way," he said, immediately regretting it.

"Oh? What's he like?"

How to explain Fitz? Stuart didn't think he could. How could he tell Angel about the rivalry that had been the overriding characteristic of his relationship with his brother, how they had fought since they were babies, first over who got to play with the red fire truck, and later over their allowances and which clothes belonged to whom? How could he tell her how he, as the older, more responsible sibling, had gotten Fitz out of trouble numerous times, with little appreciation from his brother? He didn't want to explain about the times he'd reasoned with schoolmates who were in the process of beating Fitz up and how he'd taken a few licks himself for his pains, or how he had bailed Fitz out of a hundred financial binds brought about by his brother's own bad judgment, or how he had corralled Fitz at family parties and hidden him away so that his snippy great-aunts wouldn't see his little brother when he was drunk.

"Fitz is just Fitz," he replied enigmatically. He stood up. "I think I'll check out the refrigerator, see what's handy for a snack," he said, and leaving her staring after him in openmouthed surprise, he headed for the kitchen.

If only he had been able to manufacture a more plausible excuse to get away, he thought morosely as he surveyed the few limp pieces of celery and half a key lime pie in the fridge. And now he might even have to eat something.

He didn't have to agonize over the choice for very long. He chose the pie.

WHAT IN THE WORLD had she said to make Stuart take off like that?

Angel heard him opening and closing the refrigerator and rummaging around in the silverware drawer, but she wasn't fooled. Chair legs scraped against the rough kitchen floor; she heard him sit down. There was no doubt in her mind that Stuart had started itching to get out of the room as soon as Fitz's name came up. She had seen it in his agitated expression.

Slowly she sat up and inspected the places on her legs where the man-of-war had stung her. Stuart's hands had been sure and soothing as he tended her wounds—as gentle as a woman's, in fact. They were hands that could easily comfort a child, but she didn't allow herself to hold that thought. If she started thinking in that vein, she'd start coming up with reasons why Stuart should be part of their child's life.

Suddenly her eyes came to rest on a crumpled piece of paper on the floor. Wincing with the pain, she leaned over and picked it up, recognizing almost immediately that this was the letter from Stuart's brother.

She had no right to read the letter. She knew that. But she heard the rhythmic clink of fork against plate as Stuart ate, and as long as he sat at the kitchen table, he would never know she was reading his letter. Even as she cautioned herself that she shouldn't do it, her fingers smoothed the paper flat.

She scanned the letter quickly, noting the impersonal tone and the signature that had almost certainly been mass-produced by a signature machine. Whatever she had expected of this communication from Stuart's brother, it was not this form letter signed so formally by H. Fitzroy Adams. Was this what Stuart had been so uptight about?

She heard Stuart push his chair back, so she quickly crushed the paper in her hand and tossed it to one side of the couch. He'd find it there later, none the wiser that she had read it.

Stuart came in at the same time that Caloosa entered through the pet door; the cat immediately crossed the porch and went to Angel.

"That fool cat got you into trouble. You could have drowned," Stuart said.

"But I didn't," Angel said.

"If you'll do something like trying to rescue a pelican in the middle of a bunch of man-of-wars, how can I trust you not to do the same kind of thing when you're pregnant? Or when the baby is small?" He was frowning at her, his arms crossed over her chest.

"I won't. I'll be more careful when I'm responsible for a child," she said, but she was thinking that if something happened to her on this island, so far away from other people, her baby would be all alone and no one would know it.

Stuart stood watching her with the cat, a whole panoply of expressions playing across his face. Angel, acting as if Caloosa had her full attention, pretended not to notice.

Stuart heaved a sigh and shook his head. "Sometimes, Angel, I wonder if you know what you're doing," he said.

Before Angel could reply, he turned his back and walked away. Anyway, she couldn't think of anything to say. Stuart was right. Maybe she didn't know what she was doing at all.

Chapter Eight

Not long after she recovered from her tangle with the man-of-war, Angel came in from the field to find Stuart sitting at the kitchen table, poring over one of her books on childbirth. "Did you know that only five percent of women give birth on their due dates?" he said without looking up.

"No," Angel said.

"That's what this book says," he told her. "Maybe you should read it."

"I'm saving it for later," Angel said. She took a loaf of bread out of the freezer and slapped it down on the counter. "Would you like a sandwich?"

"What kind?"

"Egg salad."

"Sure, sounds good."

Stuart flipped through other pages of the book while she made the sandwiches, and when she had finished, she sat down beside him to eat.

They had almost finished eating when Stuart said casually, "Isn't today the day your period is due?"

Although Angel was positive that she had conceived, she had no proof. She knew that she'd need to start going to Key West for prenatal checkups soon, but she wanted to postpone her first one as long as possible for fear that Stuart would find out she was pregnant. And she hadn't dared to use one of the home pregnancy test kits because she was sure that Stuart would notice it was missing. She might have known that Stuart would ask this particular question; with his sex-ed expertise, he probably kept track of her cycle better than she did.

"Nothing is supposed to happen until tomorrow," she said, getting up and rinsing her plate at the sink.

"Oh. I guess I got my dates mixed up. Days seem to run into each other when I don't have enough to do. You know, I've decided that next time I go fishing with Barky, I'll stop off in Key West and buy drafting supplies, so I can start designing that cabin cruiser for my friend Tom. He wants a forty-footer, state-of-the-art, all that kind of thing."

"Good idea," Angel said, thinking that this was a project that would keep Stuart busy and that he might want to stick around until it was finished—whether she was pregnant or not. Still, she knew that right now she should look him straight in the eye and say, "I'm pretty sure I'm pregnant." She did look him in the eye, but all she could force herself to say was "I'd better get back to work."

"Sure," he said easily. "I'll see you later. What do you say I chip a few more oysters off the dock pilings this afternoon? We'll have steamed oysters for dinner. By the way, aren't oysters an aphrodisiac?" He grinned at her.

"The last time you cooked them, they sure weren't," she said, leaving him speechlessly recalling the night before they were married when he'd tried to get her to talk about sex at a time when she didn't want to at all.

If Stuart really knew a lot about pregnant women, she told herself as she headed for the outhouse, he'd have realized that she'd been paying frequent visits there lately. Even if she hadn't had any other symptoms, to Angel, the sensitivity of her bladder would have been the real clincher.

As for aphrodisiacs, pregnancy was the best one ever invented. Angel, anticipating the evening, was sure of it.

THE NEXT NIGHT, Stuart asked casually, "Well, Angel, did it happen?"

Angel looked at him blankly. She was holding Caloosa and clipping her long claws with a metal clipper. She thought he was referring to the cat.

"Did what happen?" she asked.

He gave her a look of impatience, but it was fond impatience.

"Did you get your period?"

"Oh," she said, looking down at the cat's paws. She hesitated only slightly. "Yes," she said. "Yes, I did."

She glanced up in time to see Stuart's face fall. He looked so disappointed, as disappointed as she might have been if it was true.

"That's too bad," he said quietly.

"Yes, it is," she said in a level tone, but her heart was beating a mile a minute. She shouldn't be deceiving him this way; it was wrong, all wrong. But, oh, she wasn't ready for him to leave yet. Give her another month, one more month of nights spent making sweet love to each other, of turning to him in bed and feeling his arms go around her. Give her one more month of days on the beach, kissing until she could stand it no longer, then trying to make a baby right out in the broad daylight to the music of the surf spilling upon the sand. One more month. It would mean so much to her, and Stuart could spare the time. He had no timetable, no place he had to be.

Caloosa, perhaps sensing Angel's misgivings, leaped from her lap and chased a ball into the kitchen. The only sound in the room was the swish of the overhead fan and the chirp of tree frogs on the outside of the window, their long tongues lapping up insects drawn to the living room light.

"Don't look so sad," Stuart said, getting up and walking over to her. She sat looking up at him, hoping that he wouldn't read the deception on her face.

"I'm not," she said, and at least that was true. Or partly so, anyway.

"There'll be other chances," he said. "Lots of other chances."

"I know."

He sat down beside her and massaged the back of her neck. "Would you like me to rub your back? Valerie used to..." His words trailed off in midsentence.

"Valerie? Who's Valerie?" she said, instantly alert, but Stuart had clamped his lips together.

"It doesn't matter. Here, let me move around to the back of you... That's right. Relax, Angel. Do you have cramps?"

"Y-yes," she said, her mind reeling. Valerie must have been important to him; he used to rub her back when she had her period. So what had happened between them? Where was this Valerie now?

Stuart's cool hands on her back didn't do much to calm her active mind. She felt a sharp stab of jealousy; maybe the reason he wanted to leave her as soon as she became pregnant was because he wanted to get back to this Valerie, whoever she was.

"How does this feel?" Stuart said, close to her ear. His hands were inscribing circles on either side of her spine. It felt good.

For two cents, she would have turned to him, thrown her arms around his neck and begged to know if Valerie, whoever she was, was special to him. But she only answered quietly, "It feels fine."

He didn't speak anymore, and Angel finally straightened and stretched. "I'm really tired, Stuart. I think I'll go to bed now."

"You go ahead. I'll close up the house," he said.

She let Stuart go about the business of checking the pet door for Caloosa and turning out the lights. When she heard him leave the house, she quickly changed into her nightgown and switched off the bedroom light, knowing that he'd soon return from his trip to the outhouse. She climbed into bed and retreated to the corner, so that her back would be toward Stuart when he came in.

Soon she heard the back door close, and she listened while Stuart rummaged in the refrigerator for a snack. After a while, he walked into the room, his footsteps light, and she concentrated on breathing steadily as if she were asleep.

He parted the mosquito netting and sat down on the edge of the bed, causing her to roll slightly toward him when the mattress dipped. She stiffened, knowing that if she corrected her posture, Stuart would know she was awake.

"Angel?" he said in a low voice.

She kept breathing regularly, and soon he lay down on the bed beside her. He reached over and touched her arm briefly, but took his hand away after a moment. In a matter of minutes, he was asleep, but she lay awake in the dark for a long time, thinking over what she had done.

Her conclusion, in the moments before she fell asleep, was that she was wrong to have deceived Stuart, but if the result was that he would stay on Halos Island, then lying was worth it.

That night, or perhaps it was early morning, they were both awakened by an owl's cry somewhere close by. The owl hooted several times, then stopped. Angel, trying to get more comfortable, rolled over on her back and encountered Stuart's arm. She drew back from it and pulled the sheet up over her.

But he had awakened, and she heard him sigh, her name a mere whisper upon his lips. He slid his hand over and rested it for a moment on her hip. She froze. Sometimes, in the night, he reached for her, and often they came together blindly in the dark, linked not only by their willing bodies, but also by their pact to create a child. At those times, they eased effortlessly into and out of each other as if it were second nature. Which, by this time, it was.

"Mmm . . ." Stuart said sleepily, and she knew that he was only half-awake. His hand moved upward to cup her breast through her nightgown, a signal that he wanted to make love.

She was supposed to have cramps. If she really had cramps, she wouldn't want him to make love to her. Yet her nipple went rigid and tingled at his touch, and it was all she could do not to turn on her side and slide her leg over his.

Suddenly, Stuart's fingers became still. He had remembered. "Sorry," he said, a muffled word, and he withdrew his hand. Before she could reply, he had flopped over on his stomach and was breathing in and out, in and out, the rhythmic inhalation and exhalation of a man fast asleep.

Angel, however, was not asleep. She lay on her back, the sheet pulled up to her chin, and tears slowly seeped from her eyes.

If she had not lied to him, they would be making love at this very minute. And it would have nothing to do with wanting a baby, but everything to do with wanting each other. It would be the very best kind of lovemaking, and it made her sad that it wasn't going to happen—at least not tonight.

It was a week or so later that Stuart brought home the sailboat.

Angel was outside gathering fresh tomatoes from the garden when she saw a sail approaching far out to sea. She watched for a moment but didn't recognize the boat. It was Saturday, not the day for Toby to bring the mail. And this little craft with its white billowing sail bore absolutely no resemblance to Barky's runabout with its distinctive putt-putt motor. In fact, Angel knew no one who owned a sailboat.

She set the tomatoes aside and walked slowly toward the dock. She recognized Stuart at the tiller as the boat drew closer. He was smiling, his hair blown back from his forehead by the wind. She ran to meet him.

As the sailboat glided toward her, Stuart's grin broadened, his teeth white against his tan. He tossed her a line. "Hang on to that for a minute, will you?" he called.

She caught the line and hauled on it, then began to fire questions. "Is this your boat? What happened to Barky? Didn't you go fishing?"

Stuart jumped onto the dock and loomed over her, hands on his hips, a smile of amusement curving his lips. "The answers are yes, it is my boat, and yes, we did go fishing for a while, but we gave up and went to Key West when we didn't catch anything."

"Looks like you caught *something,*" she said, her eyes taking in the bright shiny sailboat with its polished brass fittings.

"She's a beauty, isn't she?"

"She's quite a boat, all right. Where'd you find her?"

"Barky had a friend who wanted to sell her, and when I found out that she was built by a Bahamian native, I was interested. She's made for sailing around the shallow reefs of the Bahamian out islands, so she has no centerboard and the keel's small. She should be perfect for sailing the waters in these keys."

At the moment, all Angel could think about was that the sailboat gave Stuart a way to leave the island whenever he wanted. "I don't know much about boats," she said.

He smiled at her. "I thought I'd teach you to sail."

"Me? Sail?" She laughed, genuinely amused.

"What? You think you won't like it?"

"I know I won't, Stuart. I've been sailing once in my life, and I spent the whole time ducking and dodging. This big stick swings around—"

"It's called a boom," Stuart supplied.

"And you have to keep leaning in different directions," she said.

"That's to balance the boat."

"As you can tell, I know nothing about boats, I'm scared to go sailing around in the ocean, and I'm not athletic at all."

"You look pretty athletic when you're swimming," he said.

She wrinkled her nose. "When I'm swimming, I don't think you're admiring my athletic prowess," she said saucily. It was becoming increasingly easy, now that she knew Stuart better, to tease him, and he seemed to like it.

He slung an arm around her shoulders. "Will you give it a try?" he asked.

"I don't know about a landlubber like me learning to sail, but I'd like to go out on her, if you'll take me." She liked bearing the weight of his arm; she liked the way he was grinning down at her.

"Can you go now? I've an urge to explore some of the isolated keys to the south of here."

"Well . . ."

"Come on, be an angel, Angel," he coaxed in his most winsome way, making her smile.

It was no use trying to resist him when he was so charming. "All right," she said. She glanced at her watch. "It's getting late. I could bring along the chicken I fried earlier, and some drinks, and we could eat dinner over near Fiddler's Key."

"That's the best idea you've had all day. Want me to help carry things?"

"There's not much to carry. You stay here and admire your new boat, and I'll be back in a few minutes. By the way, what's her name?"

"Right now she doesn't have one," he said.

"We'll christen her tonight. Between the two of us, we'll think of something."

"If we're going to be christening a boat, you'd better bring that bottle of champagne from the pantry. I bought it for a special occasion. We'll splash some on the bow and drink the rest."

"Oh, I don't think I'd better have any," Angel said, without thinking. Knowing that she was pregnant, she had made a conscious decision not to drink alcoholic beverages for the duration.

"Why?" Stuart asked, looking puzzled.

Realizing her slip, Angel made herself look as indifferent as possible. "I won't be drinking alcoholic beverages when I'm pregnant. I thought I might as well stop now," she said.

"Well, we already know you're not pregnant yet. In fact—" Stuart squinted into the sun as he rapidly subtracted "—at this point, you're about five days away from your most fertile period. Am I right?"

He would have been right if she hadn't already conceived. "Right," she said with reluctance.

"So bring the champagne and two glasses. And hurry up. This is a great boat for sailing before the wind, but the drift makes tacking difficult, so it's going to be slow going."

Angel turned away, wishing she could be honest. If things had been different, she and Stuart might have been able to turn this inaugural cruise into a celebration of something wonderful. But now her worry was compounded; if Stuart wanted to leave the island, he now had the means. He wouldn't even have to wait for a Tuesday or a Thursday so that he could leave with Toby on the mail boat.

A FEW HOURS LATER, Angel sat across from Stuart in the new sailboat with her feet up and a plate of fried chicken in her lap. They were riding at anchor off the coast of Fiddler's Key, the boat rocking gently on the outgoing tide.

The short cruise had turned into a glorious experience that Angel enjoyed tremendously. They'd started to eat their dinner shortly after dropping anchor, and now the bright orange crescent of the sun was sinking into the sea behind the key in an exquisite show of pink and amber and pale, pale blue.

"So what do you think about the boat?" he asked her.

"Before this, I only experienced boats as a means of getting from one place to another. Sailing is more like recreation than transportation," she said.

"Not too much duck and dodge?"

"You kept it to a minimum." She smiled at him.

Stuart unexpectedly waved his glass of champagne in the air and stood up, balancing himself as the boat rose and fell on the gentle swell of the waves.

"I hereby christen this boat *Angel's Wings* in honor of my beautiful wife. Angel, the way you looked today when we tacked into the wind made me think of it. With your hair streaming behind you, all silvery gold in the sunlight, you looked as if you'd taken flight." He moved toward the bow and tossed the contents of his glass toward it. The drops seemed to hang suspended, glinting like liquid gold before falling onto the bow.

Angel, who had taken advantage of Stuart's turned back to pour the untouched contents of her own glass over the side, smiled back. "You shouldn't have named this boat after me," she said.

"If not you, then whom? It's customary to name a boat after one's wife." He sat down beside her and draped a casual arm across her knee.

She looked down at the wedding ring on her finger. "I keep forgetting that I *am* your wife," she said in a moment of rare candor.

"I don't," Stuart said, tracing the neckline of her shirt with his thumb. His eyes were a deep, translucent blue in the shadowy dusk. She especially liked it when he looked at her like this; he made her feel like the center of the universe. *His* universe.

"You'll forget soon enough," she said tartly.

"Will I?" he said softly.

"I hear that it's really nice in the South Seas. Life can be easy there—"

"Easier than on Halos Island? That's hard to imagine."

"And the natives in their villages run around with hardly any clothes on, and—"

"So do we."

"And it's far away from everything," she finished.

"Far away from you," he said.

"And our marriage," she reminded him.

This earned a raised eyebrow from Stuart. "Shall we talk about our marriage, Angel?" he said.

She managed a laugh. "What's to talk about?" she said offhandedly, but inside, she was confused. Relationship talk had always been off-limits, by tacit understanding.

Stuart removed the plate from her lap and twined his fingers through hers. "I've learned in the past few weeks that being married is different from not being married," he said. He sounded pensive and a little amazed.

"Didn't we know that?" Angel said.

"It's one thing knowing it. It's another thing living it," he told her seriously.

Angel thought she might agree, but she had no intention of telling Stuart. All she said was "What makes marriage different from, let's say, merely living together?"

Stuart leaned back and sighed, still holding her hand. "Commitment," he said.

"Commitment?" she repeated slowly. They both knew that he didn't have any commitment to her aside from the financial one that he had made to support their child.

"Yeah" was all he said, but now his smile was uncertain.

Angel's gaze fell on the ring on the third finger of her left hand. She heard her blood rushing in her ears. "Stuart, you have no commitment to me. That's understood."

"Theoretically that's true. Contractually it's true, as well. But emotionally, well, there's something there."

"Probably it could be explained in an anthropological sense," Angel said. "In the original hunter-gatherer society, the male had a natural impulse to protect the mother of his children. Therefore, committed relationships ensued," she said.

"'Therefore, committed relationships ensued,'" he said, mimicking her. "All that stuff you learned on the way to your Ph.D. has cluttered up your brain. Do you have a scientific explanation for everything, Angel? Do you always have to try to turn personal interludes into cerebral exercises?"

"Probably," Angel said in a small voice. The moon was rising, and with it the wind. The boat bobbed up and down on the waves, and the air had cooled. The rocking of the boat should have been soothing, but instead it only enhanced Angel's growing agitation at the way this conversation was getting out of hand.

All this talk of commitment made Angel wary. She had committed—once. She had been dumped—once. She wouldn't let it happen to her again.

"Angel," Stuart said, "look at me."

She turned her head. Stuart was gazing at her with a serious expression. It caught her by surprise.

"Wh—what?" she said, her voice catching. Her gaze locked with his.

"The past few weeks have in some ways been the happiest in my life. I'll always remember them. I want you to know that."

She started to shake her head, sure that he was exaggerating, but his finger against her lips stopped the words.

"Shh," he said. "Don't talk, my Angel. Just kiss me."

She lifted her lips to his, and as his mouth covered hers, she felt as though her heart would break. The weeks since Stuart had arrived on Halos Island had been the happiest of her life, too, and she'd only realized it now. She had been only half-alive as she lived with her bees and her cat on the deserted island to which she'd fled, bruised and tattered, to recover from her disastrous love affair. Since Stuart Adams had arrived, she'd relearned what it was like to feel open and alive again. When he left, she'd be all the better for this experience, the experience of knowing a kind, caring man who made her feel like a real woman again.

When he left. She would try not to say those words, even to herself. Because when he left, Stuart would take a piece of her heart with him.

His fingers glided across her body, quickly dispensing with her clothes and then his. She felt herself giving way to it, giving in to a man in a way she had never been able to before. Her mind was filled with him, her senses overwhelmed by him, and the soft swirls of dark hair on his chest were teasing her already sensitive breasts, his hips were pressing against hers, and she was holding him tightly, as if she would never let him go.

It could have been a frenzied mating, but instead Angel felt enveloped in a deep tenderness that seemed to surround Stuart and flow into her as she molded her body to his. She was aware of her breathing synchronizing with his, of the tautness of his body tensed in anticipation. Each and every time he touched her like this, it was exciting to her, made her want him all the more. He made her feel bold and wildly sensual, he made her bloom into the woman she had always wanted to be.

"Stuart, oh, Stuart..." she murmured as his hands teased her with agonizing slowness. "What do you do to me?"

"The same thing you do to me," he whispered, the planes of his face etched in moonlight, and he entered her slowly so that they would both savor the moment. Slowly, slowly, each millimeter sending warm waves of desire fanning upward and outward, until she held him snug and tight within her.

He made a move to bury his face in her hair, but she said, "No, I want to look at you." He smiled in instant understanding, his eyes dark with passion, and wove his fingertips through her hair until they pressed against her skull. His skin against hers was like silk, slipping and sliding, pure erotic pleasure. In a burst of energy, she wrapped her legs around him, urging him to bury himself deep inside her, consuming him in the only way she knew how.

She would have closed her eyes, because she was afraid that he could see through her to her very soul, but when her eyelids started to drift shut, Stuart spoke sharply. "No. Open your eyes, Angel. I want to know more than your body."

She opened her eyes, feeling fully revealed as she watched his expression slip into transport, then abandon. And yet she knew that she still did not know Stuart Adams. She knew his body, and she might be getting a glimpse of his soul, but she could not know his heart.

He moved against her harder and faster, and she met him stroke for stroke, watching his shadowed face as he strained toward his peak. She was one with him for this brief moment in time, and it was more than physical, it was an ecstasy that she had never dreamed possible. This was beyond passion, beyond pleasure, a journey up, up, into a realm that she had never known existed. This was mating, but it was also something finer, something more exquisite, more meaningful.

When she could no longer think, when the world had receded to a tiny bright pinpoint deep within her brain, when her eyes had lost their focus so that they no longer saw Stuart's face but seemed filled with the stars whirling high above them in the dark curtain of the sky, the world and the stars and the night burst into a thousand—a million—fragments of light. She heard herself cry his name, and she heard his voice in her ear, and in that moment, she was not only part of him, they were part of the whole universe, and for once in her life it all made sense.

Woman. Man. That was all there was, and that was all there needed to be.

"Angel?"

The harmony of their breathing brought them down together. Stuart's voice pierced her consciousness, and when she opened her eyes, she realized that he was staring at her in perplexity.

"Are you all right, Angel?" His voice was tender, caring.

She couldn't speak. She could only stare up at his dear face, so familiar, and now so much a part of her life.

"Y-yes," she said. She had never been more all right in her life.

"Then why are you crying?" he asked. He touched a fingertip to her face, and it came away wet with her tears.

She could only look at him, her eyes still brimming with unshed tears, and silently she lifted his wet fingertip to her mouth and kissed it.

"I don't want to make you sad," he said in a bewildered tone.

She could not bear to talk about her feelings at that moment—perhaps she'd never be able to let Stuart know how she felt—so for an answer she only pulled his head down upon her breast and lay back in the rocking boat, the breeze drying her wet face.

"Angel?" he said, his fingers caressing her breast.

"Shh," she said, staring up at the stars. "Shh."

Chapter Nine

They fell into a routine of living together, probably the way most married people did. The fact that they were not like most newlyweds seemed unimportant in the face of what they did in their daily lives.

Angel began to feel comfortable around Stuart. He never criticized her, never belittled her. He was so different from what she had learned to expect from a man that he might as well have been a different species altogether.

He was interested in her work. He asked her questions about it. Howard had never done that, even though he was a scientist, too. She told Stuart as much about her bees as she thought he could absorb, but he never seemed to tire of hearing her talk about them. Curious, she asked him why he was so interested.

"I like the way you look when you talk about your bees. I like your enthusiasm. I find the things you tell me interesting. Hey, what can I say? I'm a honey of a guy."
He laughed at himself, but she agreed. The more she got to know Stuart Adams, the better she liked him.

He made life fun again. *When had it become so serious?* she wondered. After she came to the island? When she broke up with Howard? Once she had been a person who liked to go to movies, to dance, to sleep late once in a while. She was rediscovering that person, bit by bit, with Stuart's help.

They went to Key West and saw a play, spending the weekend in the honeymoon suite at the Kapok Tree again. He bought her a dress with black spangles, even though she protested that she'd never wear it. He proved her wrong by treating her to a nightclub where they listened to jazz and Stuart drank margaritas while he admired the way she looked in her new black dress. They danced together, and again she was so nervous that she stepped all over his feet. He didn't seem to mind. "You'll learn," he said. "You'll learn."

She *was* learning—learning to like herself and him. After only a few weeks of being married, she couldn't recall life on the island before Stuart.

They settled into a life of comfortable domesticity punctuated by the things that Stuart did to make things interesting. He was definitely no couch potato, and she learned that her suspicions about his being a complete romantic were absolutely correct. This fascinated her; she'd always thought that women were the romantic ones in a relationship, but no one, absolutely no one, could be more romantic than Stuart Adams.

"What's this?" he said one night, pulling a dilapidated, mildewed Leatherette case out of the living-room closet. Angel looked up from the button she was sewing on a pair of shorts.

"Oh, that's an old portable Victrola. Those navy guys must have left it here," she said.

"Does it work?"

"I don't know," she said, snipping the thread. She folded the shorts and set them aside. Stuart opened the lid of the Victrola to reveal a turntable and an arm, both remarkably free of dust.

"It doesn't matter whether it works or not, if we don't have any records," he pointed out in a bemused tone.

"I think there might be records in the back of the closet. Look behind the ironing board."

Stuart knelt on the floor and tugged at a cardboard box until it sat in front of him. "Look at these," he said, wiping away the dust. "Old 78 rpm records. Collector's items, some of them."

"Are there any Glenn Miller? My grandmother used to play those."

"Sure. Right here is 'String of Pearls,' and here's 'Tuxedo Junction.' We've got 'Stardust' and 'Green Eyes' and 'Pennsylvania 6-5000.' Miss Beatrice couldn't have provided better dance music at the Junior Cotillion," he said.

It always made Angel feel uncomfortable when Stuart mentioned his life in Boston or on Nantucket. He came from a life of privilege, and she did not. She couldn't even imagine living the way Stuart must have lived before he came to Halos Island.

As she watched, Stuart plugged in the Victrola and set a stack of records on the changer. When the first strains of "String of Pearls" filled the air, he stood up and held his arms out to her. "May I have this dance?" he said.

"Can't we just listen?" she implored. She was still self-conscious about her dancing.

"No sense in sitting around like lazy slugs," Stuart said, pulling her up beside him.

"I should think that you'd had enough of my dancing," she said, but she went into his arms anyway.

His voice was close by her ear, and it sent warm tremors through her. "I never get enough of any part of you," he said before twirling her around in an intricate maneuver that she could barely execute.

She was dizzy, as though she'd had too much to drink. "Stop, Stuart," she said, but he only pulled her closer. It was so enjoyable to be close to him, smelling his scent of fresh-washed cotton and sun-warmed skin, bending and dipping gracefully in his arms.

The record changed to a song Angel didn't recognize. Stuart flung her away from him, looking carefree and younger than his years. *This time on the island has been good for him,* Angel thought. As he pulled her close again, she curved her arm even farther around his shoulder, wanting to feel every contour of him, wanting to make him want her. At the moment, she felt sexy and wanton and exceedingly voluptuous, traits that were foreign to her. Or had been before she met this man who was now her husband.

Her husband. The words seemed to have taken on new meaning, new nuances.

Her husband was whispering in her ear. "You're getting it, Angel. You're a really good dancer," he said.

"Two left feet," she whispered back.

"Your feet aren't the body parts I'm thinking about at the moment," he said. He lowered his hands and rested them on her buttocks, cupping her firmly against him. She let her head fall back, caught up in the scratchy romantic music from the Victrola and in the attentions of this very handsome, exciting man whose growing excitement she could feel through her clothes. She felt her own power over him and smiled up from beneath her eyelids, giving him a long, smoldering look.

He lowered his head to kiss her lips briefly before letting his mouth drift to her throat. He skimmed his hands slowly upward over her rib cage, until they reached her breasts. She moaned. His hips ground insistently into hers, and she pressed into it, into him.

"I like this kind of dancing," he said, keeping his hands where they were and guiding her around the room.

"I think," she said unsteadily, "we should go into the bedroom."

"You do, do you?" he said.

"Yes," she whispered against his rough cheek.

"There are a few new steps that you definitely need to learn." He moved his hands and tugged gently at her nipples until she was hungry for more.

She reached for him, cupping her hands possessively around his erection. "Tat for tit," she murmured, and he laughed.

"I love it when you talk that way to me. I love doing this," he said as the shoulder of her blouse fell down her arm. He slid it down even farther as the record changed to a slow samba, and she said helplessly, "I don't know how to dance to these Latin rhythms."

Her blouse was around her waist, and her breasts were open to the cool night air. Somehow their feet were still moving, though barely. She pulled his shirt aside, and he said, "With Latin rhythms, it's all in the hips," demonstrating something that would not have been allowed on any dance floor.

"Am I ready for Miss Beatrice's Junior Cotillion?" Angel asked mischievously as she nibbled on his earlobe.

"I'd say you've far surpassed anything Miss Beatrice ever knew."

And what about Valerie? Does she know how to dance like this, too? Angel wanted to ask, but it was a question she could never ask Stuart. She pushed aside the stab of jealousy and concentrated on following Stuart's lead. He was moving them slowly and inexorably toward the bedroom.

The needle on the phonograph got stuck on part of a song that went, "thrill me, thrill me, thrill me," and Stuart said, "Thrill me, Angel," and she thought, *One advantage that I have over this Valerie person is that at this moment, Stuart Adams is here with me. And he is my lawfully wedded husband.*

"Have we practiced enough steps?" she inquired innocently as they reached the bedroom door.

"There's one more," he said unsteadily as he laid her on the bed and lowered himself over her, supporting himself on his outstretched arms.

"Show me," she said, reaching for him. And he did.

The record continued to scratch, urging "thrill me, thrill me," for hours; neither of them was listening. At least not on that particular frequency.

THE NEXT DAY after breakfast, Stuart said with a twinkle in his eye, "Since you caught on so quickly to my dancing lessons, I thought I'd teach you to sail today."

Angel shot him a look of pure alarm. "I hope you're not expecting me to have the same natural aptitude for sailing that I do for dancing."

"Your dancing," he said, leaning over to kiss her quickly on the lips, "is superb. Unequaled in modern history. I'm willing to settle for a lower level of perfection in your sailing skills. Oh, and wear shoes with rubber soles. Old sneakers or something."

Angel could tell he wasn't about to take no for an answer, nor would he listen to lame excuses. Consequently, Angel soon found herself boarding the boat that Stuart now referred to as *Angel's Wings.*

"Think of sailing the same way as you think about riding a bike. Once you learn it, you'll never forget it," Stuart said as they cast off from the dock.

This she most certainly did not believe. She had been trying to forget what sailing was like ever since earlier experience with it. "Isn't the water a little rough?" she asked anxiously. She thought she'd spotted a whitecap or two beyond the reef. Maybe she could talk him out of this if she convinced him that beginners had no business learning to sail in rough seas.

Stuart glanced out to sea. "No, it's as smooth as a mirror, and even if it were rough, you'd find your sea legs after a while," he said.

Sea legs, Angel thought dismally. *What about my sea stomach?* She hadn't dared to take a motion-sickness tablet before leaving the house. She thought it might not be good for the baby.

Stuart didn't know it, but morning sickness was now more than a quirk of pregnancy, it was a full-fledged problem that was almost impossible to hide. Never had she thought morning sickness could make her feel so awful; it hadn't the first time she was pregnant. She had felt fine. But that was then. This was now, and an unsteady now at that. She inhaled deeply, hoping the fresh air would help.

"We'll get out on the open sea," Stuart called to her as he busied himself with lines and sails and other parts of the sailboat that, despite a short lesson on the subject, Angel didn't yet know the name of. "Then I'll show you how to come about."

She swallowed and felt stupid. She had no idea what he was talking about. "Come about?" she said, trying to look interested.

"It means tacking through the eye of the wind when sailing a zigzag course to windward," Stuart said. He clapped her on the back. "You'll be a good crew member. I'm sure of it."

He seemed not to notice that she was distinctly green around the gills as they sailed effortlessly through the cut. Stuart looked as if he were in his element, his hair unruly in the wind, his hand firm upon the tiller. She would have warmed to him if she'd felt all right, but at the moment all she could feel was resentful. And sick to her stomach. How could he insist that she go out on a boat when she was pregnant?

Oops, she thought. *Almost forgot. He doesn't know.*

"When it's time to put in a tack, I'll shout, 'Ready about,'" Stuart said.

"Ready about what?" she said. She could already taste bile at the back of her throat.

He grinned. "You really are a novice, aren't you? 'Ready about' is a warning for the crew to prepare for the tack. When I start the turn, I'll say, 'Hard-alee.'"

"Hard-alee. Sounds like 'Hardly.' As in I *hardly* think I'm going to like this."

Stuart only laughed.

Angel thought she had managed to get a grip on her nausea when he shouted, "Ready about." The call "Hard-alee" came shortly after that, and the forceful turn of the boat lurched her to the center.

"That's good, Angel," Stuart said. "Stay there to balance the boat." He shifted his weight to the other side of the boat while she crouched where she was. God, she felt awful.

"Stuart, I—" she began. She wanted to go back to the island. She should have made up some excuse, any excuse, to get out of this.

"All right, now we want to—" Stuart began.

"Stuart, I can't," she said, clutching her stomach.

"What?" he said, his expression questioning.

But she didn't get a chance to tell him what. Instead, she leaned over him and tossed her breakfast into the sea.

"A MERE UPSET," she said when they were back at the house. "I get seasick sometimes."

"The water wasn't rough at all, and you've never even mentioned seasickness before. You've been on this island how long? Three years? Traveling back and forth to Key West by boat?"

"The *mail* boat, Stuart. I've never been on a *sail*boat the whole time I've been here," she pointed out.

Stuart shook his head in disbelief. "All right, all right, I can't deny that you were really sick. Listen, Angel, you'd better take it easy. I'm going to cook dinner."

He tossed a salad together, gathering the cucumbers from her garden and humming to himself as he worked. It wasn't until he started frying hamburgers that Angel's stomach revolted.

She had to eat; otherwise, Stuart would grow suspicious. She couldn't imagine why he hadn't caught on already that her symptoms were suspiciously like those of pregnancy. Stuart, unlike most men, was neither bored nor baffled by the mysterious inner workings of a woman's body. And he knew her body intimately.

Stuart brought trays into the living room, and she accepted hers without comment. He sat down in a chair across from her and gulped down his hamburger heartily, while she only picked at hers. She could hardly bear to watch him eat.

She swallowed hard against the nausea; it refused to go away. She had to concentrate mightily on each swallow, and then she had to take a deep breath and force herself to take another mouthful. She became light-headed with the effort.

"Is your hamburger all right?" Stuart said when he saw that she had eaten only half.

"Wonderful," Angel said, feigning an enthusiasm that she did not feel, and all the while she was thinking, *Lies, lies and more lies*. Why had she ever decided that honesty was the next-best policy?

Later, when she had managed to get her recalcitrant stomach under control, she sat quietly, appreciating her lack of nausea, and thinking that the poet had been right when he wrote,

> O what a tangled web we weave,
> When first we practice to deceive.

Although in her case, the poem should be altered, since she didn't deal with spiders but with solitary bees, who nest in the ground:

> O what a tumbled tunnel we dig
> When we fill it with lies so big.

And it seemed as if she were digging herself deeper into that tunnel all the time.

AFTER THE NEXT DAY, when a whiff of a rotten fish washed ashore at the high-tide line sent her running for the woods, Angel avoided the beach as much as possible. Consequently, she spent a lot of time in the field, and one day Stuart surprised her by bringing her a tall, cold drink when she was lying on her stomach in a thicket, patiently watching one of her bees build her nest.

She sat up when Stuart appeared.

"Mind if I interrupt?" he asked. He held out a thermos and she opened it.

"Mmm... What is this?"

"It's tea laced with juice from the key limes that Toby brought the other day."

"You're getting handy around the kitchen," she said. She poured some of the tea into the cap of the thermos. "Want some?" she asked, holding it toward Stuart.

He shook his head. "I drank a glassful before I left the house." He gestured at the bee, which was hovering outside the hole it had been digging. "What are you doing here, anyway?"

"Observing," she said. She never knew these days how eating or drinking was going to affect her stomach, but the tea was good; it slid easily down her throat. Stuart stared at the bee. "I often wonder how you can do this day after day. Don't you ever get tired of it?"

She shook her head. "Never."

"I would," he said, studying her. She knew he was admiring her; she liked it. She enjoyed being the focus of his attention more and more these days, even when it was focused on what she had always considered her physical liabilities, which Stuart had by this time convinced her were assets.

"I'd get tired of designing boats," she pointed out. "How's your work coming on that cabin cruiser, anyway?"

"I'm having fun with it. It's so easy to concentrate here on the island, where there's no telephone and no interruptions— By the way, the last time I went to Key West I forgot to buy that shortwave radio. Next time I'll pick one up. It'll put you in touch with the rest of the world."

"I only hope I can learn how to work it," Angel said dryly.

"No problem. I'll teach you," he said.

"Always teaching me something, aren't you?" she said fondly.

"With varied success," he pointed out as he sat down. He smiled lazily. "Why don't you teach me something? I'd like to know what you and your bees are doing today that's so fascinating, for instance."

She lay down on her stomach again. "Observe this female.... No, you'll have to come down to ground level. Lie down beside me." She patted the patch of sand next to her.

When their shoulders were touching, she said, "Okay, now watch her dig her nest."

It was silent except for the whirring of insects in the brush as the subject female bee created a subterranean home. She stood on her four hind legs and swept at the dirt with her forelegs, shoving the sand backward under her abdomen.

"I'm glad we don't have to do that to create a home for our baby," Stuart whispered.

"Stop trying to be funny. You'll disturb her," Angel said. Stuart rolled his eyes at her seriousness, but they watched in companionable silence until at last the bee flew away.

Stuart said with a certain amount of relief in his voice, "Is it over? Can we go?"

Angel looked over at him and grinned. "You go. I'm here for the day," she said.

"All day?" he asked incredulously.

She nodded and sat up, brushing the sand off her front.

"What if that bee doesn't come back? What if another bee comes back and you think it's the old bee?"

"Another bee wouldn't be interested in this one's nest, and the same bee will come back, all right. It's her instinct. Unless she is injured or killed, of course. But she knows where she started building her nest. She won't abandon it.''

"What's the purpose, Angel? Why do you spend hours watching these bees? What are you looking for?''

She looped her arms around her legs and hugged them to her. "I don't know," she admitted.

"You don't know, and yet you spend hours out here in the hot sun watching insects?''

"I observe. That's my job. I'm not sure what I'm looking for, but if we waited until we knew what questions to ask about a subject, a lot of potentially valuable information would be lost. So I continue watching this unique species, hoping that the fragments of knowledge that I gather will someday be assembled into a whole for the betterment of the world in some way.'' Angel could speak passionately about this; her work had for so long been her life, and hardly anyone ever asked about it.

Stuart was looking at her with new respect. "I wish you'd told me all this before," he said.

"I didn't think you were interested," she replied.

"I wasn't. But I am now.''

She shrugged. "This is what science is all about. It's not only about Nobel prizes or discovering new medicines or going on expensive expeditions to the Amazon. It's about little people like me, doing what they love to do, furthering man's knowledge about the world the best we can.''

"I was going to ask you to go sailing with me. Maybe I've changed my mind," he said, getting to his feet.

She looked up at him. She didn't care if she never went sailing again after her first and only lesson, but now she knew how it felt when he showed interest in the activity that was nearest and dearest to her heart.

"How about tomorrow?" she heard herself say. "I'll make time in the morning."

He grinned, and his eyes lit up. She could tell he was pleased.

"Tomorrow," he said, and he walked away whistling.

THE NEXT DAY was a beautiful day for a sail, and Angel's stomach was cooperating this time. They left the island in midmorning. Once they were outside the coral reef, Stuart began the sailing lesson in earnest. He demonstrated how to push the tiller down and away in order to bring the bow around through the eye of the wind, and he showed her how to release the jib sheets. Angel was an avid pupil, mostly because she wanted to please.

Her first test came when the boat turned through the wind, and the crew—in this case, Angel—was supposed to pull the jib sheet across, which she did successfully.

"Good!" Stuart told her. "You're doing great."

It was easy to do well as long as she felt all right, and Stuart was adept at directing her. As it grew close to noon, Angel realized that she loved swooping along on the surface of the sea beneath the infinite blue sky; on a day like this, everything seemed right with the world.

"Want to be the skipper for a while?" Stuart said.

"Oh, Stuart, I don't think—" she began.

"You can do it. The best way to learn is by doing," he said.

This was something she knew to be true, and although she wanted to learn only in order to please Stuart, she took his place at the tiller. "Having fun?" he asked her once, and she laughed. "I like this more and more," she admitted, and he reached over and squeezed her hand.

"Let's head for home," Stuart said finally. "You can take her."

All went well until they were within sight of the reef. Angel was prepared to let Stuart take over, knowing that she wasn't ready to guide the boat through the cut in the coral, but in those last few seconds before Stuart was supposed to take her place at the tiller, something happened to the wind. The tiller felt dead, so Angel compensated by giving it more action.

"The wind direction has shifted," Stuart said. "Don't let it get on the other side of the sail, or—"

The wind caught the sail and slammed at it as if it were an open door.

"Careful!" Stuart shouted, but it was too late. Angel froze as the swinging boom caught Stuart squarely on the side of the head and he fell, almost as if in slow motion, into the bottom of the boat.

Chapter Ten

"Stuart! Oh, my God! Stuart?"

He didn't answer.

The wind shifted again, and she got the boat under control. She couldn't stop what she was doing to tend to Stuart; she couldn't take the chance of capsizing the boat. As she brought the boat around, Stuart moaned and sat up.

"What happened?" he said.

"The boom came around and hit you," she said frantically, reaching for him. "Are you all right?"

"It damn near knocked me overboard," he said as he struggled to sit up. "I still feel a little woozy. I think I was out cold for a minute."

"Stuart, I'm so sorry. Maybe we'd better get you to a doctor. Maybe—"

But Stuart refused to sail all the way to Key West. "A doctor is definitely not necessary," he said as he took her place at the tiller. "I feel fine."

"*I* feel awful," Angel said, and the words earned her a keen look from Stuart.

"You're not getting seasick, are you?" he asked sharply.

"No, no, I only meant that I feel terrible that I made such a disastrous mistake," she said hastily, averting her face so that he wouldn't see her expression.

"We learn from our mistakes—remember that. Now, matey, let's take this little bucket home," Stuart said.

Still heartsick about having caused the accident, Angel scrambled to follow his instructions to the letter as he tacked through the opening in the reef and down the home stretch toward the dock.

"Are you *sure* you're really all right?" Angel asked again as she and Stuart secured the boat.

"I was all right enough to get us back here," he said pointedly, but Angel thought he looked pale, despite his tan.

"How's your head?" she asked, reaching up to finger the lump.

"I've got a slight headache," he said. "Don't worry about it. I've been hit worse."

"The boom really socked you in the head. I wish there was a doctor nearby. I wish I could be sure everything is okay," she said anxiously as they made their way up the path.

"Angel, stop dithering over me. I should have ducked and dodged a little faster, that's all. A short rest in the porch hammock, and I'll be as good as new."

"I should have been paying more attention to the wind," Angel said remorsefully. "I shouldn't have pushed on the tiller so hard."

"*I* should have supervised you more carefully. As your instructor, I'm the one who was lax." When they reached the front porch, he smiled reassuringly and gave her a brief hug. "While you're still in a guilty frame of mind, maybe you could bring me an aspirin."

Angel brought him two aspirins and a glass of water, and he swallowed both pills at once. "I'll get some ice so you won't have a big lump on your head," she said, bustling away to the kitchen.

Angel wasn't sure she believed that he was okay, especially after he'd sustained such a strong blow, but when Stuart flung himself into the porch hammock and suggested that she make a pot of conch chowder, she decided that there wasn't much more she could do for him.

As she cut up the conchs and tossed them in the big soup pot, she kept an eye on him as he rested. Just in case.

ANGEL had been handling the boat well, and then this had had to happen, Stuart thought to himself as he swung gently in the hammock. He was all right, but it was as if the incident had leached the self-confidence right out of her. Maybe she'd regain it. With more work, with more successes as she learned to maneuver the sailboat, she'd be fine. Fine . . . she'd be fine. He shifted to a more comfortable position and lapsed into a fitful doze, the bag of ice held to his forehead.

He dreamed a dream that seemed as if it were happening to him at that very instant. It took him back to his past, to a time when all things seemed possible and his future as a member of the family firm was assured. A different future, bespeaking the lifestyle that he had grown up expecting to live, a life filled with family, friends, children, privilege, position. It was the kind of life to which all Adamses aspired, and the young Stuart had been no exception.

In his dream, he and Fitz had recently arrived on Nantucket for their two-week vacation, as they did every summer. Valerie was there, too, laughing up at him, her eyes bright with the new knowledge that only the two of them shared. She was three weeks pregnant, and since they were going to be married in a month, they were both thrilled. The baby was unplanned, but as Valerie said, who would care? Ever since they had been children together, they'd known they would be married. A baby so soon was hardly an inconvenience. They'd wanted to have a baby in the first year anyway.

He planned to tell Fitz about the baby during the two weeks they'd be at the old family beach house in the village of Siasconset on Nantucket Island. He expected Fitz, who was to be his best man, to be happy for both him and Valerie. After all, Fitz had grown up with Valerie, too; she was like a sister to him. Back when they were all kids, Fitz had tagged along with Valerie and Stuart on every expedition they'd launched during those all-too-short Nantucket summers. Later, Fitz had taken a devilish pleasure in cutting in on Stuart and Valerie at Miss Beatrice's dancing school, and Valerie had even flirted with Fitz occasionally when she thought that Stuart wasn't paying enough attention to her.

Not that Stuart had ever thought those early flirtations amounted to much. He and Valerie were a pair, always had been, and when they both turned thirty, they'd decided not to wait any longer. They'd get married, they agreed, and treat their hometown of Boston to the biggest society wedding of the summer.

In that first week in June two years ago, Valerie had arrived on Nantucket sporting a new Takawa Tsunami, which hadn't yet been cited as the most dangerous new road vehicle of the year. On that first night on the island, she'd called Stuart up at the big gray-shingled house that had belonged to Adamses for generations.

"I'm at the Whale Tail Lounge," she'd said over the roar of music and loud voices at the favorite watering hole of all the young regulars on Nantucket. "Want to meet me here?"

Fitz had his car on the island, so he drove both Stuart and himself down to the Whale Tail. The brothers were in a rare mood that night, exhilarated at the prospect of two glorious weeks of sun and sand and sailing. After a couple of hours spent renewing old friendships with other people they knew at the Whale Tail, the air inside had turned blue with cigarette smoke, and along with some friends, they'd trooped outside for a breather. They naturally ended up in the parking lot to admire Valerie's new Tsunami.

"Want to take her for a spin?" Valerie said. "Put her through her paces?"

"Nah," Stuart said, because he hadn't seen Valerie in over a week. He'd been overseas on business and had just returned to Boston the night before; he couldn't wait to get Valerie alone someplace, just the two of them.

"Why not see what this baby's made of?" Fitz had said over the rhythmic rock beat floating out of the lounge. He thunked the fender of the Tsunami with his knuckles.

Valerie jingled the keys. "We'll drive out the old road to the Perkins place. We haven't done that for years," she said, jumping in. Fitz had climbed in beside her, and so Stuart, not liking the seating arrangement but deciding that it wasn't worth an objection, slid into the back seat. Their friends wandered back inside the lounge, drunk with the prospect of another lazy summer and too much booze.

Valerie, her foot heavy on the accelerator, struck out along the deserted unpaved road toward the far end of the island where the Perkins house stood abandoned by its owners. Halfway there, Valerie unexpectedly said, "Let's put the four-wheel drive through its paces." She wheeled off the road onto a rutted trail leading down to the beach.

"Slow down, Val," Stuart said when she whizzed across a wooden bridge, the boards rattling in protest, and Fitz, his teeth white in the moonlight, grinned at him over the top of the front seat and said, "What's the matter, are you chicken?"

"Stuart, chicken? Never," Valerie said gaily, and she laughed, the sound captured and flung out to sea by a rising wind that was stirring up the sand. Stuart wished he had suggested that he drive, and he was on the brink of doing just that when Valerie, swooping the Tsunami around a sand dune, suddenly clapped a hand over her left eye.

"I've got something in my eye," she said abruptly, screeching to a stop so suddenly that the tires bit into the loose sand.

"Hey, watch it!" Fitz yelped, grabbing onto the side of the Tsunami. "You'll dig the tires in so deep we'll have to call a wrecker."

Valerie was pulling her top eyelid down over her lower one. "Must have picked up a grain of sand. Fitz, will you drive?" she said as Stuart handed her his handkerchief.

"Sure. Scoot over," Fitz said, and Stuart interrupted to say, "I'll drive, Fitz. You were drinking Scotch, and a lot of it." He himself had drunk only one beer.

"Your turn's next. Anyway, I'm always drinking lots of Scotch. Take after my old man." Fitz laughed and threw the Tsunami into gear, gunning the engine so hard that sand flew up behind them and Stuart was thrown backward in his seat.

Valerie, meanwhile, was blotting at her eye. "There, I'm okay," she said, handing Stuart's handkerchief to him across the back of her seat. "See what she'll do on the curve, Fitz."

The Tsunami lurched around a dune, and they came out on the beach into the full moonlight. The scene was surreal—the moon so bright, Valerie's laugh so shrill, the Tsunami roaring along at the edge of the rolling gray ocean.

"Hey, Fitz, slow down! I'd like to live to tell about this," Stuart said, but Fitz only howled like a wolf, an eerie sound in the night, and turned sharply to the left.

"Whee! It's a roller coaster!" cried Valerie, clinging to Fitz's arm so that she wouldn't be flung out the open side of the vehicle. In her hurry to change seats, she hadn't fastened her seat belt.

"Watch this!" Fitz yelled as they came upon a rise, and Stuart started—too late—to say, "Look out for the rocks!" because he remembered that they were there and Fitz couldn't have or he wouldn't have shot over the lip of land so unheedingly.

And then Stuart felt the rocks tearing at the bottom of the Tsunami with a horrendous crunch, and they were lofted into the air for what seemed like an eternity, flying silently toward the moonlit path on the water. After that there was a sickening crash followed by a searing pain, and pressure on his back, and the wail of sirens far away.

When he came out of the coma, he was in the hospital, the cut on his back bandaged. They told him that Valerie, his Valerie, had never had a chance. She'd been thrown out of the vehicle, which had landed on top of her, crushing the life out of her and their baby—the baby that they had both wanted so very much. Stuart couldn't remember the accident at all, and Stuart's doctors told him that people often forgot those things that they couldn't bear to remember. As he lay in the hospital, weak and helpless, Stuart could only try to recall a scene that seemed just out of the grasp of his memory.

But Fitz, the only witness, had made sure that Stuart remembered. Fitz told the police that Stuart had been driving the Tsunami. Valerie's death—and their unborn baby's—was Stuart's fault.

Now Stuart woke up and sat bolt upright, rocking the hammock violently. He remembered now. He remembered all of it. All this time, for the past two years, he'd been unable to recall anything that happened after the three of them left the parking lot of the lounge in the Tsunami, and now he knew. He *knew*.

"Stuart?" Angel, wearing an apron, appeared in the doorway to the kitchen, concern written all over her face.

He only stared at her, shaken by his knowledge. It hadn't happened the way Fitz said. His brother had lied.

Angel crossed the floor and stood before him, touching a gentle hand to his face.

"Stuart? Is everything all right?"

"I didn't kill them," he said hoarsely. *"I didn't kill them."*

Angel knelt beside him on the hard porch floor, her forehead knit with anxiety. "Kill whom? What are you talking about, Stuart?"

"Valerie. The baby. I didn't do it!" He buried his face in his hands.

"Tell me," Angel said, resting her hand on his knee. And, haltingly, painfully, he did.

IT WAS DARK OUTSIDE by the time he finished talking.

"They charged me with involuntary manslaughter, and I pled guilty," Stuart said in a broken voice. "Because I'm an Adams, I only had to do community service work and was on probation for a year. You'd be surprised what money and privilege can accomplish." He said it bitterly, although he hadn't been bitter at the time. He hadn't, after all, had to go to jail. He knew he'd been more useful to society by doing what he did, which was to teach boatbuilding classes to disadvantaged youth, some of whom were now serving apprenticeships with the family firm.

"I'm so sorry," Angel said. "So very sorry, Stuart." She was holding his hand. She had held it the whole time he was talking.

"All this time, I thought I'd killed Valerie and our baby, and it was Fitz! Fitz was driving. That son of a bitch," he said. He still couldn't believe it. An Adams was supposed to be a man of honor, and Fitz had violated the unwritten code to save his own skin.

"He's your brother," Angel reminded him quietly.

"I hate him." Stuart stood up and paced from one end of the small porch to the other, his head aching, his heart hammering. He felt like pounding something, like tearing something apart.

"He's all you have in the world," Angel said in a soft tone of voice. "He's the only member of your immediate family who's left. If I had a brother or a sister, I could never hate him or her. Never."

"You're not like me, then. I'll make him pay, Angel. I'll find some way to hurt him, to make his life a living hell."

Angel stood up and walked to the place where he stood. She placed a gentle hand on his arm.

"And would that bring Valerie and the baby back?" she said.

He stared down at her. "No. But it sure would make me feel better," he said harshly. He shook her arm away, but, to his surprise, she merely moved closer and slid her arms up around his neck.

"You must feel terrible," she murmured.

His first impulse was to push her away, but he didn't. She smelled sweet, and she was pressing her body against his. He took comfort from its warmth and its closeness. Without thinking about it, he slid his arms around her waist and buried his face in her hair. It smelled like her shampoo, and suddenly he didn't want to hit or hurt or destroy. He wanted someone to soothe his pain, to make the memories go back into the dark recesses of his mind.

"Angel," he said.

"I know. Your brother did a horrible thing to you. It's natural for you to feel angry."

"I wouldn't have done what he did," he said.

She was stroking the back of his neck, and he felt himself relax. He still wanted to destroy Fitz, but at the moment it didn't seem like the most important thing. The most important thing was murmuring comforting words in his ear, was caressing him gently, was reminding him that there were other things to do besides plotting revenge.

"Stuart, come to bed," she said, taking his hand. She had to tug at it for a few seconds before he was able to move his feet; he walked like some weird kind of robot, unable to think, knowing only that Angel was offering solace and that he'd do well to avail himself of it.

In the darkened bedroom he felt her unbuttoning his shirt and slipping it down his torso, and then she unzipped his pants so that all he had to do was slide them down his hips and step out of them. He was shaking by this time, shaking so hard that his teeth chattered, and she was talking to him, easing him down on the mattress.

He threw an arm across his eyes to blot out the images of Valerie in those last moments when he'd seen her tossed through the air, and he would have covered his ears if he'd thought that would muffle her last scream. Oh, he'd been better off when he didn't remember, much better off. Now he knew that memories of that night would haunt him for the rest of his life, waking and sleeping, no matter what. The memories ground into his guts. How could he live with this?

Angel slipped into bed beside him and tucked herself close to his side, sliding an arm over his chest and resting her head on his shoulder. She was so much smaller than Valerie, and so sweet. Sweeter than Valerie, who had never had a serious thought in her life. He reached for Angel's leg, resting his hand on the soft inner skin of her thigh.

He felt unaccustomed tears pooling behind his eyelids. He hadn't killed them. It had been Fitz. The tears were about his sadness and also his release. He had been charged and he had paid his debt to society, but who was going to pay society's debt to him? He had lost two years of his life because of a crime that he hadn't committed.

All right, so he wanted a pity party. He wanted someone to say, "I'm sorry." And, of course, someone had. Angel had.

"Angel?" he said quietly. "Are you awake?"

"Yes," she whispered.

"After Valerie died, I wanted to die, too."

"I can understand that," she said.

"I thought that my life wasn't worth living without her."

For a long time, Angel didn't speak. Then she said, "I can understand that, too."

Her voice had a strange quality to it, one he'd never heard before. He mulled that over and decided that what Angel had said was merely the kind of remark anyone would make under the circumstances. Chances were it was nothing more than an expression of sympathy.

"I don't think it's possible for one person to understand what another person has been through, but thanks for trying," he said.

She lifted her head and looked at him, her face pale in the darkness. "It's true that I wasn't there when this happened to you, and I suppose you're right—no one can ever fit inside another person's heart or mind or body to feel the exact same emotions or fears or whatever. But I'm no stranger to loss," she said.

"Do you want to tell me about it?" he said. He suddenly knew that this was the key to Angel, to the reason she hid away on this faraway island, to her desire to have a baby without the interference of the father.

"I never wanted to tell anybody," she said truthfully. "When I came here, I left it all behind. But now I'd feel comfortable telling you. I think you might understand."

He slid his arm under her head and kissed her temple. "I'm a good listener," he said.

Angel stared up at the brown water stain on the old ceiling, barely visible in the faint light. She took a deep breath. "I loved a man," she said. "Howard. He was a professor at the university." And then the entire story of her love affair, her pregnancy, her breakup with Howard and the loss of the baby spilled out, the words tumbling over each other to release the hurt that had built up inside her for so long.

"I always thought I was special until I knew Howard, and after I gave him the gift of myself, he threw me away, wounding my pride and, even worse, my heart," she said. Her eyes held the ache of dammed tears, and when she turned toward him blindly, he took her in his arms and held her close. The telling of her story left her feeling like an emotional wasteland, lost and bleak, the way she had felt right after Howard left her. On Halos Island, the pain of her anguish had subsided into an ache and then a stillness in her heart; the anguish had been revived in the telling of this bit of history that she wanted to forget.

"So you've been pregnant before," he said, sounding as if he were in shock.

"Yes," she said. She felt numb, but was relieved that he knew her history. "Does it matter?"

"I was almost a father myself," he said, tightening his grip on her shoulder. "We've both lost a child, and we've both been running."

"For similar reasons," she added, with a kind of wonder. She had never imagined that the two of them might have the same kind of tragedy in common, and she felt bonded to him as she never had before.

"I was running from the pain of what I thought I did to Valerie and our child. Now that I know I wasn't responsible for their deaths, I don't want to run anymore. I want to make Fitz face up to what he did."

"It was an accident, Stuart."

"I want him to pay the price. To have to leave his career like I did and pay a debt to society. To admit what he did so the whole world will know I didn't do it. Is that so much to ask?" His voice held a barely contained fury.

"I don't know, Stuart. Is it?"

''Why should he have a wife and child and a life to be proud of? Why should Fitz have what I deserve?'' He was sick of paying for what his notoriously irresponsible brother had done. He was angry, and rightfully so. He'd never get over it. Never!

''You have a wife,'' Angel told him gently, reminding him of who she was and why he was with her. He had been so caught up in his own feelings of hatred that he hadn't thought about how she must feel as she listened to what he had to say.

Suddenly he was overwhelmed with the twists and turns his life had taken since the accident on Nantucket. He realized now that he had taken a wife as a defiant gesture, a kind of thumbing his nose at the world he knew and all its conventions, and in so doing he had involved Angel in the mess his life had become. For the first time, he regretted bringing Angel into this. He should have sailed for the South Seas after all; this baby-making scheme had been a ridiculous idea. Angel had suffered enough already, because of that miserable creep Howard.

Thank goodness she wasn't pregnant yet. They could separate amicably, admit the folly of this contrived marriage and obtain a quiet, no-fault divorce. He'd settle a fair amount of money on her to express his gratitude.

The air in the room had grown stuffy, and Angel sat up to open the shutters, pushing them to the far sides of the window so that her shape was limned in bright moonlight. He was about to get up when she said quietly, ''Stuart. Look.''

He leaned toward her, carefully avoiding touching her. Over her shoulder he saw what she was looking at—a tiny deer, no more than twenty inches long, browsing amid the gumbo-limbo trees at the edge of the clearing.

"A fawn?" he asked, though the deer didn't have a white-spotted back like all the fawns he had ever seen.

She shook her head. "It's a full-grown doe. See how rounded her belly looks? She'll probably give birth in June or July. She's part of a herd of key deer that comes to this end of the island to feed."

Stuart had read about key deer in the in-flight magazine on the plane from Miami to Key West. They were a subspecies of the white-tailed deer and lived only in the lower Florida Keys. They were known to be rare, so he'd never thought he'd be lucky enough to see one.

The little doe, ethereal in the moonlight, lifted her delicate head and pricked her ears up, perhaps listening for their voices. She moved slightly, swaying along with the leaves. Transfixed by her beauty, neither Angel nor Stuart spoke. Soon the deer faded quietly into the shadows, leaving Angel and Stuart feeling calm and centered and bathed in a cool, comforting peace.

Angel turned to Stuart. "The scenery is one of the many benefits of living on this island," she said, sliding her arms around him.

"It certainly is," he said, looking only at her.

It seemed natural to kiss her, and so right. When he released her lips, thinking that this was the time to have a serious talk, to tell her that this had been a mistake that they could soon rectify, she shifted in his arms and drew him down on top of her in the bed. Her hair slid across his forearms like molten silk, and her eyes were lustrous and lit from within.

"All the bad things that happened to us before we met are behind us now, Stuart, can't you see?" she said, and in that moment, he did see. But overlying it was his sense of shame at making her a part of his past when what he had been looking for was a future.

He started to shake his head no, but her hands came up to frame his face, capturing him, and she said urgently, "Make love to me, Stuart. Please?"

How could he refuse her anything when she had been so understanding and so kind? How could he refuse her when her body was naked beneath his and when all his senses, already primed by the fragile beauty of the little doe, were opening to take her in? Angel's heart beat against his chest, he could feel it quickening, and before he knew it he had crushed his mouth against hers, had settled himself between her legs. He felt her hands pressing against the hard ridges of his back to urge him closer, and he reveled in her greediness for him. His own palpitating need rose within his chest, transmuting his mood into one in which nothing mattered but making her totally and completely his once again.

She was his wife. She was not some casual liaison. Even if they had decided to make a baby for all the wrong reasons, they were making love for reasons that were absolutely right. During his short time on Halos Island, their sense of mutual respect had blossomed and grown. Their lovemaking had to do not only with the powerful chemistry between them, but also with increasing tenderness and understanding, caring and friendship. It had to do with the fact that Angel McCabe was his wife and he had every right to comfort her in this way, as she did to comfort him. It had to do with love.

His heart shuddered against hers as he entered her. One thought emerged as his flesh welded to hers: love. He had been thinking that he loved his wife. How could he?

He couldn't love anyone. He had killed the two people he'd loved most in the world.

No. He hadn't. Fitz had killed them. Did that leave him free to love again? Did he dare to love anyone?

"Yes!" he cried as he poured himself into her, making himself part of her now and... Not forever. Would that be fair? He'd decided only minutes ago to leave before he created even more of a problem.

Leave? No way. Feeling her body throbbing beneath him, listening to the music of her breathing in his ear, feeling her moist lips pressed into his shoulder, knowing he was still a part of her even now when his body was subsiding, he knew he couldn't leave her anytime soon. And if she became pregnant?

She would make him leave. It was in the contract. Why would she want to keep him around, him with his emotional baggage, when she could go back to being the way she was before, free to be herself on her lonely island?

He suddenly didn't want Angel to get pregnant. And tonight, which was the height of her most fertile period, he had spilled himself into her without regard for what might happen.

He clutched her to him, thinking that he'd better get a grip on himself, both physically and emotionally. Even as they lay in each other's arms, heart-to-heart, he knew he could not, in his present state of mind, allow himself to fall in love with Angel McCabe.

Chapter Eleven

In the morning, Angel was pale but determined.

"How would you feel about going to see your brother?" she asked after breakfast as they were cleaning up the kitchen.

"It isn't even a remote possibility," he said. "Unless I get an uncontrollable urge to bash his head in."

"We know all about your uncontrollable urges," Angel said slyly, swinging the dish towel at his legs. He sidestepped, hardly in the mood for her antics. She didn't take the hint, swatting him with the towel anyway.

"I can't go to see Fitz," he said. "He's avoided me ever since the sentencing. He has a wife I've never met and a child whose name I don't even know."

"All the more reason to go see him," Angel said.

"Easy for you to say," Stuart said sourly. "What do you propose I do, appear on his doorstep with a wedding present and a silver baby spoon? Monogrammed, perhaps, with the Adams family crest?"

Angel looked troubled. "If that's standard procedure when visiting a new Adams niece or nephew, that's what you should do," she said.

"Standard procedure is notifying members of the family when a new niece or nephew is born. I didn't receive any birth announcement from Fitz and his wife, whose name, as I recall from the story in the *Boston Globe,* might possibly be Jeanne,'' he said, heavy on the sarcasm.

"So why do you think Fitz was ignoring you all the time you were teaching kids how to build boats?"

"Because he felt guilty, okay? As he should."

"You're going to be eaten up by hate, Stuart, you know that? Fitz has already destroyed a couple of years of your life. Are you going to allow him to destroy the rest of it?" Her hands were on her hips, her eyes flashing fire.

"Oh, you're one to talk, all right," he said. "You ran away to this godforsaken island to get away from your wrecked life, and you're telling me how to live mine? Get real, Angel." He started to walk out onto the screened porch to cool off, but she caught him by the shoulder and wrenched him around.

"Maybe I learned something by coming here, Stuart. Maybe you have something to learn, too." Her voice was dangerously low.

He looked at her more closely. "Are you sure you feel all right? You look more tired than usual."

She tipped her head back and looked at him. "I'm not the one who was hit on the head yesterday. You were. Are you sure it didn't do more than bring back your memories of the accident? You're acting awfully touchy."

"*I'm* touchy," he said. "Coming from you, that's pretty good. What's really bugging you, Angel?"

She stared at him. "You want a baby to replace the one you and Valerie were going to have. All that garbage about carrying on your family name was a bunch of baloney."

"So isn't that why you want a baby? To replace the one you lost?" He glared at her.

"I want a baby to mother," she said. "I want the experience of rearing a child."

"I suppose that sounds a hell of a lot more noble than replacing the baby you conceived when you were with another man."

Her face fell, and her expression became somber. "We shouldn't say these things to each other. No good can come of it," she said.

"Maybe the things you're saying are what you think I need to learn," he said.

"No. The learning has to come from within yourself," she said.

"Great. And how does that happen?"

She inhaled deeply. "I don't know how it will happen for you, Stuart. I only know that I figured out a lot of things by being by myself for a long time. What I learned, in case you're interested, is that you can't run away from your feelings. You can bury them, but they surface when you least want to think about them. I learned to be self-reliant. I decided that I have what it takes to rear a child by myself and that I didn't want to wait to be a mother. That's a lot of learning and growing, Stuart."

He stared down at her, hearing her words but momentarily distracted by the thought that she looked as if she'd lost weight lately. There were hollows in her cheeks that he had never noticed before, and there were deep circles under her eyes. Well, neither of them had gone to sleep until late last night, and he probably looked pretty rugged himself.

"No one can minimize your accomplishments," he said, because that was certainly true.

"Thanks for that, anyway," she replied.

For an instant he wanted to reach out and caress the silky soft skin of her cheek. But he was still too angry with her for bringing up the things he didn't want to think about.

"I'm out of here. I think I'll go fishing," he said tightly. He stomped across the porch and went out, slamming the screen door behind him.

On his way down the path, he thought that he might tell Angel that he was going to see Fitz, and then leave the island and do whatever he pleased. Go to New Zealand. Hop on a freighter to nowhere. But he didn't want to leave the island. He wanted to stay near Angel. But, so far, she'd given no indication that she wanted him around permanently.

Nothing in life is permanent, buddy, he told himself as he swung a hand line off the dock. *Especially when you keep screwing things up.*

He sat staring down into the dark water lapping at the dock pilings. Was there a chance that Angel was right? That he should go see his brother?

His heart contracted at the thought. He couldn't imagine seeing his brother face to face; it had been so long since he'd been cut out of the lives of everyone who was important to him—friends, family, colleagues and clients...and Fitz, who had deserted him when he most needed someone in his corner.

It wasn't long before something tugged at his line, cutting his thoughts short. He pulled the fish in, cleaned it and took it back to the house. Angel wasn't there. At loose ends, he sat down with his drafting supplies to look over his preliminary sketches of his friend Tom's cabin cruiser. The design of a cabin cruiser, at least, was one thing that he was unlikely to botch. Which was more than he could say about other aspects of his life.

IN THE MEANTIME, Angel was hiding out in the west meadow, vomiting behind a palmetto tree.

She hated having morning sickness, hated the heaving of her stomach, hated the sour taste in her mouth afterward. She couldn't imagine how she had so far succeeded in hiding her nausea from Stuart, who, despite being keyed into pregnancy in a way that few men were, didn't recognize a pregnant woman when she was right under his nose.

After a while, Angel lay back in the tall grass, listening to bees buzzing in the flowers and the not-too-distant roar of the sea. The tiff with Stuart made her anxious, and she tried to forget it. All couples argued now and then. It didn't mean anything. Or did it? Was he growing tired of her? Last night he had brought her to extraordinary peaks, again and again. Based on past experience, she thought it was probably the pregnancy that made her so sensitive, made her feel as if she wanted to make love over and over again, day and night. But she'd rather think it was Stuart.

She closed her eyes, picturing this husband of hers who was supposed to be a mere convenience. Stuart Adams had turned out to be more—much more—than that. As the days went by, she had learned what he was really like, and now she knew that he had brought a new and worthwhile dimension to her life.

He had made her try things she'd never done before, like sailing, which she could definitely learn to like a lot if given half a chance. He had made her experience sex in a different way, had given her a new and precious knowledge of herself. Yet she knew better than to think he would stay with her; she wasn't part of his privileged world. She was only a humble scientist, happiest when she was with her bees.

She heard a rustle in the grass and, thinking it was Caloosa, kept her eyes closed and held out her hand. "Come here, you," she said.

She was surprised when Stuart's large hand enveloped hers. Her eyes flew open to see his face above her, and she struggled to a sitting position. Her stomach turned over, and she pressed against it with her other hand. Stuart didn't notice.

He looked as if he were over their earlier misunderstanding. "I thought you were going to go fishing. Aren't the fish biting today?" she said.

"I caught a nice big one."

"Good. We'll grill it for dinner."

He hunkered down beside her. "Would you mind if I built a tree house in the branches of that low pine tree over there? For the baby?"

"It will be years, Stuart, before our baby will be able to climb a tree," she said, touched nevertheless.

"I know I shouldn't build the tree house until I at least know you're pregnant. But until the baby is big enough to play in it, you could sit in it when you eat lunch out here. Later, you could put a cradle in it, where the baby could sleep while you're working."

"That's a sweet idea, Stuart," she said.

"I'll build the tree house in the shape of a ship. Your view of the beach and the ocean beyond should be magnificent," he said.

He had said nothing about being part of the scene. Why should he? He was probably more than ready to move on. At the thought of his leaving, her throat caught and she couldn't speak.

"Angel, I've been thinking," he said. He looked thoughtful and contrite.

Her heart almost stopped. He must be more upset than she had realized. He had been thinking...about leaving? She only looked at him, expecting the worst.

"I do want to go see Fitz. I have to confront him about what he did, or I'll never get the anger out of my system. But I don't want to go alone. I need moral support."

Angel's relief was so great that, for a moment, the world dimmed. He was only talking about his brother! He wasn't going to tell her that he had decided to leave! But suddenly she knew what was coming next.

"Will you go with me to see Fitz, Angel?" he said, his eyes anxious.

She would do anything, anything at all, for him. And all he wanted was for her to accompany him to see Fitz.

"When?" She barely managed to get the word out.

"As soon as we can. I know he'll be on Nantucket now. For as long as I can remember, we always went in June."

Angel focused on a bee burrowing into a red flower in the distance. Overhead, the palmetto fronds rustled in the breeze.

"I'll go," she said, and Stuart squeezed her hand.

He stood up. "I'll ask Toby to arrange for the tickets. Thank you, Angel." He stood staring down at her for a long moment, taking in the way she was lying spread out in the sun.

"You're so beautiful," he said, almost to himself.

She didn't even deny it, as she once would have. She was glad he found her beautiful. She was glad she was his wife.

"Thank you, Angel," he said. "For everything."

She only smiled, wishing he would kiss her, but he was so preoccupied that he started back toward the path without even touching her.

It didn't matter. Nothing mattered except that he wanted her with him when he went to see his brother. Her heart sang with the knowledge that he needed her.

Stuart showed no signs of a similar euphoria as he walked away. Even though his newly regained memory had absolved him of the crime he'd never committed, he looked as if he carried the world on his shoulders.

While she, she thought unhappily as she sat up and felt her stomach churn, probably carried the world in her stomach. Or at least it felt like it these days.

ANGEL held Stuart's hand throughout the bumpy flight. Immediately after takeoff, she reached for the barf bag in the pocket on the seat in front of them.

"Does the turbulence bother you?" he asked, and she nodded as if she didn't trust herself to speak.

He reached up to adjust the air nozzle so that cool air blew on her face, and after that she gripped his hand less tightly. Before long, they had passed the long hooked arm of Cape Cod curving into the Atlantic Ocean and were swooping in for a landing at the little airport on the island of Nantucket.

As they rode through the quaint narrow streets, he was surprised to find that Nantucket, although as charming as ever, had lost its attraction for him. The houses with their steep roofs seemed harsh and unwelcoming; the sand was an unattractive flat beige after the shimmering pink sand of Halos Island. He stared out the window, feeling increasingly apprehensive as the taxi conveyed them to the old beach house where Adamses had summered for generations.

He had almost forgotten that Angel was with him. "What if Fitz isn't there?" she asked. They were the first words she'd uttered since they'd entered the taxi.

"He will be," Stuart said.

"He doesn't know we're going to pay him a visit."

Stuart shrugged. He didn't want Fitz to know they were coming; he wanted to take him by surprise.

Angel subsided into an uneasy silence as the group of houses that included the Adams place loomed in the distance. Stuart tried smiling at her for reassurance, and she smiled back, but not with much enthusiasm. For a moment, he saw her through new eyes: She looked lovely. She had worn a soft, swingy dress in a golden shade of yellow, and she had caught her hair at the nape of her neck with a neat tortoiseshell clip. With her profusion of pale hair smoothed back from her face, her eyes took on new importance. They were enormous, the pupils large with... what? Worry? Fear? If so, it was all on his account. His heart warmed to her. He could never thank her enough for accompanying him on this unpleasant errand and for letting him know that whatever happened, she was on his side.

The taxi driver stopped in front of the sprawling, weathered gray cedar-shingled house. Its wings stretched out toward the sea, its many porches designed to catch every ocean breeze. A profusion of geraniums spilled from white window boxes, and a picket fence bordered the garden. Stuart saw a baby carriage parked outside one of the open garage doors.

"Fitz? Are you expecting anyone?" a feminine voice called from inside the garage. Stuart and Angel got out of the cab, and Stuart took Angel's hand. They started up the slate path.

A male voice replied with a few indistinct words, and a tall, robust woman with long wavy auburn hair stepped out of the garage. She was carrying a chubby pink-skinned baby, and she smiled uncertainly.

"Yes?" she said.

Stuart's mouth suddenly went dry. He licked his lips. "Is Fitz here?" he asked.

"Yes, of course. May I tell him who... ?" She smiled politely at Angel, but when she looked Stuart full in the face, her expression froze. At that moment, Stuart's brother stepped out the front door of the house.

"Fitz," said the woman in a kind of warning.

The man narrowed his eyes. He walked slowly down the steps, his expression wary. Even Stuart was aware of the close family resemblance they shared. Fitz's hair was wavier, and he was an inch shorter. Otherwise, they could have been twins.

"Hello, Fitz," Stuart said.

For a moment, Fitz looked unsure of himself, but he quickly covered his reaction and strode forward, his voice too hearty.

"Well, Stuart," he said in a booming voice, extending his hand. "Long time no see."

Stuart pointedly avoided his brother's outstretched hand. "This isn't a courtesy call. I want to talk to you," he said.

Fitz faltered, then recovered. Casually he withdrew his hand and slid it into his pocket. "All right, you might as well come in. Jeanne, please tell Rose that we'd like some light refreshment in the study." The woman with the baby, obviously Fitz's wife, hoisted the drooling baby over one shoulder and disappeared into the house by way of the garage.

"Come along," Fitz said brusquely, leading the way up the front steps and across the wide porch.

The house was exactly as Stuart remembered it from the old days, only it seemed to have grown bigger and somehow more vast now that he was accustomed to the little bungalow on Halos Island. Their footsteps echoed on the wide oak planking of the hall floor, and the place smelled of the same brand of lemon oil furniture polish that the maids there had used ever since Stuart was a baby. Angel, unaccustomed to such shabby, understated luxury, was looking around in awe, still holding fast to his hand. He gave her fingers a reassuring squeeze, and she squeezed back. He took heart from her brief smile.

The carpet in the study was the same faded Kirman that Stuart remembered from the time he was a boy. He and Angel sat on a dove-blue settee in front of the bookshelves, and Fitz lowered his frame onto a hardbacked chair across the room. On the mantel, a clock ticked, reminding Stuart that he had a lot to say and little time in which to say it. He intended to catch the last plane back to Boston in the afternoon.

Stuart said, "Fitz, this is my wife, Angel."

"I didn't know you were married," Fitz said in surprise.

"I wouldn't have known you were married, either, if I hadn't read it on the society page of the *Boston Globe*," Stuart replied sharply.

Fitz had the good grace to look flustered. "I'll introduce you to Jeanne when she returns from the kitchen," he said.

"I didn't come here to meet your wife. I came to talk about the accident."

Fitz stood abruptly and walked to the window, where he stood looking out at the garden. "I thought we had put all that behind us," he said.

"Maybe you have, but I haven't. I'm still torturing myself over what happened to Valerie. And to our baby."

Fitz remained motionless for a moment or two before whirling around to face them, his face white. "What baby?" he said sharply.

"The baby Valerie was going to have. My baby, Fitz." Stuart kept his voice even, and his eyes never wavered from Fitz's face.

Surprise flared in Fitz's eyes. "Valerie was pregnant?"

"Yes. We were happy about it. We wanted to start a family right away after we were married, and it happened a little too soon, that's all. I lost both of them when she died." He stared steadily at Fitz, and finally Fitz sat down again. He still looked stunned.

At that moment, a woman came in with a tray. She set it down on the small table beside Fitz's chair and scurried out again. No one touched the food; no one even looked at it.

"I didn't know about the baby," Fitz said.

"No one did. It was our secret. We were going to share it during that vacation, but only with you. We never got the chance."

A long silence, and Fitz finally spoke. "It was a tough break, Stu. I miss Valerie as much as you do," he said.

"I doubt that," Stuart said, his tone harsh.

Fitz looked at Angel. "Well, you have a beautiful wife," he said inappropriately.

"Yes, I do." Stuart paused and cleared his throat, deciding he'd better take the bull by the horns. "Why did you lie, Fitz?" he said.

"Lie? I don't know what you're talking about." Fitz treated Stuart to the Adams stare, a tactic they'd both learned to use when upstarts needed to be put in their place. It didn't work on Stuart; he knew that stare all too well.

Stuart leaned forward in his seat. "You told the police I was driving. It was you, Fitz. You were the one who was driving." He spoke with a deceptive calm, but there was menace in the set of his chin and in the way he punctuated his words with jabs of his fist. He wished Fitz's face was in front of his knuckles.

"No, Stuart. Valerie got a piece of sand in her eye and asked you to take over the driving. You accelerated too fast over the rise, and the rocks tore out the bottom of the Tsunami."

Hearing the blatant lie once more was too much for Stuart; he began to shake with rage. He leaped from his place on the settee even as Angel cried out, and he hauled Fitz out of the chair and jacked him up by his collar.

"You're a damned liar, Fitz! You rode in the front seat with her, and she slid over onto the passenger seat and forgot to put on her seat belt! You were driving recklessly, the way you said I was driving when you told the police about it afterward, and you flipped the Tsunami over. I'll never forget her scream that night when the car rolled over on her. It's too bad it wasn't you, you son of a bitch!"

Fitz tried to remove his hands from his shirtfront. "Let me go! Are you crazy, Stuart? You have amnesia! You don't remember! You can't prove anything!"

"I remember! I remember now, and I remember it all! I'm going to remember it for the rest of my life, the life that you tried to steal from me!"

Stuart drew his fist back and punched Fitz in the stomach, even as Angel screamed. He caught a glimpse of Jeanne's horrified face as she rushed to her husband's aid. As Fitz went down, his head pitched forward, his shoulder catching the edge of the food tray.

Sandwiches and glasses of iced tea went flying across the highly polished floor and the carpet.

Angel leaped from the settee and threw her arms around Stuart to pull him away from Fitz, who was slumped on the floor and gasping for breath amid the broken glass and the remains of several sandwiches.

"Fitz? Oh, my God, what have you done to him?" his wife cried, tears streaming down her face. She tried to help him up.

"I'm all right, Jeanne," Fitz managed to say. He was gazing up at Stuart, hangdog and pitiful, not a shred of the proud Adams stare left.

Stuart moved a few steps away and wrapped his arms around Angel, feeling nothing like the vengeful satisfaction he had anticipated. Instead, he felt an immense sense of letdown, and sorrow, and a mental anguish that was even greater than what he'd felt before. This was his brother, not a total stranger, and no matter how much he'd thought he wanted revenge, it was suddenly clear to him that taking it would be anything but sweet.

His brother heaved himself to his feet. "All right," Fitz said heavily. "Maybe I deserved that."

"I'm calling the police," Jeanne said, letting go of Fitz and reaching for the phone.

"No," Fitz said, restraining her. "Stuart is my brother. We have to talk."

Everyone stood uncertainly, looking from one to the other.

"Sit down," Fitz said.

Stuart found his voice. "I think we'd better go. I told the taxi driver to wait."

"Jeanne, tell the driver to go away," said Fitz, but Jeanne looked incapable of movement. Fitz seemed exhausted, and he closed his eyes and heaved a deep sigh.

"Jeanne? Will you please do as I ask?" This seemed to galvanize her into action, and after one last mute glance directed at her husband, Jeanne left.

Fitz shot Stuart an apprehensive look. "Look, Stuart, I might as well get this all out of my system—I've felt guilty ever since it happened. I've always feared that you'd someday remember that night. I knew that when and if you ever did, I'd be the one reviled by our relatives, and I'd be the one teaching boatbuilding to disadvantaged youth, and I'd be the one taking a leave from the company. I'd be the one, not you. I couldn't face up to it, Stuart."

"You're an Adams. You're supposed to face up to things," Stuart said woodenly. He still couldn't understand why Fitz had abandoned the code of honor that had governed their behavior ever since they were kids.

"That made it even worse. I panicked in the clinch, Stu. When that policeman came over to me in the hospital emergency room, I blurted out the first thing I could think of—that you were driving. You were in a coma, and I thought you'd never wake up. When you did, I was overjoyed—until I realized that you'd tell everyone what really happened. You can't imagine how relieved I was when I found out that you couldn't recall anything about the accident."

"How convenient for you," Stuart said. "My amnesia got you off the hook, didn't it?"

Fitz looked down at the floor, his expression drawn. "I guess you'll never understand, Stuart, but I—I couldn't face the disgrace of owning up to being the one who...the one who..."

"You can't say it, can you? You killed Valerie. And our child."

"I killed them," Fitz whispered.

Stuart wasn't going to relent, even though Fitz looked shattered. "You've never faced up to anything before, have you? I always came along and got you out of trouble. I suppose it seemed natural to you—let good old Stuart take care of it, even if good old Stuart didn't have a clue."

"I'm not proud of what I did," Fitz shot back.

"I lost everything that was important to me—Valerie, our child, my place in the family firm, even you. You didn't care, did you?"

Fitz leaned back in his chair and stared up at the ceiling for a long time. "I cared," he said softly, when he could meet Stuart's eyes again. "I felt so guilty and so afraid that you'd find me out that I couldn't deal with seeing you anymore."

"I protected you too much. I should have made you suffer the consequences of your acts years ago, when we were kids. I should have made you grow up, but it's too late to change any of that now," said Stuart.

Fitz lifted his head. "What do you want from me, Stuart? I can't bring them back. I can't say anything that will make you feel better."

"I want to hear one thing from you before I leave this house, Fitz," Stuart said steadily. "I want to hear your apology."

Fitz's face flushed. "If it will help, Stuart, I am sorry. Honestly." He hesitated. "I feel like a jerk for asking, but now that you know the truth and now that I've admitted what I did, what are you going to do about it?"

Stuart stared down at his shoes. He could go to the police. He could demand that charges be brought against Fitz as they had been against him two years ago, a lifetime ago. But what good would it do?

Jeanne chose that moment to come back into the room. She was carrying their baby, a little round butterball of a child with bright blue Adams eyes, exact replicas of his and Fitz's. When Stuart looked at Fitz and Jeanne and the baby, he saw a family like the one he had always wanted with Valerie, but, strangely enough, it didn't matter that Fitz had achieved this for himself, nor did he feel any longer that his brother had achieved it at his expense.

"Well? What are you going to do?" Fitz said. He stood and pulled the still-perplexed Jeanne to him, and the three of them faced him, waiting to hear what he would say.

"I'm not going to do anything," Stuart said, looking down at Angel. He was rewarded by her smile, a smile that outdazzled the sun.

"What?" Fitz said, as if he couldn't believe it.

"I don't condone what you've done, but you've lived an exemplary life since the accident, with your attention to the Maritime Charitable Trust and your marriage and...oh, a lot of things."

"I've tried," Fitz said. "I've really tried. All this time, while I've had to live with my guilt, I've wanted to be like you. To model myself after you, the way you were... before." Tears shone in his eyes, and he blinked them back.

In that moment, Stuart made his decision. "Exposing what you did won't bring Valerie and the baby back. What I really need is my brother," he said, and he offered Fitz his hand.

At first it seemed that Fitz wasn't going to take it, but that was only because Fitz was too stunned to move. Then his brother was moving toward him, clasping his arms around him, embracing him.

In that moment, Stuart could have cried. But any tears shed would have been happy tears, because the worst chapter in his life was now closed. Closed and locked, and the next and perhaps the best chapter was just beginning.

The baby reached out and touched the tip of Stuart's ear with a tiny fingertip. When he and Fitz broke apart, Stuart said, "Maybe you'd better introduce me to this little tyke."

"This," Fitz said, unsteadily but with great pride, "is my daughter. Candace Jeanne Stuart Adams, meet your uncle."

"Mfgmph," said his niece, and Stuart thought, *Perhaps soon I'll be able to introduce Fitz to my own little son or daughter.*

THAT AFTERNOON, despite being invited to spend the night at the house on Nantucket, Stuart and Angel flew back to Boston, where Stuart checked them into an elegant room at an expensive hotel.

Angel was glad they hadn't stayed with Fitz and Jeanne. It had given her pause to see Stuart on Nantucket, in surroundings where he so clearly felt at home. The big house had bespoken permanence and old money, Stuart's usual milieu. Now that she had seen him there, she couldn't imagine how he could possibly feel comfortable in the broken-down bungalow on Halos Island.

Stuart ordered a big dinner from room service, complete with candles and a carnation-and-baby's-breath centerpiece. They sat down across from each other and stared at the food, unable to do more than pick at it.

"What did you think of Fitz?" Stuart asked.

Angel shoved a black bean into her rice pilaf. "Do I have to say?" she said.

"No," he said, but he looked wounded, as if she had compared them and found Fitz more attractive. That wasn't the case, but she ate a forkful of carrots and considered her answer.

"I think I could like him in a limited way," she said finally.

Stuart lifted his eyebrows. "What do you mean by that?" he said.

"I could never trust him after what he did to you."

"Ah," he said. "I see."

"I could exchange Christmas cards, see him once in a while for dinner and to catch up on family gossip, and talk on the phone occasionally, I suppose," she said.

"If you were me, you mean?"

"Yes, of course."

"And if you had to get along with him—you, yourself—could you?"

"He's likable enough. Maybe I could eventually learn to trust him. But it's not going to come up, is it, Stuart?" More than ever, Angel knew now that she was not part of Stuart Adams's world.

Stuart threw down his napkin and stood up. "I guess not," he said, walking to the window. It overlooked downtown Boston, including Boston Common. It was dark, but the Common was well lit, and they could see people strolling along beneath the trees on the winding paths, enjoying the balmy summer night.

Angel put down her fork and got up from the table. She went to Stuart and linked her arm through his. "I can't imagine growing up like you did, Stuart, among people of wealth and privilege. Seeing that house, those people—I couldn't help but realize how different our child's life will be. How do you feel about that? About your son or daughter's growing up far away from here and not attending the right schools or learning to dance at Miss Beatrice's Junior Cotillion and ... well, all the other things you took for granted?"

Stuart considered it for a long time before he spoke. "The things I took for granted aren't the important things. What a child needs—and what I want my child to have—is a full-time parent."

She noticed that he didn't say "a full-time mother and father." She leaned her head against his shoulder, so solid, so strong. Was she mistaken, or was there a faraway glint in his eyes, a light that bespoke other places, other dreams? For a moment, she thought about what it would be like to travel with him, to leave her island and her bees, to let the four winds carry them away to some special place where all they would have to do was eat and sleep and make love, never worrying about the world they'd left behind.

But she could never do that. Not now. She was going to have his baby, and babies tied you down. And besides, he had never hinted that she could go with him when he left.

Suddenly she needed to be reassured. She was the one who had provided all the support he needed; she had been cheerleader and hand-holder and friend, and all at a time when she wasn't feeling tip-top. And he wasn't paying any attention to her, and she was tired, and her head ached. All she wanted was for him to put his arms around her, and here he stood staring out into the night, ignoring her completely. Tears flooded her eyes and began to drip down her cheeks, falling to the pale gold fabric of her dress, where they left dark, ugly stains.

Something must have clued him in, because he looked down at her and saw the tears. His eyes widened. "Angel, what's wrong?"

"I...I..." she began, but she couldn't express her feelings or her physical exhaustion without telling him she was pregnant. For one brief moment, she considered it. But she knew that if she did, maybe Stuart wouldn't bother coming back to Halos Island with her, and she didn't think she could face going back alone. She wanted to walk along the beach with him again, their hands swinging between them. She wanted to sleep with him at night and wake up beside him in the morning. She wanted to lie on the beach under the stars and make love with him. For as many days and nights as she possibly could.

"Angel?"

"I'm tired, that's all," she managed to say.

"Let's go to bed," he said, his arms circling her. She rested her forehead on his chest for a moment, and his lips brushed the top of her head. Before she knew what she was doing, she was tugging the buttons of his shirt through their holes and he was unzipping her dress, and his pants fell away and so did her slip, and soon they stood unclothed together in front of the wide window, in full view of downtown Boston.

They had both grown accustomed to complete privacy on the island; it seemed strange to have to worry about people. "I think we'd better get away from this window," he said, and he swung her up in his arms and carried her to the bed, where he tumbled the bed covers aside and laid her down very gently. He straddled her, his lean body seeming to float above her, his dear face so familiar. In that moment, she wanted to pretend that she wasn't really pregnant, that they weren't really going to part, that they had just met and all was fresh and new and exciting.

It was precisely because they hadn't just met that it was exciting, she thought hazily as he touched his lips to each nipple in turn and slid down her body, kissing the gentle curve of her abdomen where the baby was growing. Because they had done this so many times before, he knew exactly how to extract the most exquisite sensations from every part of her body, knew exactly when to increase contact, when to draw back, when to part her thighs and fit himself into her as if that were where he was meant to be.

Tonight he made her lie back and enjoy what he did to her; he expected nothing from her but that she lose herself in pleasure. And she did, giving herself up to him, surrendering her body and her mind and her spirit so that she hardly knew where she ended and he began.

In those moments, she pretended that she was his and he was hers irrevocably. *Forever,* she thought, even though there was no forever for them. In her moment of climax, she cried out, cried his name, sobbing as though her heart would break, and he soothed her, kissed her, calmed her as he would have a small child.

Afterward, he didn't fall asleep right away, but lay staring at the ceiling; she was awake too, but neither of them spoke.

The only forever for us, Angel thought, *is in the child we have made together.* And she curved her hand protectively over her abdomen, keeping her secret, keeping it safe.

Chapter Twelve

Stuart wished he could figure out a way to take precautions.

It would be easy for a woman. She could take birth-control pills. She could use a diaphragm. For women, there were foams and spermicides and gadgets. But anything a man could use would be obvious.

Not that he wanted to renege on the deal. He only wanted more time. He couldn't leave her yet, not when they were establishing a relationship that meant more to him than anything in the world, even more than the baby-to-be.

After their return from Nantucket, Stuart knew when it was time for Angel's period to start. He watched for the signs on the day it was due, but Angel didn't mention it. And on that same day, when she came back from her swim, she walked nude and determined to where he was sitting in the living room and, with one passionate look that seemed to contain a whole universe of longing, drew him down on top of her on the couch. She had never initiated lovemaking before. And this time was exceptional, a sublime blending of two souls. He had never known such lovemaking, had never reached such peaks until he made love with Angel McCabe, his friend, his lover, his wife.

Afterward, still damp with perspiration, Stuart splayed his fingers out over Angel's belly, imagining what she would look like when she carried his child. He had always thought pregnant women were beautiful, and he knew that she would be more beautiful than any other. He pictured Angel voluptuously swollen, her breasts heavy in his hands, their veins a lacy blue network beneath her golden skin, and it turned him on again, and when he gathered her into his arms she was willing and eager and very, very passionate.

And the next day and the next went by, and Stuart still didn't mention her period. He thought of asking her if it was time to use one of those six home pregnancy test kits in his dresser drawer, but thought better of it. If Angel were pregnant, he wouldn't want to know.

ANGEL'S BREASTS were so enlarged, the areolae so dark, that she thought Stuart must know that something was amiss. But then, he had impregnated her so soon after he arrived on Halos Island that perhaps he'd never really known how her breasts were supposed to look. They tingled, they hurt and she could hardly stand to wear a bra anymore, so she didn't—allowing her breasts to swing free under her clothes, thinking that Stuart would surely notice, but he never said a word about it. Maybe he thought she did it only to titillate him, and if so, that was all right, too.

He didn't talk about the baby anymore. He'd mentioned the baby often before they went to Nantucket, but now it was as though he had blotted the idea of having a child from his mind. Maybe he had wanted a child only to show Fitz that he could father one; maybe now that he and Fitz had reconciled, the baby wasn't important anymore.

She wanted to talk with him about it, but she didn't dare. What she did dare to do was make love with him day and night, anytime and anywhere, hoping that this physical intimacy would bring about the emotional intimacy for which she was becoming desperate. She wanted to say *Talk to me;* she wanted to say *Love me.* Stuart seemed distant and unreachable. And she only grew more and more worried that he would leave.

Maybe it was her own guilty conscience. How could anything be right when she was living a lie? It seemed as if she and Stuart edged around each other now, avoiding each other as much as was possible in such close quarters.

"Your period should have started by now," Stuart said one night a week after it was due.

"It did," she said.

Of course, it had not. She held her breath and observed him covertly from under her eyelashes.

He looked surprised—and was that a flash of relief flitting across his face? Perhaps he was thinking that she couldn't get pregnant, that she wasn't capable of bearing his child, which would let him off the hook. Did he want to be let off the hook? She began to feel panicky.

These were the weeks during which the baby grew from a mere tadpole swimming and somersaulting inside her into a recognizable human with arms and legs and eyes. Angel could now feel her swelling uterus as a solid little lump riding low in her abdomen when she pressed her fingers right above her pubic bone. And suddenly she had a craving for foods she had never cared about before, like guavas and cilantro and spinach with vinegar on it. It was all so exciting, so wonderful, and she wanted to share her news with someone. No, not just anyone. With Stuart. But the days went by one after the other, and she could never bring herself to even hint at the truth.

Stuart, who drank orange juice every morning, took to bringing a glass of it to her in bed before she got up in the morning. As nauseated as she was, orange juice was the last thing she wanted. Stuart thought she drank it, but what he didn't know was that as soon as he left the room, Angel poured it out the window. This didn't help the gumbo-limbo trees growing there.

One day, an oppressively hot one, Angel went outside to inspect the gumbo-limbo trees, wanting to know if their leaves were turning brown because of their daily watering with orange juice, and she froze when she saw the little female key deer that she and Stuart had spied that night not long ago. The doe was standing in the shadows, panting hard, and for a moment Angel thought that she was hurt. But then she realized what was happening.

She ran down to the dock to get Stuart. He was mending old nets that he had decided to use for casting for bait fish.

"Stuart! Stuart!" she said. "Come quick! The little doe—she's having her baby outside our bedroom window!"

Together they crept around the house and, transfixed, watched the laboring doe as she heaved to bring her baby into the world. Finally, tiny feet appeared at the birth opening, and then a small head, and finally, as the mother grunted, the whole fawn. It was wet and breathing, and Angel, thoroughly entranced, reached over and took Stuart's hand.

The doe had a radiant look about her, as if she knew she had produced something really special. She bent and licked the little bundle, which rested for a while before trying to lurch to its feet. Finally it made it, with a helpful nudge from its mother. As the newborn fawn began to root around beneath her for milk, Stuart said, "Let's let them have their privacy." Quietly he and Angel crept away.

Inside the bungalow, Angel sprawled on the couch in the living room and brushed her damp hair from her forehead. "Wow," she said. "Having a baby looks like really hard work."

"It wasn't as hard for us as it was for the deer," Stuart said.

"It makes me think..." she said, and then her voice trailed off.

"Makes you think what?"

"That I'd better attend a childbirth preparation class in Key West."

Stuart shot her a look that could have meant anything. "Isn't this discussion slightly premature? You have to get pregnant first."

That stopped Angel cold. With her living so close to Stuart, sharing so much of her life with him, it often seemed impossible that she hadn't told him yet. She was two months pregnant. How long could she keep him from finding out?

She knew that in order to maintain the status quo, she shouldn't rise to his bait, but lately she felt restless and argumentative. "Are you, um, intimating that perhaps it's my fault that I'm not pregnant?" she ventured.

"Hell, no," Stuart said, getting up. "It's no one's fault. We've certainly been trying hard enough. I told you in the first place that it might not be as easy for you to get pregnant as you thought it would be. It could take a long time. A long, long, time, Angel.'' He looked fierce, as if daring her to contradict him.

She was unprepared for his combative attitude. What had triggered it? She held her breath, waiting for him to say something else, but he seemed to think better of it.

He heaved an exasperated sigh and ran his fingers through his hair. ''I don't know what's gotten into me,'' he said in bewilderment.

Angel got up and pressed her hand to her back. Her center of gravity was already shifting, which was something of a surprise. Suddenly she was sick of the whole idea of being pregnant.

''I have some household chores to do,'' she said abruptly, and went into the kitchen.

Stuart stood there looking confused as she stalked out of the room. Poor guy, he really didn't have a clue about her condition. And what would she say to him if he happened to guess that she was pregnant, that, in fact, she was already two months gone?

She didn't want to think about that now. She wouldn't think about it. She'd keep busy with other tasks, she'd read a book, she'd—

''Have you seen Caloosa lately?'' Stuart said, leaning his head into the kitchen with his hands on either side of the doorway. ''She was acting kind of funny this morning.''

''Oh, that's because she's going into heat,'' Angel said distractedly. ''Happens all too often. I should have her spayed, since there's not a tomcat around.''

''Why don't you advertise for one in the personals ads?'' Stuart asked mildly.

''What kind of a crack is that?'' she said, annoyed with him.

''Nothing. It was a joke.''

"That's not something I care to hear jokes about," she said.

"What's the matter, Angel? Lately you're always making mountains out of molehills."

That almost made her laugh. A mountain was what was growing right in front of him, and he hadn't even noticed. Suddenly she wanted him to notice so that she could abandon this whole silly charade. She wanted him to bring her saltines in bed for her nausea in the morning, not orange juice. She wanted him to hold her when she felt tired, rub her back when it ached. What had ever made her think that she could handle being pregnant all by herself? Her cheeks burned with resentment, resentment not toward him, but at her condition.

"Leave me alone, Stuart. Just leave me alone," she said, bearing down hard on the sponge she was using to wipe the countertop.

"I only asked you what's the matter," he said in an aggrieved tone.

"Nothing," she said viciously.

He was too close behind her; she felt his breath on her neck.

"Don't touch me, Stuart. I'm not in the mood," she said.

"Who said I was going to touch you? I only want to get the ice cream scoop out of the drawer. Would you mind moving over?"

She moved over, but she was suddenly overwhelmed by her deception and remorse and the fact that she was going to lose her figure. And now Stuart crowding her at the sink. Everything seemed wrong; nothing seemed right. Tears welled up in her eyes, and one dripped down her cheek and fell on the back of Stuart's hand.

"What the ... *Now* what's wrong?" He sounded exasperated.

She lifted her head and looked into his eyes, his beautiful blue and very puzzled eyes. She shook her head, unable to speak.

"Angel? Have I done something that upsets you?"

"Yes, *you* upset me!" she cried, slamming a pot lid into the sink.

"How? Why?"

"Oh, God, can't you tell? I'm pregnant, Stuart! Pregnant!"

He stared. She wiped her face with the back of her hand and turned back to the sink, letting the tears come full force.

It was a long time before he spoke. "How pregnant?"

"It happened on our wedding night, I'm pretty sure." She didn't dare look at him.

"You can't have a baby. You had your period," he said. "Twice."

"I didn't. I made that up. I didn't want you to know I had missed it."

"You lied? You *lied?*" He sounded incredulous.

She nodded, ashamed to look him in the eye. "Yes," she whispered.

He ran a hand through his hair. "You don't know for sure that you're pregnant. You haven't been to the doctor. Or have you?" His eyes narrowed.

"No, of course not. But I know I'm pregnant." Now she looked at him; his face was ashen.

"I'll have to think this over. I don't know why you would ... I don't know what your game is. Your purpose. Oh, hell, I don't know anything anymore!"

"You know that I'm going to have your baby. Isn't that enough?"

"My baby. You're going to have my baby." He spoke in a voice of wonder, then shook his head as if trying to clear it. "I can't deal with this. I want to think about it." Without another word, he wheeled and rushed out of the room and out of the house.

Angel slumped against the refrigerator and covered her face with her hands. He was leaving her. What else had she expected?

Why, oh, why, had she told him?

PREGNANT. Angel was pregnant.

Stuart had to admit that women were mysterious, with their cycles that waxed and waned with the moon. But there should have been signs! Belatedly, in shock, Stuart realized that he had seen the signs but hadn't recognized them for what they were.

Nausea. Morning sickness. Irritability. He'd hardly given Angel's symptoms a second thought.

And here he had been thinking about dropping birth-control pills in her orange juice. The only thing that had stopped him was that he couldn't obtain the pills without a prescription; he'd discarded the idea as impractical.

He had to get away from her, had to think. The air on the island hung thick and heavy today, stifling him with moisture. He thought about heading inland, where the breeze was minimal, then decided against it. Instead, he walked down to the dock and stared into the water. When at last he looked up, he saw Angel watching him from the porch, and that annoyed him. It occurred to him that the perfect escape was right in front of him; *Angel's Wings* was tied up at the dock. Why not go for a sail?

The sea was rising and falling in powerful swells beyond the reef, making him think that it would be a rough ride. Rough water had never deterred him in the least, however. He was in the mood for a struggle, and it would be better to fight the sea than to fight with his wife. She would ask him to leave Halos Island for good now, he was sure of it. And he didn't want to go.

It was only after he cleared the reef that Stuart noticed the high-flying mare's-tail clouds advancing from the west. Taking note of them, he pointed the bow toward the east.

ANGEL THREW HERSELF into a fury of housecleaning after she saw Stuart guide the boat through the cut. She hated herself for blurting out the truth. Of course Stuart would leave Halos Island now; that was their agreement. Anyway, who would want to live with a woman who acted the way she did? He didn't even seem happy about the baby. Maybe that was because of his shock at her announcement. Or maybe it was because he didn't want the baby anymore.

"Well, I want you," she said to the baby. And then she burst into tears again. Were all pregnant women so temperamental?

Toward dinnertime, right after she finished cleaning the bedroom closet, the wind rose. She went outside to see if Stuart had returned, but his sailboat wasn't at the dock. That was when she saw the bank of angry-looking clouds piling up in the western sky, where earlier there had been only a shimmering silver band on the horizon.

Not that she was particularly worried. Stuart, old salt that he was, could be counted on to keep an eye on the weather.

As she went back in the house, she noticed that the air was even more humid than usual, and she had a hard time pulling it into her lungs. And the baby wasn't even big enough to push against her diaphragm yet; imagine how hard it would be to breathe when it was.

She decided to look for Caloosa. When she stepped back outside, she noticed that no birds were singing. There was no sign at all of the angry pair of mockingbirds who nested in the banyan tree.

"Caloosa?" she called, but the cat didn't come, nor did she answer.

Angel went back in the house and busied herself folding clothes, all the while keeping an ear tuned to the rising wind.

STUART ANCHORED near a tiny key that served as a tern rookery and waited, watching the birds.

He had visited rookeries in the Bahamas, and he knew that the terns laid their eggs directly on the sand around this time of year. The rookery should be a whirlwind of birds alighting and taking flight, but there was little activity going on at the moment. It puzzled him. The birds on the beach were huddled on the sand, alert and vigilant.

He couldn't make himself think about the birds. *Angel is going to have my baby,* he told himself. It was what he had wanted. He buried his face in his hands, trying to think. She hadn't actually said that he had to leave Halos Island. Maybe she'd let him stay until the baby was born. At least he ought to see his own baby before he headed to the South Seas.

Should he ask her if it would be possible for him to stay until the baby was born? No, it would be better if Angel suggested it. Would she? Or should he tell her that he was going to stay whether she liked it or not?

The boat rocked on increasingly deeper swells as he lost himself in thought, contemplating his next action. When, after a long while, he looked up, he caught his breath.

The clouds in the distance were an odd grayish green, billowing high in the sky. *Looks like trouble,* Stuart thought. He abruptly hauled anchor and started back toward Halos Island, hoping he could make it before the storm struck.

THE FIRST DROPS OF RAIN hit as Angel was closing the windows. She wished Stuart had already bought that shortwave radio he'd been promising; she would have liked to talk to somebody, anybody, and check on storm warnings.

She went outside again, her eyes straining for any sign of approaching sails. She saw nothing.

She walked around the house calling to Caloosa, here and there pulling aside the shrubbery to see if the cat was sleeping somewhere. She was really beginning to be worried about her.

Angel stopped looking for Caloosa when she realized that the swiftly rising wind was beginning to strip leaves from the gumbo-limbo trees. *Let Caloosa get wet,* Angel told herself. *See if I care.* But she did care and she didn't stop looking for Caloosa until she was totally drenched by the rain.

As she dried herself off with a towel inside the kitchen door, she began to hope that Stuart had sailed all the way to Key West. That way, at least, he would be safe from the storm.

ANGEL'S WINGS dipped into a trough, and when she came up, Stuart could no longer see the rookery key.

The seas were high, but not so high that he couldn't manage. It was exhilarating to be sailing into the teeth of the storm, and Stuart threw his head back, letting the rain hit him full in the face. As long as he could see, he didn't mind it.

He wasn't concerned about the boat's being able to hold up in this kind of weather. He had bought her because she was such a sturdy little craft, full of spunk. She'd make it back to Halos Island all right, after which he'd treat himself to a good stiff drink.

The wind blew steadily, grew vicious. He thought he had Halos Island in sight when visibility fell to a hundred feet or so. He hung on to the tiller and swore under his breath. The downpour was now torrential.

Stuart couldn't see a thing. He usually had a pretty good sense of direction, but it was possible that he had been blown off course. He reached for a life jacket, which he had removed earlier when he'd anchored at the rookery. As he pulled the life jacket toward him, the boat flailed and lurched, and the life jacket slipped over the gunwales to be lost in the raging sea.

Then, almost as if in answer to a prayer, the curtain of rain parted and he saw Halos Island, with its distinctive bungalow on the rise above the dock. That was when he heard a sail rip in the wind.

STUART HADN'T COME BACK.

Angel paced from one end of the little bungalow to the other, listening as the wind tore the shingles off the roof one by one. She hadn't realized what the steady *whap! whap!* was about until she looked out the window and saw the shingles flying past.

These were gale winds, if she wasn't mistaken. The winds bent the small trees almost double and hurtled palm fronds through the air. Bolts of lightning split the sky, and thunder crashed until the floor of the house shook. Angel had never experienced a storm like it.

When the wind tore the overhang from above the back stoop and tossed it into one of the banyan trees, she began to know the true meaning of terror.

Where was Caloosa? And where, oh, where, was Stuart?

STUART TRIED to hang on to the boat when it capsized, but he was tossed away from it by the surging sea. Through the cascading rain, he saw the hull of the boat pitch skyward, and then he saw nothing. He tried to orient himself, and after struggling against the water, he decided to let it buoy him up so that he could save his strength.

He was borne swiftly along on the crashing waves, and when he reached the peak of one, a flash of blue-white lightning illuminated Halos Island. Now at least he knew in which direction to swim.

If he could keep his wits about him, perhaps he could reach it. He struck out, glad to have a goal in sight. He heard a crash; the boat was breaking up on the coral reef. Well, he couldn't do anything about that, and he could always buy another boat.

He was making real progress when a piece of flotsam struck him on the shoulder; he flinched and cried out.

The pain was terrible, and there was no one to hear his cry.

ANGEL HUDDLED in the kitchen, paralyzed with fear as she listened to parts of the house being ripped away. The screen on the front porch was one of the first things to go, and after that a large loose branch rammed through the kitchen window. She ran to find dry rags to mop up the water, and she found a large piece of cardboard that she taped over the hole. It didn't help much; within minutes the cardboard was soaked through, but at least no more debris came flying in.

For the first time, she realized that she might die. And the baby—Stuart's baby? It would die, too.

Suddenly she knew that she would fight to live. She would do anything she had to do to survive, and not only for herself, but for the child that she carried within her.

The wind howled around the bungalow, and Angel ran to get a pot to shove under a leak in the roof. She wished Stuart were there, but surely he was safe in Key West.

And when he came back, she had to be here waiting for him. "Please let me live," she prayed. "Please."

The rain gushed through the hole in the roof, which was now so big that she could see outside. She ran to get another bucket, her heart sinking with each step.

She had to get through this. She had to!

STUART GRABBED HOLD of the large piece of debris, which looked like part of the hull of *Angel's Wings*. He didn't care what it was as long as it would float. Thank goodness for the lightning, which provided some illumination. He could still see the island, and he was making progress. At least he was a strong swimmer.

If only the life jacket hadn't gone over the side of the boat! Never mind that he had once been a collegiate swim champion; the life jacket sure would have been a big help. Maybe if he kept an eye out for it, it would float past and he could snag it.

He wondered how Angel was faring. He wondered if she worried about him out in this storm. He wondered if she even cared that he hadn't come back.

All his wondering only underscored his desire to get back to her. Now, at the height of this storm and with his survival uncertain, it seemed to him that during the past weeks he had found heaven on earth on Halos Island with Angel, and he wasn't about to give it up. He kicked with great determination, thinking about how good it felt to hold Angel in his arms. He didn't think he could bear to die without holding her again.

And the next time he held her, dammit, he was going to tell her what he should have told her weeks ago. He was going to tell her how much he loved her.

ANGEL SCRAMBLED to gather her research notes together and stuff them inside plastic bags. Years of work could be lost if they got wet, and she felt sick at the thought.

Her hands trembled as she worked, and she could hardly think. If only Stuart were here, there would be two of them to fight this storm. If only... But she couldn't start thinking that Stuart belonged here. He didn't.

What if Stuart hadn't gone to Key West at all? What if he was out there in the storm?

I can't think about that, she told herself as she threw plastic bags into the drawers of her desk. Water began to pour out of the ceiling above her, and she struggled to push the desk out of its way. It was too much effort, and she collapsed onto a chair, breathing hard, listening to what remained of the house rattling and groaning around her.

I have to be careful, she thought. *I don't want to lose this baby.*

THE SEA cast Stuart into a twilit place; it smelled of seaweed.

When he opened his eyes, he was still clutching the

piece of the sailboat's hull. Slowly he unclenched his fingers and sat up.

The caves, he thought. *I'm in the caves on the north side of Halos Island.*

His shoulder hurt like hell. He rubbed it carefully and decided that there was no serious damage. It was only bruised.

Outside, the sea was rampaging over the beach, and rain lashed in at him from the entrance. Cautiously he looked out. The tide was low, and that meant that he could stay in the caves until it started rising. It might be long enough for the storm to abate.

But he couldn't stay away from Angel. She was alone in the bungalow, and the storm was ferocious. He feared for her.

It didn't matter that the wind was howling or that he might be swept into the sea or struck by a wind-driven tree branch. What mattered was that he had to reach Angel. And her baby. *Their* baby. He had lost everything once, and he wasn't about to let it happen again, not while he had a breath left in his body.

He stumbled out of the cave, right into the teeth of the storm.

EVERY MUSCLE in Angel's body ached with the effort of pulling mattresses and couch cushions to stuff in the broken windows; every fingernail was broken. But she was losing the battle. The furniture was soaked, her belongings and Stuart's were tossed around inside the bungalow, and she didn't think that its flimsy construction was going to hold together much longer.

She paused to consider her options. Should she flee the house before it was torn apart and she was crushed by a falling wall or beam? Or should she hunker down in a protected corner, hoping for the best?

The door to the porch flew open, sending lamps and pictures crashing to the floor, and she ran to close it. And that was when she saw the figure staggering up the path. As she watched, the man was thrown to his knees by the wind, but that didn't stop her from recognizing him.

"Stuart! Oh, Stuart!" Heedless of the wind-lashed rain and the bolts of lightning that were now almost constant, she ran outside.

"Angel," he gasped, clasping her against him. The wind was so fierce that it almost tore their clothes away, and she knew that they had to get to shelter immediately. She put her arms around him and steadied him so that together they were braced against the wind, and they made it to the house. Inside, it was a shambles, but she didn't care. They were alive!

"I thought you weren't coming back," Angel said, burying her face against Stuart's chest.

"The boat capsized and broke up on the reef. When I was afraid I wouldn't make it, I thought of you here alone, and I knew I had to get back to tell you... to tell you..." He stopped talking. "I don't know of any way to say this except to come out and say it," he said.

Her heart stopped. She thought he was going to tell her that he had decided to leave the island.

"Angel, I had to come back so I could tell you that I love you," he said. "I've loved you almost from the moment we met. I wanted to tell you long ago, but I thought you'd make me leave, and—"

"Make you leave?" she said unbelievingly. "I loved you so much, and I thought you'd want to leave if... if..."

Her words were lost in the crash of the wind tearing the roof from its anchors. The roof flew off into the storm, and the rain beat upon them so furiously that they found it almost impossible to breathe.

Stuart was exhausted; he could hardly stand. Angel quickly tried to think of what to do, where to go, and she thought of the old brick icehouse. It wasn't big, but it would afford some shelter.

"Follow me!" she screamed close to his ear. He nodded, and she kept a tight grip on him as she led him out the back door of the bungalow. Once they were outside, it was impossible to remain upright, and she dropped to her knees. Stuart followed, and she lowered her head against the wind and rain and began to crawl.

The storm had reached its full fury, battering at them, tearing at them as they made their way across a clearing littered with tree limbs and coconuts and shingles torn from the house. Angel's hands groped ahead of her, sometimes gripping mud, sometimes debris. Before long her palms were scraped and bleeding and she couldn't see a thing. She knew she was headed in the direction only by instinct.

When she reached the icehouse door, she and Stuart combined their strength to force it open against the wind and fell into the moldy, dark space within. It was a welcome shelter—for her, for Stuart, and for their baby.

The wind slammed the door behind them, and, gasping, they wrapped their arms around each other in the tiny space, thankful to be alive. They had to sit with their knees drawn up; it was impossible to stretch out in the limited space. With her fingers, Angel felt Stuart's face, the fine nose, the full lips. She couldn't see him, it was too dark. Outside, the wind and rain ravaged the island, but they would be all right.

"I was so worried about you," Angel said, tears mixing with the rain on her cheeks.

His hands found her head and positioned it in the dark. She felt his breath upon her cheek. "I never want to leave you," he said. "Never."

"I don't fit into your life, Stuart," she said.

"What life? I didn't have much of a life left when I came here, Angel. The only life I want is the one I share with you. Here, on Halos Island." And then his lips found hers, salty and wet, and he kissed her so passionately that when it was over, she was gasping for breath.

"Hold me tight, Stuart. Never let me go," she said. She tried to get comfortable, resting her head on his shoulder.

"You're hurt," she said, feeling him flinch.

"Only a bruise. Put your head where it was. I want you close to me," he said.

She felt laughter rising in her throat. "As if we could be anything but close in this tiny place."

"Good thing you're only a couple of months pregnant. Otherwise we'd never fit," he said.

She grew suddenly still. "Are you happy about the baby, Stuart?"

"I'm overjoyed. It's what we both wanted."

"I didn't know if you'd still want... I mean, I was worried that you wouldn't..."

His mouth was close to her ear. "I love you, and I love our baby. Why didn't you tell me you were pregnant?"

Angel was beginning to feel slightly hysterical, and she'd have given anything at the moment for a guava. Unfortunately, the guavas had probably all been ruined by the storm. But she shouldn't be thinking of guavas; Stuart deserved an answer.

"What was more important, Stuart? To tell you I was pregnant, or to try to make something of our relationship? I had to give us a chance. I wanted you to love me, and I was afraid that I'd lose you before I even knew what it was like to be loved by a man as wonderful as you." Now she was grateful for the darkness and glad that he couldn't see her face. It was frightening to open herself up to a man in this way. A few months ago, she could never have imagined it.

His arms tightened around her.

"I should have known. I saw the symptoms, knew what they meant. Maybe I didn't want to know. If I'd admitted to myself that you were already pregnant, I would have had to face leaving you."

"Then you're not angry? You'll forgive me for keeping it a secret?" she asked anxiously.

"How can I be angry when we're going to have a baby? I can hardly believe it! We're pregnant!" His voice was filled with awe.

"I feel as if I should ask you to marry me," he said after a while.

"We're already married," she reminded him happily.

"Do you think it will last?" he said.

"I don't know. But we've got the rest of our lives to find out," she said.

"The rest of our lives is not nearly long enough," he told her, and she lifted her lips to his for a kiss.

Epilogue

Eight Months Later

"She looks like an Elizabeth," said Stuart, looking critically at the baby he held in his arms.

"Her name is Elizabeth Stuart Adams," Angel said. "And with her eyes turning a bright, sparkling blue, it's easy to see that she's every bit a member of your family."

"Agreed, but I wish we had named our first daughter after you."

"We'll name our *next* daughter after me," Angel said, gazing at them fondly. Behind them, a big picture window overlooked the vista of Halos Island's pink sand beach; gulls spiraled and dipped overhead. Stuart had insisted on building this enormous new house to replace the demolished bungalow. The new house had five bedrooms and four inside bathrooms, adjoining offices for Stuart and Angel, and a huge master bedroom. Every room featured an ocean view. It had been completed barely in time for Elizabeth's birth two weeks ago.

"What if our next baby is a boy?" Stuart asked, kissing the top of Elizabeth's head.

"Don't ask me. I'm still trying to name all those kittens."

Two of Caloosa's half-grown first litter napped at the foot of the big king-size bed, kneading the blankets with their six-toed feet; Caloosa herself purred in a box in the closet, nursing her second litter. The strapping big tomcat, who had providentially washed ashore in the storm in time to assuage Caloosa's lust, snoozed on a ledge outside the window, the proud patriarch of a many-catted clan.

Stuart sat down beside Angel and transferred Elizabeth to her arms. Angel opened her gown and put the baby to her breast, watching the tiny rosebud lips root at her nipple until the milk began to flow. Angel's gold wedding band, as beautiful and as suitable as Stuart had said it would be, gleamed on her finger. She was so happy, so content. Soon she would resume her research with the bees, and Stuart would design custom-built sailing yachts for his wealthy friends, working from his office in the house. Life could not be more perfect.

Stuart slid an arm around her shoulders. "Do you know how beautiful you are, Angel? And how much I love you? Do you have any idea?" he asked.

She looked up at her husband, her heart in her eyes. He had always made her feel beautiful. And womanly. And loved.

"Show me," she said, and he kissed her, and it was the way it always was between them, exciting and wonderful and very, very sweet.

"How long before I can make love to you properly?" he asked, nuzzling her cheek.

"A few more weeks," she said. She was as eager as he was to resume their love life.

"Promise you won't keep it a secret? Promise you'll let me know when it's time?" His eyes danced, and he smiled down at her.

She loved him so much. Loving him, desiring him as she did, she wanted to make love with him as soon as possible, wanted to fill their beautiful new house with cats and kids and happiness.

"Oh, I'll let you know, all right. Bee-lieve it," she said, and she kissed him once again.

HARLEQUIN®
AMERICAN ◆ ROMANCE®

Once in a while, there's a story so special, a story so unusual,
that your pulse races, your blood rushes. We call this

AMERICAN ROMANCE heartbeat

CLOSE ENCOUNTER is one such story.

With all the black holes and barren and uninhabited planets in the universe,
Kristiana crash-landed on Earth—right into the strong arms of Derek Carpenter.
But though they experience an encounter of the closest kind they are worlds
apart. Destiny bridged galaxies to unite the two—could they break the rules
to stay together?

#604 CLOSE ENCOUNTER
by
Kim Hansen

Available in October wherever Harlequin books are sold. Watch for more
Heartbeat stories, coming your way—only from American Romance!

You asked for it…You got it! More MEN!

We're thrilled to bring you another special edition of the popular MORE THAN MEN series.

Like those who have come before him, Ambrose Carpenter is more than tall, dark and hansome. All of those men have extraordinary powers that made them "more than men." But whether they are able to grant you three wishes, or live forever, make no mistake—their greatest, most extraordinary power is of seduction.

So make a date with Ambrose Carpenter in…

#599 THE BABY MAKER
by Jule McBride
September 1995

MTM4

OFFICIAL RULES

FLYAWAY VACATION SWEEPSTAKES 3449

NO PURCHASE OR OBLIGATION NECESSARY

Three Harlequin Reader Service 1995 shipments will contain respectively, coupons for entry into three different prize drawings, one for a trip for two to San Francisco, another for a trip for two to Las Vegas and the third for a trip for two to Orlando, Florida. To enter any drawing using an Entry Coupon, simply complete and mail according to directions.

There is no obligation to continue using the Reader Service to enter and be eligible for any prize drawing. You may also enter any drawing by hand printing the words "Flyaway Vacation," your name and address on a 3"x5" card and the destination of the prize you wish that entry to be considered for (i.e., San Francisco trip, Las Vegas trip or Orlando trip). Send your 3"x5" entries via first-class mail (limit: one entry per envelope) to: Flyaway Vacation Sweepstakes 3449, c/o Prize Destination you wish that entry to be considered for, P.O. Box 1315, Buffalo, NY 14269-1315, USA or P.O. Box 610, Fort Erie, Ontario L2A 5X3, Canada.

To be eligible for the San Francisco trip, entries must be received by 5/30/95; for the Las Vegas trip, 7/30/95; and for the Orlando trip, 9/30/95.

Winners will be determined in random drawings conducted under the supervision of D.L. Blair, Inc., an independent judging organization whose decisions are final, from among all eligible entries received for that drawing. San Francisco trip prize includes round-trip airfare for two, 4-day/3-night weekend accommodations at a first-class hotel, and $500 in cash (trip must be taken between 7/30/95—7/30/96, approximate prize value—$3,500); Las Vegas trip includes round-trip airfare for two, 4-day/3-night weekend accommodations at a first-class hotel, and $500 in cash (trip must be taken between 9/30/95—9/30/96, approximate prize value—$3,500); Orlando trip includes round-trip airfare for two, 4-day/3-night weekend accommodations at a first-class hotel, and $500 in cash (trip must be taken between 11/30/95—11/30/96, approximate prize value—$3,500). All travelers must sign and return a Release of Liability prior to travel. Hotel accommodations and flights are subject to accommodation and schedule availability. Sweepstakes open to residents of the U.S. (except Puerto Rico) and Canada, 18 years of age or older. Employees and immediate family members of Harlequin Enterprises, Ltd., D.L. Blair, Inc., their affiliates, subsidiaries and all other agencies, entities and persons connected with the use, marketing or conduct of this sweepstakes are not eligible. Odds of winning a prize are dependent upon the number of eligible entries received for that drawing. Prize drawing and winner notification for each drawing will occur no later than 15 days after deadline for entry eligibility for that drawing. Limit: one prize to an individual, family or organization. All applicable laws and regulations apply. Sweepstakes offer void wherever prohibited by law. Any litigation within the province of Quebec respecting the conduct and awarding of the prizes in this sweepstakes must be submitted to the Regies des loteries et Courses du Quebec. In order to win a prize, residents of Canada will be required to correctly answer a time-limited arithmetical skill-testing question. Value of prizes are in U.S. currency.

Winners will be obligated to sign and return an Affidavit of Eligibility within 30 days of notification. In the event of noncompliance within this time period, prize may not be awarded. If any prize or prize notification is returned as undeliverable, that prize will not be awarded. By acceptance of a prize, winner consents to use of his/her name, photograph or other likeness for purposes of advertising, trade and promotion on behalf of Harlequin Enterprises, Ltd., without further compensation, unless prohibited by law.

For the names of prizewinners (available after 12/31/95), send a self-addressed, stamped envelope to: Flyaway Vacation Sweepstakes 3449 Winners, P.O. Box 4200, Blair, NE 68009.

RVC KAL